I0520061

Lily

T.M. Linville

Copyright 2018
T.M. Linville
ISBN 978-1-7337-0881-4

Cover by Lee Copeland
leecopeland.com

To Kim.
For putting up with me, for always believing in me and for
being my best friend.
I love you more than you can imagine.

Table of Contents

INTRODUCTION

The vampire species was declining. Over the centuries, the blood of the Elders was getting weaker. The Elders, the original vampires with the purest blood, have always been responsible for continuing the vampire line. There were originally ten vampire Elders, vampires that have been alive for over 4,000 years. These vampires created other vampires at their discretion. For centuries, any vampire could create another but it was highly frowned upon by the Elders as they were responsible for keeping the numbers in check.

Only two Elders remained. But their blood had gotten too weak to change humans to vampires without killing them. The process to change a human is excruciatingly painful. If the process didn't happen quickly enough, the human would succumb to the pain. In the past five hundred years, the existing elder's blood has been able to change fewer and fewer humans into vampires.

In the beginning, the blood was strong and could change a human in only a day or two. Although the process did require a strong human, the change was relatively quick and the human would survive the change. Back then, the vampire's numbers soared. And it continued to soar for another thirty five hundred years and the vampires flourished. But there hadn't been a successful change in decades.

A vampire scientist had created a human/vampire hybrid, Lily, using a mix of various blood, including that of an Elder. A hundred and twenty years later, the humans created a test tube baby, LaShay, using a changing human's blood. Together, their blood could save the vampire species. But would the two find each other? Would the vampires learn the secret to their blood in time? Would their blood be the saving grace of the vampires or its downfall?

THE BIRTH OF LILY

Circa 1925, in what is now Ashland City, Tennessee

I t was just after dusk and torches illuminated the mouth of a small cave. Four vampire trackers, two guardian wolves and Vincent, the leader, stared into the blackness before them. The stench of rotting flesh had brought them to this place and by the odor, it was not only a human that had been killed within the confines. They heard the rustle of movement within and the wolves leaped forward.

"Don't hurt it!" Vincent yelled after them.

Vincent walked in front of the trackers, wanting to guarantee that the creature they had come for was not hurt. He knew that the task at hand was new to everyone involved, for they were seeking a newborn vampire.

This vampire was born from the womb of a human, but not a normal human. This human was over one hundred and twenty years old and had given birth to dozens of offspring. But none like this. This offspring was the result of an experiment with vampire blood and human eggs, and for reasons still unknown, this child had survived to birth. The scientist, Jack McGregor, had been working on a vampire/human hybrid for decades. He had finally succeeded.

The human's name was Mary Honeycutt and she was one of the oldest feeders the coven had created. As vampires, they needed human blood to survive and over centuries, had worked to perfect the immortal human by giving them the right amount of vampire blood. Too much and they would begin to change and too little they began to age. Humans have very short life expectancies and Mary was the first to live past one hundred years but looked like she was in her twenties. It was a pity that she had to die, as Vincent knew she could not have survived the birth of a child with fangs and claws. Mary had only been pregnant for twelve weeks when she disappeared from the security of the coven five days before. Looking as if she was carrying triplets into the tenth month, she would've given birth any day. She disappeared in the middle of the night and wasn't missed until it was way too late to help her. She took a horse that no one would miss and since she was pregnant, her feeding duties had been postponed. No one even knew she was gone.

The horse that Mary had taken to escape lay on the ground before them, not twenty feet into the cave. It was drained of blood and some of its flesh was left hanging in places and completely missing in others. Apparently the newborn was hungry. As they rounded a small bend in the cave Vincent stopped at Mary's broken and bloody body. She had surly not survived the birth. Her body was bent and broken and it appeared to be half eaten. The child had, as he had feared, clawed its way out of the womb and fed on the only thing it knew.

There was a small hole in the ground with charred wood in a pile less than three feet from the remains. Mary had obviously been here more than a day. Hides and various clothing were strewn across the dirt floor of the cave. A wooden bowl and cup lay next to the fire pit. Echoes of dripping water could be heard in the distance. Vincent listened closer as the sound echoed off the dips and crevices in the rock.

He saw motion from the corner of his eye. He looked beneath a low overhang and he froze then turned his body slowly to his right. Crouched on all fours was what looked to be a five year old child. A female. But this was no ordinary child. This was a vampire in its purest form. A form never before seen in his four thousand years. She was the product of centuries of testing, trial and error and countless attempts to create a true human/vampire hybrid.

She was pale white. Ice blue eyes peered from beneath thin brows. Her tiny teeth were bared and her sharp, pointed canines clearly visible. Her hair was blond and matted with blood and dirt. Pearly white claws protruded from under her fingernails and toenails. Her nose wrinkled and the near silence of the cave was replaced by a guttural growl then she darted around Vincent and out into the forest. The wolves and trackers followed.

"Do *not* hurt her!" Vincent yelled again as he followed.

As he exited the cave, he noticed three white lilies growing among the brush and thick weeds.

"Lilies? Here?" he mumbled then smiled. "We shall call her... Let's go find Lily."

They tracked her for nearly three hours and dawn was only an hour and a half away. She had apparently climbed a tree and was now eluding the wolves through the canopy of the forest. Smart, and she's no more than five days old.

She was growing very quickly and her intelligence with it. Her instincts were already very strong. All vampires have the natural instinct for survival, just like all living things, but with vampires, it's the one instinct that they could not always control. Controlling the instinct to kill or be killed was the toughest thing new vampires had to learn. If they didn't learn to control this quickly, they could become a risk to the coven and ultimately have to be put down. Covens obviously don't like to, but the safely of the species depends on secrecy and indiscriminate killing is

4

never tolerated by anyone, especially the Elders, the oldest and purest of the vampires.

Vincent heard one of the wolves yelp and then heard a struggle in the brush ahead of him.

"We have her, sir!"

She was fighting against the deer hide tied around her and biting at anything that came close, including the coven leader. Her eyes were fixed on him and they had changed colors. The retinas were still pale blue but the sclera, the normally white part, had changed to a blood red and the claws on her fingertips had grown since he saw her in the cave. In fact, *she* seemed to have grown since he saw her in the cave.

"Why are her eyes red?" Titian asked. "They weren't earlier."

"I don't know," Vincent answered. "Maybe they change like yours when she's upset or angry. She *is* part vampire."

Vince knelt down beside her and grabbed Lily's lower jaw. He turned her face toward him. She struggled but he didn't let go.

"Calm down, child," he said softly. "We're not going to hurt you."

"Why not?" Arius asked. "She'll kill every feeder we have if we take her back!"

"We're taking her back," Vincent said, still looking into the blue and red eyes of this growling little girl. "Shhhh." He said as softly and kindly as he could, never looking away from her eyes.

He loosened his grip slightly on her jaw and she stopped struggling. He let her go completely but left his hand within biting range. She opened her mouth but she didn't bite him, she only continued to stare back at him and growl.

She growls, but she doesn't bite, Vincent thought. *Will she bite the person who caught her?*

"Who caught her?" he asked the trackers.

"I did, sir," Rader answered.

"Come here," Vince said to him.

Lily began to growl louder when he approached.

"Put another hide around her," he said when he was in front of him.

Rader started to walk around her to drape the hide over her head from behind.

"No, from here," Vince told him. "Where she can see you."

"But she'll bite me!"

Vince raised his hand slowly to her face and wiped a piece of dirt from her cheek and she didn't bite him, but she never took her eyes off of him.

"Put the hide around her," he said again.

Rader began to reach up and as soon as he was within reach, Lily took a chunk of flesh out of his arm. He raised his hand to backhand her and her growls grew deeper. Her lips were pulled back from her teeth and she snapped at him again. Vincent grabbed his arm before he could hit her.

"She bit me, Vincent!" he said and tried to jerk his arm from his grasp.

"You *will not* hit her," the leader ordered.

He lowered his arm and huffed his disapproval as he walked away. Vince slowly lifted his hand to Lily's face once again. She stared into his eyes as he ran his hand slowly down her cheek. She didn't even attempt to bite. He smiled as he picked her up.

Vincent wrapped his arm around her and no sooner than he got her off the ground he jerked his hand away from her back to find that he had a row of puncture wounds across his palm. He turned her around to see what had stuck him.

"Oh my!" he said, smiling. "She has spikes."

"Spikes? How can she have spine spikes? Only the elders have spikes." Aiden snorted as he walked over to see Lily's back. "Pft! She *is* a sideshow."

Vincent pulled Aiden's arm closer to Lily intentionally so she could reach him. She took two swipes and left two sets of parallel gashes on his arm. Then Vincent pushed him away so he wouldn't strike her.

Arius laughed, "Aiden, and apparently her claws are sharper than yours,"

Vincent lifted Lily's hand to get a better look at the claws then turned her around again to see the spikes. He had never had a chance to examine spine spikes before. He had them himself, but seeing them was no easy task, and he had never met anyone else who had them. The spikes worked the same as their fangs and claws. Tendons, connected to the bottom of the crescent shaped spike, wrapped around the spine on both sides and then connected to specialized muscles in the back. The claws had tendons wrapped around the bones of the fingers and toes and then to muscles in the back of the hands and feet. They all worked independently of each other muscle group in the hands, feet and back. The muscles worked the same way any muscle works, and the claws automatically retracted when no pressure was applied. The top of the nail sheath was actually the fingernail, but under it was a hollow opening where the claw rested. They were retractable and like a cat's claws, are sheathed when relaxed. The skin that covered the fingertip grew back as soon as the claw was retracted. The muscle and tendons worked together to pull on the bottom of the crescent and rotate the claw out of the sheath. The fangs were connected to tendons under the mid cheek and then to muscles further up around the temple. But the spikes, he had never been able to examine them like this.

It was believed that only the original 10 vampires, The Elders, had spikes and they didn't pass them on to anyone they created. They were the first of the species as they are known today and the first 10 that had completely lost the ability to reproduce naturally. The spikes had been a product of evolution, devised as a defense against attacks from predators in the trees. Tens of thousands of years ago, very nearly after homo vampirus had split from the homo sapiens species, a vampires only real threat came from up in the trees. A large tree dwelling cat, Panthera onca augusta, also known as the giant jaguar was their only threat. Now extinct, the cats lived during the Pleistocene Epoch and died out before the end of the last Ice Age. It is said that it only took four generations for the vampire's spikes to become fully functional. But also in those four generations, a mutated gene was introduced to the DNA and had changed it. It stripped the species of the ability to reproduce but it also gave them immortality, a super-fast healing process and a vampire skin that can only be compared to Kevlar. Only a vampire or one of their wolves could physically harm another vampire.

A parasite, some believe it was a mutated virus, attempted to reproduce itself completely inside its host. Homo vampirus, not yet susceptible to the sun, fought the parasite and was able to stop the internal attack, but not before the invader had changed the DNA code. The free flowing stem cells in their blood were the first part of the parasite's attempt to replicate itself. In the process of using the stem cells to the vampire's own benefit, it made them vulnerable to the sun and unable to have children by compromising the internal reproductive organs by shrinking them to make room for a small organ that reproduced and filtered the stem cells.

Also shortly after the split of the Homo sapiens and Homo vampirus, humans lost their ability to see in the dark. Since they began to hunt in the daylight they no longer needed the ability. Vampires hunted humans at night while they slept and thus retained the night vision. Vampires remained nocturnal, making their sensitivity to the sun more profound since they slept while the humans hunted and vice versa. The two species rarely had contact with the other during daylight hours, and after tens of thousands of years, humans assumed that vampires had become extinct. They believed that it was a wild animal that would attack them while they slept. Since humans sustained the entire vampire population and because humans were scarce then, vampire numbers were low. Humans outnumbered vampires one thousand to one. The natural order of the food chain had been sustained through the centuries. Lily was only one of thousands of attempts to combine the species so the vampire bloodline would live on indefinitely. It was also an attempt to make vampires less susceptible to the sun and less dependent on human blood.

But the blood of the vampires had weakened over time and in the past two hundred years only the blood of the Elders could change a human to a vampire. But the excruciating process was taking longer and longer to perform. In recent decades even the Elder blood was only able to change the strongest of humans. The others died during the transformation as the pain can be unbearable. So the hope was to create a hybrid whose blood would be stronger than the Elder's and be able to once again create vampires with less risk of them dying. Lily was that hope but the trackers had no idea what she *really* was.

Lily finally retracted the spikes and Vincent picked her up and cradled her in his arms. He draped a dark coat over her and began the trek back to the coven. After about ten minutes he took the hides off of her. She even retracted her claws, and to his surprise, she wrapped her arms around his neck and laid her head on his shoulder.

Is she more human than we would have thought, Vincent wondered?

She was sound asleep when they reached the main entrance to the coven.

From the outside, the coven would have appeared as just another neighborhood. The houses and roads were no different than that of any other in the surrounding towns. The difference was that under this neighborhood there was a labyrinth of hallways and rooms, laboratories and libraries. The property of the coven covered about seventy acres and most of it was reserved for farmland and grazing land. The labyrinth below covered nearly thirty of those acres.

The entire coven lived here, including all of their human feeders and the feeder's children. The vampires needed them to survive. The feeders were treated as if they were one of them. They could come and go as they wished, but there were always a lot of extras if they devoted themselves to the coven. They all knew that they could easily be replaced, but vampires too get attached to others. They had seen so many humans come and go in their time that they finally, as early as the 1700's, began experimenting with vampire and human blood in order to extend the lives of the feeders. Mary was one of the most devoted feeders they had ever had. She truly loved being with the vampires and they loved her. She had agreed to help the vampires by carrying offspring to term if she were allowed to raise the children as her own even though they were not. Early on, she would get pregnant by another feeder and then raise the child. Then later, the offspring were the product of selective breeding and later, genetically engineered from eggs harvested from a number of others and implanted into a womb to carry to term. As a gift, Vincent had granted Mary three children that she called her own, Samantha, Robert and Sidney.

She also had given birth to Eric and Erica but they were for Alexa, Vincent's wife, from conception. She had always wanted a child, but as a vampire could not conceive so Vincent allowed her to adopt a baby to raise. She had only wanted one, but when they turned out to be twins, she was ecstatic. Alexa raised them both as her own from the moment they were born.

Eric had always been arrogant and thought that since his parents were the King and Queen of the coven, that it made him the heir to the throne. He was poorly mistaken. He was careless and spiteful and was always rubbing someone the wrong way, usually Erica. Eric had always been bigger than Erica and he never let her forget it. Eric was six foot one and about one hundred and sixty pounds to Erica's five foot eight and one hundred and thirty pounds.

He and his sister couldn't be any more different if they lived on opposite sides of the globe. Erica was smart and levelheaded. She was always thinking, always trying to make things better for the coven, the vampires and for the feeders. Everyone loved Erica, except her brother. But Eric didn't really like anyone, and there was no love lost on him either.

On two separate occasions, the entire coven had to uproot and move to another city or risk detection or worse, action from the Guardians, the vampire overseers that governed the vampires. Eric felt that since he was the 'prince', he could go out every night and rape, kill and feed. Vincent wanted his last such infraction to be his last. Vincent was going to put him down because he was just too much of a risk to everyone. But Alexa refused to let the orders be carried out. She reminded Vincent that before they met, he had once been a part of a murdering horde and that he too had risked the safety of the species.

Vincent and Alexa had lived in London in the late 1800's. The world was very different then. There was no extranet cameras, no television, not even phones or radios. It was much easier then to get away with murder. London is where Vincent met Dr. Jack McGregor, the scientist responsible for the creation of Lily. He had messy sandy blond hair and a moustache of the same color. He stood about six feet tall and weighed about one hundred and sixty pounds. He was a brilliant scientist and had experimented with vampire and human blood for over a century. He was also a very twisted individual, and still was. He was better known in the coven as Dr. McGoo. Vince started calling him that shortly after the turn of the 19th century, after his curiosity had gotten the better of him and he went on a killing spree in the Whitechapel area of London. The spree became known to history as the Whitechapel Murders, but everyone that knew anything about them knew them as simply 'the work of Jack the Ripper'.

Jack McGregor was still alive and well and lived with the coven in what is now West Nashville. It was there from which Eric forced them to leave. This was after Lily's arrival and how the coven ended up being residents of Atlanta. They had to leave Atlanta after about twenty years because Eric had killed an Atlanta police officer. He said it was a mistake, but that was doubtful.

On that day, it was also Eric that woke the sleeping dragon, also known as Lily, in the early morning hours on the day of her arrival at the Nashville coven. Vincent entered the front door of the meeting hall and was planning on a quiet trip to the tunnels where he would put the little sleeping vampire in a cage until he could figure out what she was, how she was going to react and how to move forward from there.

He wasn't so much as to the bottom of the steps when Eric shouted out from the other end of the hall.

Lily's eyes shot open and Vincent felt spikes erupt down the length of her spine. She clawed at his chest and managed to wiggle and claw her way out of his arms. She shot down the hallway and Vince shot after her. Her claws tinked and tapped against the floor as she ran from hallway to hallway.

The black coat Vincent had placed over her had fallen away as soon as she was out of his arms so she was a naked five year old running down the brick-lined hallway with one inch canines, two inch spine spikes and claws on her hands and feet. It was very near dawn, and the vampires were settling into the underground area for the day. As Lily, Vincent and Eric ran past, each one looked at them as though he were chasing a purple unicorn.

"What the hell is it?" Eric asked Vincent as he ran behind.

"A child," Vincent answered calmly.

Vince was still annoyed with his son for waking her in the first place. When they finally reached a hallway that ended in a heavy locked door, Lily turned and attacked. Instead of stopping her, Vince simply stepped out of the way. She took Eric completely by surprise and before he could get her off, she had clawed him up rather badly.

When Eric finally got his hands around her, Vince promptly took her and held her out in front of him. He turned her around to face him and she clawed at his arms and took swipes at his face. He only held her out, away from him and stared at her. She either realized that he was not going to let her go or that he wasn't going to hurt her, or both, because after only a short time, she calmed down. She retracted the claws and relaxed. Just as he was going to cradle her again, Erica's voice came drifting down the hall. Lily turned quickly in her direction.

Vincent's daughter, Eric's twin, was walking down the hall toward them. She had long flowing brown hair. She was about five foot eight and was a solid one hundred and thirty five pounds.

"So I take it you found Mary," she asked as she approached. "And what do we have here?" She smiled and brushed Lily's hair out of her face.

"This is Lily," Vincent answered.

Lily did nothing to attack. Erica's smile was apparently contagious because Lily smiled back. Eric came up behind Erica and pushed her into the wall as he walked toward Lily and Vincent. In a split second, Lily was on the full offensive once again. Her arms pawed the air after Eric but Vince turned so his back was toward Eric and was between him and Lily.

"Go away!" Erica said as she punched Eric in the jaw.

Lily strained her neck to look past Vince. Erica then simply walked around him, took Lily from Vince and began walking back down the hall in the direction she had come.

"What the hell?" Eric asked, shrugging his shoulders.

"If you threaten her, she attacks, dumb ass," Vincent said then followed Erica and Lily down the hall.

Eric just stood there, his hand rubbing his jaw, and watched as Lily snuggled into Erica's arms. That was the moment that Eric's hate for Lily began. She had embarrassed him but took immediately to Erica. *Everyone* always *takes to Erica,* he thought. He looked down the hall toward the others.

"You just wait, Lily," he mumbled under his breath.

Erica carried Lily to the only place Vincent could have planned to put her. A cage that was designed to house werewolves. It was a few doors down from the laboratory in what everyone called 'McGoo's hallway'. Most of the rooms off this particular hallway were used by the doctor to do his experiments.

The room was well lit and had a small table with two chairs sitting behind a large cage. Erica walked past the table, took the key off of the far wall then unlocked the heavy cage door. It was a simple cage, rectangular in shape with heavy steel bars spaced about four inches apart. There was a makeshift bed on the floor that was made of straw and grass with a heavy quilt on top.

Erica put Lily down on the bed and then sat down beside her. Instantly, Lily spotted the large wolf laying against the outside of the cage. Lily pointed to him.

"Wolf," Erica said, looking directly at Lily.

"Woooof," Lily mumbled while still pointing to the huge animal.

"His name is Onyx, and he doesn't like anyone," Vincent said from the doorway of the cage.

"He just protects the premise. Not the people in it," Erica corrected.

"Can you say, Onyx?" Erica asked Lily. "Aaaa nix."

"On-ix," Lily sounded out.

"Very good."

Onyx was a solid black Guardian Wolf. He was huge, He was over three hundred pounds and like Vince had said, he didn't like anyone, not even Vincent. Most wolves choose who they would protect to the death when they were just pups. But Onyx, the offspring of Vincent and Alexa's wolves, Venom and Snowball, had chosen no one. He protected the property of the coven and did it quite well, so Vincent let it slide that he had no vampire of his own to protect.

Erica pointed to the dress she was wearing. "Dress."

"Dwess," Lily said with puckered lips.

There wasn't much in the room but Lily pointed at everything that was around and Erica gave her a name for it, from the broom in the corner to the cup on top of the table.

As soon as Vincent was out of sight, Erica carried Lily down the hallway and then upstairs to her house and straight to the bathroom. Onyx only lifted his head when the door to the cage clanged shut.

"Ok little girl, it's bath time. You are absolutely filthy," Erica thought aloud.

Erica smiled at the naked little vampire in her arms and Lily smiled back. She was relaxed and after a moment her fangs began to descend. Lily obviously hadn't done it on purpose and raised her hand to feel the protruding canines. Then she got this look of deep concentration and Erica felt the spikes erupt down Lily's back as she watched shiny white claws slide from their sheaths under Lily's nails.

Lily arched her back so the spikes scraped against Erica's hands then she looked down at her claws and wiggled her fingers. She looked up into Erica's eyes and flashed a big toothy grin as she showed Erica her clawed hand.

"That's very good, little one," Erica cooed. "Usually takes new vampires months to have that kind of control. And usually they have to get really mad for the defenses to surface."

Erica decided to test Lily's control so she sat Lily on the floor and knelt in front of her. She took one of Lily's hands and pushed on the tips of the claws, in the hopes that Lily would get the idea to retract them. At first Lily just pushed her claws against Erica's hand in a playful way. Then Erica laid her hand on top of Lily's palm and revealed her claws to Lily. Lily grinned and pushed against the tips, which prompted Erica to retract the claws. Lily giggled aloud and pressed against Erica's fingertips. The claws came out once more and then Erica pushed her claws against Lily's. Lily quickly retracted her claws then pushed against Erica's who did the same. Lily laughed out loud as she began to understand the game. Erica taped Lily's fingertips and instantly the claws were out. Another tap and they were gone.

Erica couldn't help but laugh with Lily, not only by the game but by how quickly Lily caught on. Erica then ran her hand down the spikes on Lily's back and they disappeared below the skin.

Erica knew of some that had been a vampire for a year that didn't have the kind of control Lily did. And Lily wasn't even a week old. But she supposed that being born with the ability was a lot different than being changed into it.

"Whew, you stink little girl," Erica whispered.

Erica held her hand in front of Lily. "Stay."

Luckily, when Erica returned with warm water, Lily was still in the room, just looking around the empty room and then followed Erica to the bathtub.

Erica poured the water into the tub then went to get more water. Lily followed and Erica didn't stop her. She followed her to the living room and watched

Erica pour steaming water from a large pot over the fireplace. She then refilled it and took the hot pot to the bathroom. It took several trips but Lily just followed along behind.

When the tub was nearly full, Erica lowered Lily into the water, not sure of what her reaction would be. When Lily's lower body was in the water, she tried to lift herself out by wrapping herself around Erica. Erica only smiled and let Lily hold on to her.

Then she slowly tried again to lower Lily into the water.

"It's okay, Lily," Erica reassured.

After the fourth try, Lily finally loosened her hold on Erica's neck and settled sleepily into the water. Erica grabbed a washcloth and soap and began to clean the dried blood and dirt from Lily's arms and legs. When Erica dropped one of Lily's arms and the water splashed in Lily's face, Lily actually audibly gasped.

"Aww, I'm sorry," Erica cooed, wiping the water from Lily's eyes with a dry towel.

But then Lily lifted her hand and dropped it on her own, this time splashing Erica's clothes. When she looked at Lily to reprimand her, Lily was smiling. A full toothy grin and Erica just couldn't be mad. Then Lily splashed again and again. Erica used the splashing to wet Lily's filthy hair. It worked. Then Erica lathered the matted hair with soap and began to massage the suds around. Apparently Lily liked it because she cooed and grinned and just let Erica wash her hair. Then she splashed Erica with water again.

When Erica tried to lay Lily back to rinse her hair, Lily was having nothing of it. She wrapped her little arms tightly around Erica's neck and wouldn't let go. Erica tried to pry her off but Lily was not leaning back into the water. Erica finally got Lily to let go but was right back when Erica tried to lower her in the water again. The third time, Erica simply leaned forward and dunked Lily into the water and rinsed as much of the soap out as possible. Now they were both soaked. Lily let go of Erica's neck and Erica went to get a cup from the sink then rinsed the rest of the shampoo from Lily's head just by leaning her head back and not her whole body. This worked better.

Erica wrapped the towel around Lily then they sat on the floor beside the tub. Erica worked through the tangles and after about 20 minutes was finally able to get a comb through Lily's shoulder length, blond hair. She then went and fumbled through a few drawers to find the smallest shirt she had, slid the shirt over Lily's head and, as if Lily were any ordinary child, said "Boo" when Lily's head popped out of the shirt. Lily laughed.

Steven, Erica's husband, walked into the room, curious as to where the laughter was coming from.

"Who's that?" he asked.

"This is Lily," Erica answered. "Remember the experiments that McGoo does? Well, this time it worked and here she is."

"The first true blood vampire, *born* with fangs and claws," Steven acknowledged. "At least she'll never have to experience the change."

"True," Erica said as she combed once again through Lily's hair. "She seems pretty tame, considering what she is."

"I would definitely keep an eye on her though. You know how temperamental new vampires can be," Steven reminded her.

"Vincent wants her under lock and key for the time being."

"So why is she here?"

Erica smiled shyly and shrugged her shoulders. "She needed a bath?"

"Erica! You have no idea what she's capable of." Steven paused. "Vincent doesn't know she's here, does he?"

"She's just a little girl," Erica reassured.

"She's still a newborn vampire," Steven reminded her.

"It will be fine."

Erica picked her up and held her for a little while but decided that it would be really bad if she was caught with Lily out her cage. She kissed Steven then carried Lily downstairs and back toward the basement and the cage. Lily began to doze off in Erica's arms.

They were almost to the last turn at the last intersection of halls when Eric rounded the corner from the opposite direction and stopped. He glared at Erica with a smirk on his face.

"What are you doing?" Eric yelled.

Lily jumped and was instantly awake and on the defensive. Erica tried desperately to keep Lily in her arms but she wasn't fast enough. Lily hit the ground running and shot down the hall to the left toward McGoo's hallway. The next second there were six vampires and two wolves after Lily. Eric's doing.

Erica chased after them and managed to throw one of the vampires into the wall.

"That's one down," Erica mumbled to herself.

Lily turned the first corner, claws scratching against the stone floor trying to get traction. A long corridor lay in front her with door openings on either side at varying intervals that lead to houses above or research labs or storage below. She ran past the first couple of doors that smelled like vampires but entered the hallway that smelled like humans, McGoo's hallway. She scurried, nearly on all fours down the hall. She entered the first opened door and ran to the other side of the room, through an opened door, through another room and finally through a pair of opened double doors, into a very large white room with thick glass windows overlooking other rooms all around but with no exits. On the right wall was a long metal table. Lily could smell the blood that had seeped through the cracks over the years in the white tiled floor.

She slid on all fours, turning as she slid until her side hit hard against the far wall. Lily had ended up in the laboratory that was used for the experiments. The smell of blood was so strong that Lily actually felt lightheaded for a moment.

She growled and hissed, her eyes blood red with fear. She faced her would be attackers head on as they were only seconds behind. Eric didn't like Lily, thought she was a threat to his ego and wanted to see her dead. The wolves, Venom and Zeus on Eric's orders, stood on each side of him. They all approached slowly, meticulously calculating every move that Lily might make. When they were halfway across the white tiles, Venom stopped cold in his tracks. The ratta-tat-tat of wolf claws on stone, then on tiles, reverberated through the opened door of the lab. Lily thought the sound was coming for her and watched as everyone's attention turned toward the opened doors.

As everyone turned to see which wolf it was, Onyx knocked his way through the crowd at the door and over Zeus's head, nearly hitting his own head against the ceiling.

The huge black wolf landed a few feet from Lily, his momentum sending him sliding into the wall over her. Everything had happened so fast, Lily only had time to duck and cover. She knew that the wolf was coming for her and she ducked and waited for the bite.

Onyx stood over the child, making her look so incredibly small under his huge frame. Eric took a step closer and Onyx lowered his head, his nose wrinkled, his ears flattened against his head and his white teeth flashed brightly against his solid black coat. His yellow eyes were fixed on Eric.

Eric looked down at Venom and shrugged his shoulders as if say, "Well, what *are* you waiting for?" but Venom didn't move. He was Onyx's sire but even he knew that nothing could take down Onyx. And Onyx was not backing down.

After a few seconds, Lily slowly opened her eyes and found that no one had moved since she had closed them. A low, guttural growl rumbled in Onyx's throat and Lily ducked, not quite realizing that Onyx was standing directly over her with his teeth bared, daring anyone to make a move against her.

Lily slowly looked up to see the massive wolf above her, protecting her from her would be assassin. Her claws slowly retracted as her tiny hand wrapped around Onyx's front paw.

Eric heard footsteps behind him and turned around just in time to receive a hard right hook from his sister.

"Dammit, Erica!" he grumbled as he grabbed his jaw.

"Ass hole!" Erica spat back. "She's not dangerous. She's only protecting herself, dumb ass! You would've done the exact same thing!"

"So you get *Onyx!?*" Eric asked.

Erica didn't answer, she just walked past Eric and right up to Lily and Onyx. She scratched Onyx behind his ears and knelt down to see Lily. Erica put her arms out. Lily leaned out to look around her.

"They are not going to hurt you, honey," Erica said softly. "I promise. Onyx and I will never let anyone hurt you, ok."

"Why did you get Onyx?" Eric asked again.

"I didn't get anyone!" Erica spat. "He was apparently waiting for me to bring her back when you went after her."

Onyx and the wolves had the ability to change into human form. They were werewolves, genetically engineered by Dr. McGregor. Jack was a genius and over the years had used his knowledge to create protectors for the vampires. He did so by attempting to change a timber wolf into a vampire. The introduction of the vampire blood into the canine host transformed the wolf into a very hairy human with some vampire characteristics. Then the werewolf was able to change back into the wolf form. A very large wolf form. It took decades to find the right wolves though. Most were defiant and refused to obey their vampire masters. Some escaped into the forests of northern Alaska and although a huge effort was put forth, they couldn't be found. It is assumed that they have dispersed all over North America and even into South America. Stories will occasionally pop up about a horrible murder that left humans ripped to pieces and half eaten. It's believed that the humans got too close and were killed by werewolves refusing to be detected.

The wolves were allowed to choose which vampires they would protect but Onyx had never chosen, until now.

Lily slowly reached out and let Erica pick her up but Lily never took her eyes off of Eric. Lily's claws erupted from under her fingernails when Erica walked past the other wolves and her brother. Onyx followed closely behind.

When they reached the basement cage, Erica walked inside and sat down on the bed, putting Lily in her lap.

Lily fell asleep in Erica's lap and after an hour and a half, Erica finally left to talk to Vincent. Erica and Onyx both visited him that night to talk about Lily.

"Dad, Eric needs to be told to stay away from Lily. She is no threat to him or to any of us."

"What has he done now?" Vincent asked.

Erica explained what Eric had done. She told him that Lily had finally calmed Lily down and that earlier, she had taken her out of the cage to give her a bath. It was then that Erica agreed to raise Lily as her own and Onyx vowed to protect them both from Eric or anyone else that might threaten them. Vincent agreed to speak to Eric about his behavior. He should've done it right away, because apparently Eric was one step ahead of everyone.

Eric walked into the room with Lily's cage and Onyx nearly took his head off.

"Onyx! Stop!" he shouted. "I'm only here to apologize. I'm sorry for the misunderstanding. I thought she was dangerous and didn't want her killing any of our feeders."

Onyx only growled. Eric looked over to Lily and his expression changed.

"Onyx? Does Lily need to be feed? She looks hungry," he said. "Go get a feeder for her."

Onyx looked at Eric and refused to go.

"Onyx! I promise you, I won't hurt her,"

It was against the rules not to follow direct orders from the leader's children. Onyx dropped his head and walked toward the door. He looked back and Eric held up his hands, palms facing forward and fingers spread wide.

"I promise, I won't touch her," he said

Eric walked up to the cage. "We're not going to hurt you Lily," he told her. "Erica sent me down here to send you and Brian downtown to pick up a horse for you. You're going to need one soon and she has been kind enough to arrange one of your very own. Brian will take you downtown so you can be at the stables early. You get to pick which one you want and the biggest selection is early in the morning."

Eric didn't even know if Lily could get near horses because they have a natural fear of vampires. They can sense the predator and they usually react violently. But it didn't matter, Eric had arranged for a vampire assassin to be waiting for Lily.

The assassins are werewolves trained specifically to hunt and kill vampires. They were created to protect the coven against outside vampires, rouge vampires that kill feeders and cause havoc within the coven. The werewolves came from the same stock as the guardian wolves. Creatures that can change from a wolf to a werewolf but not into a human. They don't contain enough human DNA to become a full human so they usually preferred to be a wolf instead of the half wolf, half human monster they were created to be.

Finally Eric felt that Lily was calm enough so he unlocked the cage and let himself in. A few steps behind him was a thin human that stopped outside the cage. Lily's fangs and claws erupted as Eric came close to her

"We're not going to hurt you," Eric said just before Lily leapt toward him.

He pushed her back and quickly stepped out of the cage and slammed the door.

"Maxwell will be back for you later," Eric said as he locked the cage. "Don't get comfortable, you're not going to be here very long."

Lily hadn't stopped pacing in the cage for nearly four hours. She was growling and hissing and making attempts at talking. She was actually getting better at it. Most of the coven had been by to see the new baby vampire and she was clearly not happy being the center of attention.

"Maybe she's hungry?" Jack suggested to Erica. "She is part human, maybe she needs food, too."

Dr. McGoo left for about ten minutes then brought a thick, raw steak to Lily's cage. He dangled it outside the bars in front of Lily. She took a few big whiffs and then grabbed it from his hand. She sat on the bed and ate the meat from off the bone, chewing slowly. For a little while, she calmed down.

It had only been about an hour, and she was pacing the cage once again. Erica watched her pace, watched her eyes and subtle variations in her expression, trying to figure out what was wrong. With each passing hour, Lily became more and more agitated. It almost looked like she was in pain at times.

Erica and McGoo sat at the table and watched. Lily started to claw at any vampires that happened past but paid no mind to Onyx laying against the outside of the cage or any other wolf for that matter.

Finally Erica walked up to Lily and Lily took a swipe at her. Erica took a step back but Lily continued to claw at her.

"See what she'll do when she gets a hold of you," Jack said as he walked up to Erica. "Worse case, you'll have some claw marks for a few minutes. Best case, we'll see if she just wants out."

Erica turned to look at Jack.

"Do you really think it will be that simple?" she asked.

"Well, she doesn't claw at the wolves," he said. "And the wolves didn't put her in here."

Erica took a deep breath and took two steps toward the cage. As soon as she was within reach, Lily grabbed her arm and pulled it to her mouth. She sank her teeth into Erica's wrist and drank deeply. McGoo's forehead wrinkled as he contemplated her actions.

"Why would she want our blood?" he said aloud.

As Lily continued to drink, she began to stretch her legs and arms. Her face wrinkled and contorted as she was in obvious pain. She tilted her head back and forth slowly, stretching her neck. Finally she let go of Erica's arm and stretched both arms above her head then arched her back. Erica and Jack watched as the shirt Erica had put on her began to shrink. At least it looked like it was slowly shrinking.

Lily was growing, literally in front of their eyes.

Over the next eighteen hours, her legs grew longer as they filled with muscle. Her arms grew longer and the muscles in her upper arms and shoulders filled in, giving an older, more toned appearance. Then her face began to age. Her cheekbones lifted and her eyes grew apart slightly. Her mouth stretched and her lips became fuller and more deeply colored. She opened her mouth to stretch her facial muscles then stretched her fingers, exposing her claws. Her hair slowly changed from blond to black. She bent over and stretched her back. The spikes that lined her spine slowly appeared. They had grown longer and thicker.

She had grown from an eight or nine year old to a twelve year old in a matter of hours.

Erica and Jack just stood in front of the cage and stared.

"Well, I guess we know why she wanted our blood, now," Erica said, still in shock.

"Is that Lily?" Vincent asked.

No one even noticed that he had walked up.

"I've only been gone a day, what the hell happened?" Vincent nearly yelled at McGoo. "What did you do now?"

"What do you mean, 'What did I do now'?" McGoo snapped.

"Stop!" Erica yelled. "You two can yell at each other later."

Erica grabbed the key and unlocked Lily's cage. Lily looked worried and had sit down on the bed and was now looking to Erica for comfort.

Erica pushed Lily's dark hair behind her ears and kissed her forehead. Erica reassured Lily that everything was ok. She stayed in the cage a couple of hours until Lily fell asleep. Erica was sure that Lily would continue to age through the night. So she locked the cage, hung the key back on the wall and finally left for bed herself.

DOWNTOWN

After everyone had finally left Lily alone to sleep, Eric and Maxwell, the feeder that was taking her downtown to get the horse, returned. Onyx woke when the lock on the door clicked open. In a flash Onyx was all teeth and headed straight for Eric. Eric just stood there.

"No!" Eric yelled and pointed to Onyx. "You know you can't hurt me, Vincent would put you down and you know it."

Eric had assumed that Onyx would defend Lily. He also knew that Onyx couldn't hurt him. The guardian wolves were forbidden to do harm to any member of the coven.

"Maxwell is going to take Lily to get a horse from town. Vincent said so," he said to Onyx. "They'll be back by late morning, I promise."

Eric lied and to make sure Onyx didn't ruin his plans, he lured Onyx into the cage, quickly locked the door and took the key. Maxwell was careful to be quiet as they walked through the halls of the coven. He led Lily outside and they took a horse and buggy to town. One of the coven's Model T's would have most certainly been missed but the horse and buggy would not.

Maxwell had taken her to town as Eric ordered. He had just put his horse in the stable and down some hay when he noticed that Lily was gone. He ran outside and looked around. She was about forty yards down the street when Maxwell saw her disappear behind some buildings.

Lily looked around but didn't see anything but a dark alley that was cluttered with garbage and rats scurrying about. She turned around to walk back to the street when she saw something disappear behind a trash pile. She crouched down and waited for it to show itself again. When the rat ran out of a hole at the base of the wall not two feet from her, she lunged. It scurried away quickly and she chased after it for about half a block, still crouching, her hands outstretched in front of her.

"Ugh!" She mumbled under her breath. She took a small quick lunge forward and brought her hand down across the back of the rat's neck, effectively breaking it. Instinct told her that it was food and she began to rip the hide off of the dirty pest when another movement in the shadows caught her eye. She froze as she stared into a pair of red eyes looking back at her. She wasn't the seven or eight year old the assassin was expecting but she still smelled the same. The werewolf looked up at her from his first evening kill.

The werewolf was more wolf than human. Thick fur covered the entire body. Hands and feet that were still webbed ended in heavy claws. His muzzle was full of teeth that protruded from exposed gums as he growled at Lily from his crouched position. His eyes nearly glowed red as a low rumble echoed off of the brick walls of the alleyway. He stood slowly, never taking his eyes off of her. The limp arm of a dead woman that was draped across his shoulder, fell to the ground as he stood. Blood dripped from the corners of his mouth and he sniffed the air.

The rat draped limp across Lily's hand, its tail still swinging back and forth as she watched this creature take a step toward her.

He was crouched forward as he took another step. He was thirty feet from her when he began to run. Lily threw the rat down and turned to run. She was fast but apparently not faster than him. At the end of the alley, he caught her by the shoulder and hurled her toward the ground, head first. Lily's instincts took over. She had been thrown at full force. The impact should've killed her instantly and the assassin knew that. But as she careened toward the ground she felt her body change. The vampire completely took over. Claws, fangs and spikes broke through the surface as she put her arms out, tucked her chin to her chest, did a complete roll and bounced onto the balls of her bare feet, facing the werewolf that now froze in shock. He sniffed the air again and stared at her, confused. He could smell the human blood but he was looking at a red eyed vampire.

Lily could feel the burn in her eyes and she knew they were as red as his. Her pulse quickened and her heart pumped harder, forcing blood through her veins and driving the werewolf into a near frenzy. He could smell blood but she wasn't going to be as easy to kill as a human.

Lily just stared at the assassin, not knowing what to do. He knew that Lily was all alone and that no one was coming for her. No one would be venturing down the alley at this time of night. Eric had given Maxwell orders to desert Lily at the alley connecting 2nd and 3rd Avenue and now Maxwell was gone. A growl escaped Lily's lips and turned to a feral hiss. Then he lunged at her but she saw it coming. She dodged his attack, springing off the wall and flipping back onto her feet. He lunged again, and again he missed. He was getting irritated now. He couldn't believe he was being outsmarted by something that smelled human.

When he attacked again she wasn't as fast. Unfortunately for her, the assassin had all night and he was hell bent on having Lily for dinner. She did after all have part human blood flowing through her veins, regardless of what else she was.

The assassin grabbed her in mid-air by the shoulder and dug his claws through her human skin, through her vampire skin, then through the muscle and around the inner bone. Lily roared in pain and kicked at her attacker. He flung her against the red brick wall and grabbed her hip with his other hand. He held her back against the wall horizontally at the height of his head. He sank his teeth into her side and she screamed and kicked with everything she had. He took a bite out of her side and the pain was almost unbearable. He almost seemed to laugh as he took another bite. Then suddenly he dropped her. She was running before she hit the ground.

She was now running for her life but her life was slowly draining away. She was absolutely exhausted and loosing blood. She ran for what seemed an hour. She slowed to a walk and looked down at her baggy clothes. They were saturated with blood and the smell was so strong to her that she wanted it off of her. She remembered the bath.

She found a stream and splashed into it. She fell into the water and started to frantically wipe away the blood. She striped out of her torn and bloody clothes. Her shoulder and her side were nearly healed but she didn't have any energy left. She crawled to the bank of the stream and started to feel dizzy. The trees faded in and out and she felt the red begin to fade from her eyes. She lowered herself to the ground and closed her eyes.

She was floating through the air and something cold was against her bare skin. She felt safe and horrified at the same time. She wondered what was happening as her conscience faded again.

It was nearly 3 AM when Vincent found Lily. He had gone to check on her and found her missing. He immediately went to find Eric when he saw Onyx locked in the cage. Fortunately, Eric's plan to have Lily killed by a vampire assassin had failed. He did on the other hand, succeed in having Maxwell killed.

The entire ordeal only lasted about three minutes and while Lily was able to stay alive, But the bites from the assassin had taken way too long to heal in her growing body. She was going to have scars from that day for the rest of her life.

Lily opened her eyes to bright sunrays streaming through curtains hung over an open window on the other side of the room. The curtains swayed slightly in the breeze and she could smell fresh running water from a stream, something sweet and the faintest hint of horses. They must have been far in the distance or maybe there was an old barn nearby. She knew it was a horse because it smelled like the cave where she was born.

She was lying in a small bed and was covered up to her chin by a thin blanket. It was warm in the room and with the breeze it was quite comfortable but there was something about the smell of this place that she didn't like.

She threw back the cover with her right arm and looked down at what had been a large open wound. Now there were just light colored scars. She ran her fingers across the healed skin. Before, while in the cave, her human skin had been easily torn or scuffed on the rock walls or the floor, but it always healed quickly and completely, leaving no trace of any injury. The layer of vampire skin had been torn by the vampire assassin. Only an assassin, which was once a guardian, a guardian wolf or another vampire could penetrate this layer. Since this layer had been breached so deeply and remained unhealed for so long, a scar remained. She lifted her other arm and rotated the recently injured shoulder. Only light scars remained there, too. Four tear drop shaped scars in the front and one, slightly larger on the back where the assassin had dug his claws into her shoulder. There were two large sets of bite marks on her side. Werewolf bites.

She was startled from her thoughts as someone walked into the small room. In an instant she was crouched on the balls of her feet, claws to the floor, her eyes beginning to burn as the vampire half of her DNA took over.

The woman that walked into the room stopped suddenly and smiled at her.

"It's okay, Lily," she said in a soft, soothing voice. "I won't hurt you, I promise." She took two steps forward and sat a plate on the bed and a glass of something on the floor. "Thought you might be hungry since you were finally awake," she smiled. "You've been asleep for over sixteen hours, dear. You must be famished."

But Lily never relaxed her stance. After the week she'd had, she didn't trust anyone

"Erica?" Lily asked in a harsh voice. Her mouth and throat were bone dry.

"Vincent brought you here," she said, still smiling. "He just told me that he had some business to take care of before he took you home."

Then the smell hit her. There was blood in the cup on the floor and it smelled so good. On the plate she could smell animal blood in the rare steak.

"My name is Ashley," she said. "You need to eat something, Lily. You've been asleep for a while. You must be hungry."

As she began to relax her stance, she felt the spikes in her back retract, but the holes didn't heal quite as fast as they had in the past. She retracted her claws slowly and stepped closer to the cup.

Ashley walked over to the bed, straightened the blanket then patted it for her to come back to the bed. Lily hesitated then figured that if this human were going to hurt her, she probably would've done it by now. In Lily's brief experience, if something wanted you dead, it didn't spend much time talking and it never smiled.

Lily climbed onto the bed and Ashley handed her the glass. She drank it quickly but pushed away the plate of steak when Ashley offered. About three minutes passed and she began to feel dizzy. The room began to slowly fade.

Lily felt hands on her sides and started to swing her arms in protest. She was not going easily this time. If someone wanted to take her they were going to have to work for it.

"Ugh!" She grunted, struggling to get free.

"Shhh, Lily, it's okay. It's okay," a woman's voice purred.

Lily felt the breath against her hair as the words were spoken and could feel the cloth of a blouse in her fist and against her face.

She slowly lifted her head and opened her eyes. She was in another room. She was awake, but barely. Her body stiffened instantly and before she could even focus her tear filled eyes, her claws were out and she was swinging at whatever was near her. Then she felt strong arms wrap around her and hold tight.

"Lily, you're safe," said the voice as the arms held her.

When her eyes finally focused for a second through the tears, her face was inches away from Erica's. She looked down at her and smiled. She wiped the tears from Lily's face and wrapped her hand gently around the fist that had a grip on her shirt.

"Erica," Lily grumbled roughly and let go of the shirt.

Lily was still half asleep and could barely hold her eyes open.

"Yes, it's okay," she said and held her hand to her chest. "We're away from Eric for the time being. Vincent had some pretty harsh words for him and threatened to do physical harm if he ever did something like that again."

Onyx growled lowly and head butted Lily's leg with his head.

"Lily, you are the only person that wolf has ever liked," Erica laughed talking about Onyx.

Erica let Lily go and let her play with the wolf. Apparently he did like Lily. He kept licking her face every chance he got and Lily kept trying to stop him.

"He doesn't make it a habit of licking people's faces," Erica laughed. "But he likes you.

"Vincent went after the assassin as soon as he heard it was supposed to kill you. And then "Onyx put a bloody end to one werewolf vampire assassin. Don't you worry, Lily, you have a very solid personal force of your own. Onyx comes with his own pack if he needs one and apparently, earlier you needed one. You're going to be with Onyx and me for a while. Alexa will be meeting us in the morning in the city along with two more wolves. Lily, stay with Onyx. That will be the safest place for you until everything is finalized." Erica said, pushing Lily toward Onyx. "Don't worry, Eric rarely ventures out into the open country, he's more of a city kind of guy and stay's pretty close to the city. He won't come looking for you here."

Lily just stared at Erica, thinking about being bit by the werewolf in the alley.

She walked up to Onyx and he head butted her again, nearly knocking her down. They walked to another part of the house, where it smelled like the place she had been days ago.

"Ash-lee?" Lily asked hoarsely.

"Ashley's dealing with some husband issues," Erica answered. "She'll be back in little while."

LILY DAY THREE

L ily later found out that she had been taken to Ashley's so Vincent would have time to make room for her in Erica's house and move Eric's residence to the opposite side of the coven. Vincent was furious with Eric and had it not been for Alexa, Vincent would've done a lot more than just relocate him.

After leaving Ashley's, Erica, Sarah and Lily went shopping. Sarah was a feeder that Erica brought along in case Lily got hungry. No one knew what her feeding schedule would be, so Erica brought a feeder in case she needed blood. They loaded in the horse and buggy and headed to town. There was a lot of pointing and calling off words. Lily picked up quickly on the nouns, it was the verbs that gave her trouble, at least at first. Erica was very patient with her, though. They stopped by to see the seamstress and she took all of Lily's measurements for new dresses. Then they actually went to go look at horses. Apparently Eric wasn't lying when he told Lily that she would need a horse. Like Eric, Erica was curious as to whether or not she could ride one.

The horses had grown accustomed to pulling the buggies carrying vampires, but they still would not allow any vampires to ride on their backs. When they arrived at the stable, Erica didn't go in. Sarah and Lily went into the stables cautiously, not wanting to spook the horses in such a small enclosure. Sarah pointed to a strong bay mare. Lily walked over to her and stroked her neck. The mare lowed her head to Lily but didn't seem to mind her presence. That was a good sign.

Sarah paid the man for the horse and a saddle. Then he loaded the saddle into the buggy, tied on the horse then they headed home. Lily guessed that riding lessons would come later.

Weeks passed and it would seem like years. Lily's intelligence grew leaps and bounds very quickly. She looked like she was 20 years old and soon acted like it, too. Her education continued with Erica. She caught on quickly to grammar and mathematics but it was the sciences that fascinated her the most.

Lily started spending time with Dr. McGregor and learning about genetics and DNA. It was amazing at how much he knew just by his experiments and testing.

Hi-tech gene splicing machines, neutron cameras and hi-powered microscopes didn't exist yet. McGoo managed to create his own equipment with the materials he had and he did quite an amazing job. He taught Lily about genes and how they were passed from parent to child, how dominant genes would dominate recessive ones and how she had ended up with the crystal blue eyes. He simply made sure that all the gene choices were blue. He told her that her mother had blue eyes. She didn't ask which mother, the one from which part of her DNA was taken or the one that carried her. Maybe they both had blue eyes.

Lily always quizzed McGoo about what she was and how she really existed. The best explanation Lily had gotten was that she was genetically engineered from various vampire, werewolf and human DNA. She did find out that the human DNA was from feeder stock, who had blue eyes, and the vampire DNA was from more than one source but she couldn't get any specifics. But obviously, one of the sources was an Elder.

Erica spent countless hours with Lily. Teaching her not only about the social sciences, but she also taught her what it was to be a vampire. She told her their history and how they had survived undetected for so long. They had human allies outside the covens that helped them remain discreet. Every coven had its own people working in local law enforcement. They did a lot of covering up and shredding of files where sightings or interactions were involved.

Erica was like Lily's mother, her best friend and sister rolled into one. She made sure that Eric stayed at a distance and she was usually successful. But on more than one occasion Eric and Lily had exchanged blows. Yes, they fought, claws, teeth and all. It took years for Lily to learn to control her temper but occasionally she still had problems remaining calm when Eric was around.

Eric and Lily simply hated each other. They couldn't be in the same room without a fight breaking out and many fights resulted. On one particular occasion, Eric decided that he was tired of always being second best when it came to their scuffles. He surprised Lily early one morning and he nearly took her head off. Literally. He hid inside Lily's house, behind the door to her room and waited for her to come home. When she walked into the room he attacked. She was taken completely by surprise and he nearly sliced her in two with an ax. He went straight for the kill and aimed his swing at her neck. She saw him just in time to duck out of the way.

As she ducked she took a swipe at his legs with her claws. She cut through his trousers and clean through his legs down to the bone. The pain caused him to lose his grip on the ax and it flew across the room. That was the last major encounter before Vincent threatened to turn Eric over to the Guardians for discipline or kill him. Alexa was the only reason Eric was still alive and with the coven.

UNDERGROUND

That was over one hundred and fifty years ago and a lot had changed since then. Lily had learned a lot since then, too. She had matured into one of the coven's most trusted vampires but still, on occasion, her temper would flare. Usually something got broken when that happened and Eric was usually the direct cause. The coven had moved twice since Lily was born and both of those times were the result of Eric's murderous tendencies. He always seemed to find the worst possible crowd to run with, no matter where they moved. And since he was Alexa's son, he usually got away with murder because she wouldn't let Vincent turn him over to the Guardians for discipline.

It wasn't that Eric went out and killed at random. It was usually another vampire he killed and not a human, although, it had happened. Eric's problem was that he always chose the wrong vampire friends in each city they moved to.

Every city had what the vampires call, the Underground. It's a place where vampires that chose not to belong to a coven went to congregate. They weren't a very good place to be, not for vampires and especially not humans. It was a very cut-throat environment. In each city, there were storefronts that doubled as entrances to the Underground. Every vampire had a general knowledge of each city's coven, as there was only one coven for each city, some bigger than others, but there was always only one. Lily had been with the coven for almost eight years before Erica introduced her to the Underground and its practices. It was definitely *not* like a coven.

On Lily's first visit, she learned very quickly to never let her guard down. The worst of the species resided in the Underground. And it was literally *under ground*. Networks of tunnels and caverns ran for miles under the city, crisscrossing the sewer lines as well as gas lines and phone cables. It was a city under ground. They still lived near Nashville when Erica took Lily downtown for her first visit to the tunnels and her first encounter with the undesirables. And Erica took Lily for good reason.

Lily had been increasingly defiant at the coven and had been fighting with the other vampires. She was just bored and wanted attention but the confrontations usually led to some kind of scuffle. It wasn't the fighting with the other vampires that bothered Vincent and Alexa. It was her picking fights with the younger feeders that had begun to wear on them. The older feeders would just blow her off and that was no fun, but the younger ones, the 15 to 17 year olds would argue back and eventually it would come to blows. Lily never meant to hurt any of them, but she did hurt one pretty badly. He healed rather quickly but that wasn't the point Vincent reminded her. That was the interaction before the visit to the Underground.

Vincent had warned Lily on several occasions to cool her temper and to stop picking fights or there would be consequences. He never told her what those consequences would be, just that there would be consequences. So of course, she didn't take it very seriously. She was like a daughter to Erica and since Erica was Vincent's favorite, he had always been very lenient on Lily. And Eric too for that matter. Eric and Lily would get into vicious fights. They simply did not like each other. Since her very first day at the coven, he had wanted her gone and he's tried ever since then to make that happen. He hated that Lily was faster than him. She was stronger, too. And once they nearly killed each other trying to prove which one was the best fighter.

It was shortly after that serious fight that Eric had made himself scarce. Lily asked Erica where he had been and that's what led to the visit to the Underground in Nashville. She had no idea what was in store for her.

Erica, Onyx and Lily drove one of the coven's 1933 Chevrolet downtown, parked it in a nearby vacant lot and walked into the south end of Centennial Park. After walking about half a mile through the park and past the Parthenon, the three of them ducked into a wooded area just off the main walkway. They walked to a rock overhang, pushed some vegetation to the side and walked into a pitch black cave.

They walked for a few minutes in complete darkness until they could see a faint light coming from a crack in the wall. Erica grabbed hold of a rusted handle and pulled. A heavy metal door creaked open and they stepped through and closed the door behind them. Then they walked another ten minutes through what felt like an empty hospital. Plain white tiled hallways with lanterns placed every fifteen feet or so. There were heavy doors at varying intervals of the hallways and Lily wondered what could possibly be on the other side of so many doors. There were doorways that opened to unfinished passageways, doors to large empty rooms, even doors with more doors inside. After about fifty yards they came to an intersection. The hallway to the left was tiled for about twenty feet, then there were bare dirt and rock walls supported by wood four by four timbers. The hallways straight ahead had finished walls but the lighting was more spaced out, making it appear darker. They took the hallway to the right and after only a few yards Lily could hear commotion up ahead. When they got to where the noise was coming from, she wasn't sure if she wanted to be there.

The hallway opened up to what could only be described as a modern day shopping mall. An enclosed space that was lined with stores on each side and an open sitting area in the middle with chairs, tables and benches. The chatter silenced and there were at least two dozen vampires staring at them when they got closer to the businesses. Some of the vampires in the center area were smoking cigarettes, others drinking from whiskey bottles and two draining the last few red drops at the bottom of a shot glass. Lily could see knives and guns attached to most of the vampires that were congregated. Leather was the preferred attire. After a few moments they returned to their previous conversations and the chatter grew loud again.

Most of the storefronts were glass with displays in them. One of the shops sold leather clothing, and another sold blood. The storefront they walked toward had a sign that read 'Fights' above the door and on the glass in bold white letters it read: GUARDIAN APPROVED FIGHTS EVERY FRIDAY, SATURDAY AND SUNDAY NIGHT. GUARANTEED TO HAVE AT LEAST ONE TOP RANK FIGHT A WEEK. ALL FIGHTERS WELCOME. In smaller print it read: All fights supervised and rated. Erica led Lily into the "Fights" store and they walked into what looked like a three ring circus.

The rings stood about two feet off the floor, had four ropes on four sides and a concrete slab for a bottom. In each ring, there were fighting vampires. It was a bustle of commotion and people yelling, "Go for the chest", "Dodge to the left," and then a bell rang.

A woman in a leather skirt walked up to them and asked which one was fighting.

"She is," Erica told her.

"Fighting?" Lily mumbled as the lady stopped in front of them.

"Has she fought before?" the woman asked in a monotone, unenthusiastic voice.

"No, she's new to the fights."

"Do you want warm up matches or do you want to jump right in?" the woman asked as she turned to face Lily.

Lily looked at Erica and shrugged her shoulders and Erica only shrugged back.

"Jump right in, I guess," Lily said to the woman with a little uncertainty in her voice.

"Do you prefer a male or female opponent?" she asked as she walked toward a desk between the second and third ring.

"Male," Lily answered as she and Erica followed.

The woman picked up a thick pile of papers filled with a list of names and lots of numbers. She wrote something on a sheet of paper, tore it off and held it in front her.

"Really. Pretty sure of yourself for a first time fighter, aren't you," the woman said, handing Erica the piece of paper.

Erica only smiled and took the piece of paper.

"We don't fight wolves here, you'll have to go over to the east side if you want those fights. Too bloody for my taste. You can place bets on the fights here if you like," the woman said. "The weekday fights are less controlled than the Friday night and weekend fights, less monitored, too. So if you would like to make your debut on the day after tomorrow, you can."

"No," Erica said. "She'll start today."

There were two other wolves in the room and they seemed tiny compared to Onyx. They watched him closely as he followed Lily and Erica. The woman led them into one of the three secondary rooms. There was only one ring in this room. It was bigger than the ones outside and had a mat made of patchwork leather on the floor.

"Your first opponent will be close to your size and build," the woman said in the same monotone voice, like she has said it a thousand times before. "As you progress, *if* you progress, you will be given increasingly tougher opponents. You are only allowed three fights a day as long as you fight with this group. Other groups offer more fights, but they don't offer the supervision of *our* fights. All of our fights are supervised by a medical professional and a trainer, the referee. The medical professional is there for obvious reasons, the referee is there to make each of you better fighters and to make sure you don't kill each other. The higher the fighter is in rank, the better the weekend crowd. The bigger the weekend crowd the bigger the bets. I'm in this for the same reason every other gym and group owner is in this, to make money. Big crowds bring big money.

"The only rule is 'No killing'. No direct claw penetration to the heart area and no crushing of the sternum. If you kill your opponent, you will be sentenced to two weeks in confinement for your first offence. If you kill again, the Guardians will deal with you personally. No exceptions. Each fight is three minutes long and the best fighter wins. Simply put, the fighter that gets wounded the most, loses. Any fighter that is knocked out, also loses. In weekday fights, the trainer and referee judges the fight and therefore decides who wins. Do you have any questions?"

Lily looked over at Erica and waited. She wasn't sure what she was waiting for but there seemed to be something missing. If it were this easy for her to blow off steam and pent up energy, why did everyone wait so long to introduce her to it? Erica raised her eyebrows and gave a quick shrug. She was about to take a step back when she remembered something. She leaned over and whispered in Lily's ear.

"Don't use your spikes."

"They're going to know sooner or later," Lily whispered back. "They occasionally have a mind of their own, you know."

Then Lily nodded, removed her shoes and turned toward the ring. Her opponent was just entering the room as she stepped through the ropes. He was her height and was wearing a leather vest with black pants and no shoes. His fangs and claws were already out when he faced her in the ring. Two other men walked into the room and sat on stools against the back wall.

"Do you have a name?" the trainer asked Lily.

"Lily," she replied.

"Fight is Lily versus Tyler in three, two," the trainer announced.

A bell rang and Tyler instantly took a swipe at Lily's face. She stepped back and leaned away from the blow. Then before she could blink he was swinging again. She ducked and came up swinging. She took two swipes at his chest and made good contact with one. His leather vest then had four slashes across the front.

"And I liked this vest," Tyler said as he looked down at the torn garment.

Apparently he wasn't accustomed to being hit because he looked at his chest until it healed then he came at her again. They danced around the ring for a minute then he came at her even harder and just as before, she dodged his blows. She had landed four strikes before he finally got in a good lick. He froze when he smelled the blood on Lily's shoulder.

"Time," Tyler yelled. "Since when are fucking humans allowed to fight? I may not be a high rank fighter, but I'll be damned if I will resort to fighting humans. Lily, how did you get the claws and fangs to work?"

He looked at Lily as he tasted the blood from his claws.

"I'm not human," she said, pointing to the wound on her shoulder that was visibly healing. "I'm just as much vampire as you are."

The referee examined Lily's wounds as the slashes closed on her shoulder. He wiped away the blood and looked closer at her arm.

"They're superficial cuts, Lisa, and healed like they should," the ref said, looking toward the woman in the leather skirt.

Lisa looked at Erica and then at Lily.

"What are you?" she asked. "Part human, part vampire?"

Lily nodded. "I have a layer of human skin, and that's about the extent of the likenesses. It heals almost instantly, like your skin, there's just a slight hint of human to the blood's scent."

"Your blood does smells human," Tyler affirmed.

Lisa nodded and grinned. "The smell of human blood? That should bring quite the crowds."

"Then let's continue," said the referee as he stepped to the side.

Lily was pretty amazed that they simply took her word for it and let the fight go on.

The remaining minute and a half consisted of her ducking and dodging flying claws while landing the occasional four claws across a chest or shoulder and once across his face with all five claws. That pissed him off. He flew into her just as the bell rang. He stopped in his tracks and let his arms fall to his side.

"Dammit! I lost that one," he mumbled as he ducked through the ropes. "Next time, Lily."

"Fight goes to Lily," the ref called.

"That's all for today," Erica said.

"Aw, come on!" Lily whined. "I can do three a day, she said. We just got here."

"And now we are leaving," Erica ordered.

There was no use arguing.

As they walked through the dreary, asylum-like hallway toward the exit point, Erica explained to Lily that Eric had joined the same fighting group and that's where he had been keeping himself lately. She also told her that this particular group was one of the most respected.

"Respected?" Lily asked. "It just looks like a place for vampires to nearly kill each other."

"Yes, respected," Erica confirmed. "Their fights are supervised and all activity is monitored by the Guardians."

"Oh," Lily replied.

The Guardians were the overseers of the vampires. Like law enforcement for humans, vampires had their own laws to follow, their own code of conduct. Vampires and their activities were monitored by both human law enforcement agencies and by more closely by the Guardians. Yes, the existence of vampires was known by the government. The departments were paid very large sums of money to keep it quiet. There were also vampires in every branch of the government. They made sure that the existence of vampires was kept quiet. Those who knew about them and helped them remain discrete were paid very well to keep it to themselves.

The coven in each city had at least three human law enforcement officers as feeders. They were responsible for covering up sightings or rumors of the vampire's existence. But the Underground was rarely monitored by local law enforcement. It just wasn't a place that humans wanted to be or should have been, for that matter. It seemed bright and organized but it wasn't a nice place. But apparently Erica seemed to think it was a good place for Lily to vent some pent up energy.

For the first few weeks, Lily was accompanied by Erica on her visits to the Underground and she learned how to get into and out of the tunnels without detection. There were multiple places to enter and exit the tunnels and Erica taught Lily all of them.

Lily moved up the ranks quickly and soon became a favorite among the betting crowd.

HISTORY TO PRESENT

There had been a whole lot of changes with the Underground and with the world in the one hundred and sixty years since Lily was born. There have been two world wars. The Race Wars of 2022 and what everyone now refers to as the God Wars that began in 2030 and lasted nearly ten years.

The Race Wars were probably the most ludicrous thing humans have done since Hitler thought he could create the perfect race. The thought of a superior race is as ludicrous as trying to improve the horse. You simply cannot improve perfection. There is, after all, no such thing as race. All humans are the same. The color of their skin does not make them different. They all have the same DNA, the same number of chromosomes, and at one time, had the exact same defects as the next. It made no more sense than killing someone because they had small ears or long fingers. Vampires tried to sit back and let the humans figure it out themselves, but after four years of pointless killing, the vampires finally had to intervene. It wasn't that their food source was being killed, they had their own supply of humans, it was that it just got so out of hand. Native Americans and Aborigines believed they were the truest human and the African population believed they were the oldest and truest humans. Then the Caucasian population had to get their two cents into the pot and before you knew it, the world had gone completely crazy. But the planet probably benefitted by the decrease in the population.

And then just four years after the Race Wars, the God Wars began as an argument between two groups at a Unison Rally. Then, over the next two years it grew out of proportion as more and more wanted to voice their opinions. This was another pointless war that humans created because they thought one idea was better than the other. For the most part it was a war against the Christians and the non-Christians. It got really ugly, really quickly. It spread like wildfire through the United States then Great Britain, the Middle East and eventually consumed every continent and corner on the planet. The first cities destroyed were Tokyo, Jakarta, Mumbai, New York, Los Angeles, Delhi and Cairo. But it wasn't like wars of the past. This was a bioweapon war. Sometimes the attacks were obvious right away but in most cases no one would even know that there was an attack until hours or even days later. The world as a whole had gotten smarter and biology and genetics were two subjects the war leaders focused on. Everything needed to engineer a weapon could be bought on the extranet. Everything from a non-lethal strain of the latest flu virus to a living sample of the pneumonic plague or even Ebola, although pricy, could be ordered and shipped to anywhere in the world in only a day. Scientist and genetic engineers created deadly strains of everything, e coli, staph, even common bread mold was engineered to attack human lungs. At first, the war was quiet, no bombs, no F-22's whizzing by overhead, no citizens walking the streets with rocket launchers. If you were outside, no one would've known the dangers had it not been for the overcrowded hospitals and headlines on the news every day. In one day, the water supplies for 35 major cities were hit with an artificially engineered virus designed to kill only humans. It was well coordinated but not well thought through. Everyone in the city who drank tap water was infected. That's a lot of people. That's when the war became indiscriminate. It soon turned out to be the scariest and most deadly war the world has ever seen.

For the first 5 years, the Atheists, the Jains and the Jews took cover and let the others fight it out. But when the water supplies were tainted, the killing became indiscriminant. And anyone that was in range, regardless of religious beliefs, were attacked. Everyone that was trying to stay out of it, started fighting back and making their own weapons. That is when the war turned into 'who has the best bioweapons' and 'where are the biggest crowds of people'. Hence, more major cities were all but wiped out. Public activities ceased. Anyone not already affected by the weapons stayed inside but life on the outside continued only with far less crowds. People still worked in spite of the threats, but the majority worked from home. Security for manufacturing and shipping facilities used genetically engineered dogs who could detect even the tiniest amount of contaminated matter. Equipment that monitored brain waves and body language were used to detect persons that just acted suspicious. They didn't catch everything, but they came close. Commerce continued throughout the world but the economy suffered drastically.

After 15 years of constant, pointless killing, the vampires finally got involved. The vampires were like the most bad-ass special ops unit the world had ever seen, or never seen, for that matter. They went in at night and completely wiped out the engineering labs that harbored the bioweapons and the people that created them. It took two years to get the point across. And the point was, "If you kill, you will be killed". Finally the war ended quietly and what emerged was a better planet.

At least in a sense, it did help the planet by decreasing the world population by more than 60%. But that is a whole hell of a lot of bodies. The planet reeked of decay for a decade after the killing stopped but all that decay left behind a very fertile planet. Since only humans were killed, everything else thrived. Plants grew twice as fast and were more resilient. More plants meant that the amount of oxygen in the air increased which also meant that the carbon dioxide levels needed to increase to sustain the abundance of plants. Animals grew larger and bred more rapidly. The increase in both plants and animals lead to more food and the world, for perhaps the first time, was never hungry. Humans still consumed meat but slaughter houses and the meat packing industry had changed so dramatically that it was now considered cruel *not* to kill animals. The natural reproduction rate was so high and there were so few natural predators, that animal populations had to be kept in check. Farms and ranches no longer killed animals at the prime of their lives. All animals were now free range and allowed to live their lives without very much human involvement. They were looked after and treated for any illnesses or injuries, but the natural order of the animals were left to its own devices. The older animals were painlessly euthanized then the meat was processed by machines. And there was no shortage of older animals either. Just like a natural predator, the old, weak or badly injured animals were killed for food while the strong, young animals were left to breed.

The humans on the planet also changed. The Earth's atmosphere thinned, offering less protection from the sun. In a very short period of time, human skin became darker, less easy to burn in the stronger UV rays. Light skin and blond hair were a lot rarer. There were still blue, green or hazel eyes, thanks to the Aborigines, and when light eyes were combined with the dark hair and dark skin, it makes for some really beautiful people. Lily's skin was naturally far from tan but she still had the pale blue eyes and although born blonde, had jet black hair. Although she would doubt *beautiful* would be the description Vincent would've given of her when he was chasing the newborn Lily through the forest so long ago.

People still wore cotton clothes although they were a lot more expensive than synthetic material. The plant that produced the cotton was engineered to grow continuously, instead of having to be planted and harvested every season. They grew into trees like in an orchard and bloomed yearly. Machines tended the fields, cared for the trees and did all of the production. Clothes hadn't changed very much. Although, the materials they were made out of went through different stages throughout the years. But the old favorites were still jeans and a tee shirts or sweats and a hoodie.

Cars drove themselves and auto accidents were extremely rare. Public transportation was fast and inexpensive. Single railed trains that ran on solar power, called Monos, crisscrossed over and between every major city. They were built on elevated platforms, thirty feet off of the ground. They reached speeds of over two hundred miles an hour when traveling long distances between cities. A Mono could be ridden from New York to Los Angeles or Miami to Seattle in a day.

The humans also managed to find a cure for cancer. Well, not really a cure, but a complete elimination of the disease. Scientists had found the gene that was a precursor to developing cancer. 100% of all cancer patients had the gene, but only 90% of humans with the gene developed cancerous tissues. So it stood to reason that there had to be another gene that turned off the cancer gene. It took 20 years to find it, but humans did indeed find the gene that turned it off. The only problem was, when the 'off' gene was introduced into DNA that didn't have the cancer gene, the 'off' gene would cause problems with the normal growth of the developing fetus. So after finally figuring out the 'off' gene was related to normal human growth, they still couldn't figure out why there were no growth issues in DNA that had the 'off' gene and the cancer gene. So after years of trying to find a happy medium, the humans finally got smart and just added the off gene *and* the cancer gene to the DNA. It worked. Today, only one person in approximately every two million will develop cancer. And that's due to some other DNA defect that had nothing to do with the cancer gene or the 'off' gene.

The United States bared very little resemblance to what it had been a century ago. All the rules had changed. Thanks to the God Wars, public school buildings were eliminated and children attended classes at home via the extranet. Extra, as in extraordinary net. What was once known as the internet, a web of supercomputers that linked millions of computers together via hard wired connections, was replaced with massive structures constructed to send free wireless communications out to the world. There was an extranet hub for every one thousand square miles. Not a whole lot if you stop to think about it. Everyone, no matter their income, had instant access to endless information.

Hackers and computer viruses were stopped in their tracks by bio-passwords. At birth, your DNA code was recorded, then your fingerprints and a retinal scan were taken and added to the DNA code database. This became your bio-password. There was no longer a need to have to remember fifty different passwords for fifty different accounts. Computers came with retinal and handprint scanners and DNA analyzers. *You* were now your password and in order to use any computer, you first had to be positively identified. This eliminated hackers completely. Since every program, code or data of any kind that was created was bio-marked, nothing could be done anonymously. Nothing could be faked because the creators DNA was programmed into anything and everything they did. Cyber-bullying also ceased to exist. Turns out, people aren't so tough when everything they say can be linked directly back to them.

And if someone still managed to drug or kill someone else for their password, there were no longer prisons, only holding facilities for euthanasia. Crime was no longer tolerated. One strike and you were out. But one of the best things that the US did was to eliminate the need for private and personal injury attorneys. The courts consisted of a trial before a six party peer review. Part of every child's education, was an early understanding of the law. In the lower grades, K through six, children were taught the laws, why they existed and how to protect themselves against others. In the upper grades, seven through twelve, the court process and sentencing processes were studied. Then, since every student was required to have a bachelor's degree before their graduation, grades thirteen through sixteen taught not only practicing the law but in order to graduate, every child had to score a passing grade on the state bar exam.

Education was one of the main focuses for children in most countries, especially the United States. Since every home was granted free communication and had access to any and all digital records, information could be accessed instantly. Since everyone had the extranet and the government issued readers, to everyone, regardless of income, school was no longer out of reach for any child in the US. And soon other countries followed. Readers were once known as a personal computer or tablet. A device on which to exchange information through the extranet.

Schooling became a critical part of a child's life all over the world. Knowledge was power and every nation wanted to be powerful. Although every child learned at their own pace, they were introduced to medicine, mental health, and phycology around grade five and higher math, chemistry and physics began in their seventh year. Biology was taught as soon as the third grade and other languages began in first.

And then there were the "Elites". Gifted children that had begun their studies of the upper subjects early and exceled. Some graduating with the bar as early as age twelve. These children were put into yearly international competitions, not unlike a mental Olympics, were children of each age group competed for the gold, silver or bronze medal for their country in every subject.

Poor parenting was no longer an excuse for unruly children, and unless there were serious disabilities involved, even a child convicted of a crime was represented by themselves or a parent in court. If children were convicted of a crime, they were given a second chance but the parents were charged a fine and in extreme cases, were sentenced to public service. If the child was convicted of a second crime, the parents were once again fined and had to contribute to the community for a set number of hours, depending on the crime. The child was also given community service and also put under house arrest and forbidden from using the extranet except for education. The punishment was brutal as their readers were taken away. Without the extranet, they couldn't communicate with friends or entertain themselves in the usual way. Children who were sentenced were forced to do activities by themselves.

Corporations still had lawyers, but they had a lot less power than before and were unable to initiate a claim on anyone's behalf. They could only defend against anyone who filed charges against the company or a person within the company.

Technology soared. Computers and robots not only manufactured nearly everything, from clothes to light bulbs, they also cleaned houses and even walked the dog. They built cars as well as washed them. They were babysitters and companions, even musicians and house builders.

After the war, nano-technology had cured almost all of the known diseases. Tiny robots that would be injected into the bloodstream were programmed to kill and dispose of everything from athlete's foot to the Zika virus. The diseases were still around but were losing ground every day. Soon, the human race would be free of every known contaminant. Except of course for the common cold. People still got sick on occasion but the duration was only a day or two, much shorter than the one miserable week it used to take to fight it.

There was a global bird flu pandemic that began in the US, known as H12N9, in 2035. It was thought to have originated in a shipment of rare birds shipped from a newly discovered island in the South Pacific. The virus jumped species and mutated rapidly in the new human hosts. Twelve hundred people died from the disease before scientists were able to program, reproduce and distribute enough antivirus and nanovirus to the world. The antivirus was to prevent infection and the nanovirus was to attack and kill the virus once it had been contracted. Not bad, considering that in the end, nearly one quarter of all humans contracted the virus before it was finally stopped nearly two years after the first reported case.

In the past century, privacy was also, for the most part, a thing of the past. The extranet and its cameras recorded everything that was not contained within a private residence. All public places were recorded twenty four hours a day, seven days a week and since information storage was virtually limitless, everything was kept on record. A terabyte of information could be stored on a chip no larger than a period on a screen. And because of this, anything ever recorded could be saved and then viewed by anyone who knew the time and the coordinates. The government said that they would start deleting records after 100 years, but they won't. Someone will argue that it's all part of the historical record and keep it all.

THE BIRTH OF LASHAY

Two men in white coats stood in the middle of a large laboratory. One stared into a microscope and the other stared at a large monitor displaying what was being done. On the monitor, a needle pierced the outer membrane of a clear bubble.

"So that's it?" Martin asked.

Martin Black was a billionaire. He owned dozens of television stations in the US, Canada and Britain. He had his hand in a little bit of everything and today at his lab, he wanted to be a dad.

"Not exactly," answered the other man.

"So now what?" Martin questioned.

"Now, we do this another half dozen times to make sure that one begins to divide."

"Then what?"

"Then we wait."

Martin Black did not like waiting. He was there with one purpose. To make a child. He had wanted a baby ever since he was with his late wife. She had been killed in a tragic helicopter accident. She was twelve weeks pregnant when she died. Martin didn't take the loss well and vowed never to love another woman, So, over the next eight years, he acquired laboratory facilities that specialized in genetics and DNA splicing. If he couldn't have a child the old fashion way, he'd just make one for himself. He didn't care about the legalities or ethics. He wanted a child and he'd do anything to get one. But he wanted one that was his, so he couldn't just have someone go steal him one. He wanted a daughter that was part of him and part of his wife.

"How long before you'll need the surrogate?" Martin asked.

"It will take a week to know whether or not these took," Tom, the other man in the lab coat answered. "Then another two weeks to know if they can be transplanted into a womb."

Martin sighed.

"So three weeks," he said.

"Give or take," Tom said.

Martin walked out of the lab, dropped his lab coat on the floor outside the door and walked to the elevator. He pulled his cell phone from his shirt pocket and pressed a few buttons.

"Mr. Black," answered the man on the other end.

"You have three weeks to find a surrogate," Martin informed him then hung up.

It had been two and a half weeks when Martin returned to the lab. With him was a young woman around twenty years old. She had dark hair and dark eyes. She looked around the lab and then to Martin.

"I thought this was a testing facility?" she asked.

"It is," Martin answered.

After about three minutes Tom entered with a clipboard in his hands. He handed the clipboard to the young woman and said, "Sign it."

"What is it?" she asked.

"Release forms stating that you will carry an embryo to term, which is about nine months, give or take, with no legal recourse for adoption or custody," Tom answered.

"OK," she said. "That's what we agreed to."

Tom handed her a pen and she signed the forms. Martin smiled. Two other men in coats came and escorted the girl through the lab and out the back door.

"So the embryo is viable?" Martin asked.

"Yes sir," Tom asserted.

"So it will be implanted into the girl and then in nine months my child will be born?"

"Yes sir,' Tom said again.

Martin left. Tom didn't tell him that two of the embryos had become viable. He had put the second in cold storage just in case something went wrong with the first one but he never told Martin.

The surrogate's name was Andrea and she was a homeless runaway that had been found in a shelter. Martin wanted someone that would not be missed. He had no intention of letting the girl walk away from this pregnancy. Martin had already arranged for the surrogate to be in an "accident" once she had given birth and left the lab. He wanted no one to interfere with his child. And although Andrea had agreed to let the child go with no strings, Martin wasn't chancing her coming back later and trying to get some sort of custody. The courts felt that biology was stronger than contracts and would often overturn the signed documents in favor of the biological parent, which technically, the surrogate would be, since Martin couldn't exactly say the baby was his since it was created illegally. If the courts were to take DNA from the child and compare it to Andrea and Martin, it wouldn't have any markers from the mother. That would prove that the baby was not a naturally conceived, which was against the law. Martin will make sure that that would never happen.

Martin visited the lab every other day to see his daughter. The 3D ultrasound showed a phenomenal picture of the child in Andrea's womb. He loved seeing his little girl curled up and peaceful. On more than one occasion he didn't even speak to Andrea, just took the ultrasound print and left. He was cold toward her to say the least. But she couldn't complain. She was getting one and a half million dollars to carry the child within the confines of the laboratory.

Seven and a half months in, Andrea had pushed the emergency button. Tom rushed to her room and there was blood all over the bed and was dripping onto the floor.

"Something's wrong!" She yelled.

"Oh my God," Tom panicked and ran out.

He returned about five minutes later with an obstetrician. She squirted gel on the bulge in Andrea's belly. She slid the ultrasound around and let out an audible sigh. She examined the girl and looked over to Tom.

"You had better call Mr. Black," she said.

"What's wrong?" Andrea and Tom asked at the same time.

"She has a placenta abruption. Which means that the baby is coming. Now."

"I have a what? Andrea asked.

"There is a serious complication with the pregnancy and the baby needs to come out before you both bleed to death," the doctor answered.

Tom ran out of the room to call Martin.

"You need an emergency C-section, right now," the doctor told Andrea.

The doctor fumbled through drawers and cabinets and collected the necessary equipment. She made a phone call from her cell to have neonatal ready and waiting. The baby was coming now and she was only at thirty weeks. She was going to need very special care for at least a month or so.

Andrea continued to hemorrhage. More blood ran from the bed onto the floor and Andrea was beginning to feel light headed.

Martin arrived at the lab and didn't even close the car door when he got out. He ran to the elevators and swiped his hand across the reader. The door to his personal elevator opened immediately. He pressed the seventeen repeatedly as the doors closed. He ran through the lab and to the room where Andrea was staying. The doctor had just made the cut across Andrea's lower abdomen. Blood poured out as she reached into the opening and felt around. She wrapped both hands around the baby and pulled. More blood flooded the floor and the doctor. Andrea screamed in pain and grabbed at the nearest person. It was Tom. She gripped his hand so hard he called out and jerked his hand away. Only a few seconds later she passed out.

"What's wrong with her?" Martin yelled. "She's not moving."

The baby's lips were blue and no sounds came from the tiny blood covered form. The doctor clamped the cord then cut it as fast as she could. She placed the baby on the neonatal cart that a nurse just rolled into the room from the Neonatal Intensive Care Unit two floors up. The nurse began to wipe the baby off as the doctor suctioned the baby's nose and mouth. The doctor started CPR with two fingers on the tiny baby's chest. The nurse placed an oxygen mask over the face.

Martin was pushing against the nurse to see the infant.

"What's wrong?" He asked frantically.

"She's in distress," the doctor answered calmly.

"What the hell happened?" Martin yelled. "There weren't supposed to be any complications. The girl was examined and was in perfect health."

"Sometimes it doesn't matter. Things happen Mr. Black. We can't predict everything."

Martin's eyes welled with tears as he saw the tiny figure move its arms and legs. It let out a tiny whimper and then began to cry. The doctor took a deep breath and looked at Martin.

"You sir, have a beautiful baby girl. She's going to need round the clock care and feeding for the next month or so. But she appears to be strong and healthy."

"Can I hold her?" Martin asked the doctor.

"Not for a couple of weeks, I'm afraid," she said. "She's going to be hooked up to machines and a feeding tube for a little while. But you can touch her and be with her, and I suggest you do. It's important to the bonding process. And since you're her only parent..."

Martin nodded and looked down at his little girl. He put his finger on her tiny hand and began to tear up. He wiped the tears and hoped no one was watching.

"What are you going to name her?" The doctor asked.

He smiled.

"LaShay Michelle Black," he said proudly. "After my wife."

Martin stayed at the lab facility and never left. He slept, ate and showered there. He even made the NICU bring a bed into the unit for him to sleep next to LaShay. After six days, when the IV was taken out of the umbilical cord, Martin finally was able to hold his daughter. The nurse asked him take off his shirt.

"What for?" He asked.

"Skin to skin contact helps with the bonding process. It was proven many decades ago and we suggest all parents do it frequently with newborns."

Martin shrugged, unbuttoned his white log sleeve shirt then took it off. Then the white shirt that was under it. He was in good shape. No one had ever seen Mr. Black without a shirt and the nurse stared until Martin gave her a look.

"Sorry," she mumbled and looked away.

The nurse had Martin sit on the bed and raise the bed to a sitting position. Then she handed him his baby girl for the first time. Shay cooed and wiggled in his arms. Tears fell down his cheeks and this time he didn't care if anyone saw him.

Martin had been at the laboratory since the day Shay was born. He hadn't had time to finish the nursery in his thirty thousand square foot estate. So he made some phone calls and had someone else finish it. He gave them every detail. He never does work himself, but the nursery was special to him and he wanted to be the one to paint the walls pink and hang fairies and unicorns on the walls. But since the day Shay was born he had been with her.

Everyone in the lab was astonished. They didn't think Martin had a kind bone in his body but he proved them wrong when it came to Shay. She was everything to him. She was created just for him, after all.

He had spent billions of dollars for the labs and the research and everything he needed to create a child. When is wife died carrying their baby he swore that he would still have that child. Maybe not *that* child but a child from him and his late wife. Eggs had been harvested from his wife when they were in the fertilization stages. She had had trouble getting pregnant the natural way so they went to a fertility clinic for help. They ended up getting pregnant without the help of the facility but they kept the eggs in cold storage just in case.

LaShay was the end result of a man's determination to defy the law. The laws were very strict about creating human life. It had begun with stem cell research. The need for more stem cells led laboratories to create their own. They were creating fetuses just to harvest the umbilical cord. When the pro-lifers realized this, the fight was on. Eventually the government deemed it unconstitutional for anyone to create human life from a tube. Except fertilization clinics. So Martin bought a fertilization clinic. He had worked with Tom for years to create the perfect child. DNA splices of only the best of genes were put into making Shay.

Tom had a doctorate in Biology and Chemistry. He used his knowledge to create a front for the government that hid what he and Martin were really doing. DNA testing and gene splicing had become his specialty. He used the best DNA he could find to splice into Martin's. Hazel eyes and Elite intelligence was only the beginning. He perfected Shay's DNA down to the smallest detail. Tom had found a blood sample from a dying man that was near perfect. There were no diseases; no Alzheimer's, no dementia, no cancers of any kind, not even a gene that made her eyesight deteriorate over time. She was going to be perfect. He had failed to examine the blood under an electron microscope where he would've seen the virus.

Little did Tom know that the perfect blood he had found was from a man that had begun the change into a vampire. A lesser vampire had tried to change a man into a vampire. The man, only known as John Doe, had learned about vampires and he wanted more than anything to be one. So after searching for years he had found the Underground. He convinced a vampire that he was strong enough to make the change. So they began the process in a hotel room. Two days in, he was found, near dead by the hotel staff. He was taken to the hospital and there he died the next day. But not before, Tom, who was an intern there at the time, had taken blood. Tom had tested the blood himself and realized it was like no other blood that he had ever seen. He kept the blood in cold storage until the day he may have needed it. When Martin Black came to him about creating a perfect human, he thought of the perfect blood he had found. He wasn't aware that freezing the sample, killed the vampire virus. But left everything else.

Martin raised LaShay by himself. He rarely even had anyone babysit her. He was with her day and night, nearly her entire life. He helped her with her school work and made sure that she had the best education. He would have teachers and tutors come in and teach LaShay things that didn't come with the extranet curriculum. Things from art history to gene splicing. He joined her for martial arts training and they would spar together, that is until LaShay got too good to challenge her dad. She was taught to draw and paint and she loved it. It was all done on computers and she learned very quickly. She took a special liking to her father's television stations and the broadcast graphics. So Martin brought in the top designer at the local station and had her train LaShay personally.

When Shay was old enough she went to work for her father. They remained close until Shay started dating a guy named Todd. He was the first guy that she felt serious about. She had dated a few others but she didn't feel a real connection to them. Even the guy that her father introduced her to. He wasn't happy about it, but he never pressured her to date anyone she didn't want to. Until she brought Todd home one night. He had long hair, a scruffy five o'clock shadow and wore clothes that looked twenty years old.

"Is he a bum?" Her father asked her.

"No! He works in the mail room at NY26. You're TV station," she gleamed.

Martin made a mental note to update the hiring policy in the mail room.

Luckily for Martin, Todd turned out to be a two timing ass hole and Shay dumped him after three months, but not before she had moved out of her father's estate and into her own apartment. He knew that it was inevitable so he let his baby girl go out on her own. He had a body guard follow her for the first year. She hated it and it took that long for her to talk her father into getting rid of the twenty four hour surveillance.

She moved into a nice one bedroom apartment on West 70th street. It was across from a nursing home so she was glad she wouldn't have to worry about rowdy neighbors.

She dated various men and most were approved by her father. She dated one guy for about five years before they just grew apart. Nick was a great guy. He was a fellow designer at NY26 and his office was just down the hall from Shay's. They had gotten pretty serious early on. They talked about marriage and having children and moving outside the city. They could talk about anything and they often did. They were like best friends with benefits. The sex was great and frequent but Shay still felt there was something missing. They stayed together for eight months after he proposed.

After three months, Shay had a nice long talk with her father about marriage. She wanted to know what her mother was like and how he knew he wanted to spend the rest of his life with her.

"How did you know, Dad?"

"I just knew," he said. "I knew because I felt like I would die if I didn't marry her. I couldn't picture her not being in my life. It's like a part of me died when I wasn't with her."

He had told Shay since she was old enough to understand that her mother had died during childbirth. He wasn't referring to Andrea, the surrogate, but the wife that was killed in the helicopter crash. He never told LaShay that she was created in a lab. He told her that her mother was his late wife and that it was her that died delivering Shay.

Martin had told the story so many times it was almost like telling the truth. He never told Shay that he had just let her biological mother die. He didn't have her killed, he just denied her any further care after Shay was born and she hemorrhaged to death. Her death was considered a tragedy and no one bothered to look into it any further.

"So you just knew?" Shay asked.

"Yes. It's like that was the only option for me. I loved her so much."

"So what if I don't feel that way?" She asked.

"Then don't marry him," her father said flatly.

Nick and Shay's relationship fizzled out shortly after that conversation. There were no hard feelings or broken hearts involved, at least Shay didn't think there was.

About eight years later she met Josh. He was a corporate lawyer for her father's many businesses. He handled things like people trying to sue for whatever reason. From falling in the parking lot to wrongful termination. She really liked him.

He was funny and kind and was a perfect gentleman. Her father was ecstatic when Shay brought him to dinner at his estate one Saturday night. He knew Josh in passing and was proud that his daughter had finally made a good choice in the man she was dating. Josh was a little older than Shay, about twelve years, but her father didn't seem to care.

HYBRID

Lily was a vampire like no one had ever seen before or since. She was part human, part vampire and a small part of her DNA was from a wolf. She had jet black hair, crystal blue eyes, stood five foot six and weighed all of one hundred and twenty pounds. She had a thin layer of human skin over her vampire skin, but like any other vampire, she had a reaction to the sun. She had to cover up or wear sunblock like any other vampire if she went outside. Without it, the outer layers of skin would slowly tan like any human's but the burn accelerated very rapidly after only a short time. McGoo and Lily figured that she could last probably twenty minutes in direct sunlight without protection, but she never wanted to test that theory. If she had sunblock on, she could almost guarantee to be burn free as long as she didn't miss any spots. She had learned to cover every inch of her skin every single time when Robert, Mary's oldest son, began to train her to hunt. Since she could eat meat, wild stock like deer, salmon, rabbit or squirrel could be killed and she could sustain herself if the need ever arose. Robert, with the help of Onyx taught her to hunt in the wild. Onyx lived on meat alone and they would share the kills they made. Erica also thought it wasn't a bad idea to teach Lily how to hunt for her own meat. Erica was more like a mother to Lily than anything else and of course she would be all for something that would give Lily any sort of advantage. Say, if all of the feeders decided to protest against the vampires. What would the vampires feed on? Lily wouldn't have that problem since she could hunt, at least that's the way Erica saw it.

Onyx would go along with Robert and Lily and would help chase prey back in their direction if they missed the kill. He would also go to hunt for his own food. They usually had an uneventful day in the woods, hunting various prey but the day that Lily chased the wild boar had to have been the day that she got her hunting stripes. It was a big boar, two hundred and forty five pounds with four inch tusks. Yeah, he was big and thought he was making her his dinner. Robert made the first shot with an arrow and glazed the shoulder of the pig so it would start chasing one of them. Since Lily closer, the boar thought she was just great for the taking. She wasn't. After chasing her just under a half a mile she decided that it was time to stop and fight. She was half the boar's weight but she thought could take this dumb animal. She wasn't spending all day wearing him down just to let Robert put an arrow in the worn out pig's head. If she was going to hunt for her food, she was going to need to do it efficiently. Onyx was always her backup plan, because even if she just barely missed dinner, Onyx was right behind her setting up another chance.

Onyx and Lily just knew where the other had to be in order to make a kill. Sometimes she missed an obvious takedown but rarely did Onyx miss. They preferred to hunt deer but the day they killed the boar was one she'll never forget because the thing actually got a piece of her. She was attacking him from the side when he whipped his head around and his long snout and protruding canines caught Lily in the thigh and threw her to the ground. Onyx didn't wait for her to recover. He was on the boar and had broken its neck before she had barely even hit the ground. At the time she was pissed because Onyx didn't let her fight, but he was only doing what he was supposed to do. Protect her from danger and apparently really pissed off wild boars was on the top of the list. She did get a chance to fight one of equal size and nearly the same ferocity only a few weeks later. That time, she's the one that broke its neck.

Erica did a very good job of raising Lily. Although Lily looked like a child for only a short amount of time, Erica made sure that she had time to be a kid, time to make mistakes to learn from them. Like any child in the coven, she was given a formal education. Reading, writing and arithmetic was only the short list. Biology and chemistry where also part of program and computer sciences came later. She caught on quickly and excelled in every subject. Erica taught her at the coven since Lily was unable to attend school. Lily looked eighteen when she was only nine and that would not have gone over very well in the classroom in the 1930's. Erica also made sure that Lily could do other things, like sew, mend clothes, ride a horse, and cook. Erica taught her everything a mother would teach her child.

She also protected her from Eric during this time. Since Erica was the daughter of the leader, she and Lily both got away with more than most. Skipped curfews, missed work days and forgotten task assignments were all too often overlooked.

Eric and Lily were always fighting and one day, when they were living in the Atlanta coven in '95, he got the upper hand. It was Lily's week to help with trash collection for the coven, which she absolutely loathed. She was trudging along, picking up a bag or two at a time, carrying them to the four wheeler they used and then took them to the dumpster on the outskirts of the coven. At least they had four wheelers. It beat the hell out of the horse and cart that they had started with so many decades earlier. But Eric was waiting for her, hiding in the brush just beyond the edge of the coven's property. While Lily was unloading the trash bags into the dumpster she felt a sharp pain and a burning on her cheek. Almost instantly she literally saw fire. Eric had shot a burning arrow at her and had hit her in the face. Without thinking, she ripped the arrow from her cheek and went after Eric. It was a bloody fight, all claws and fangs ripping at each other at almost blinding speed. Lily finally had him pinned, with his face to the dirt under her claws when Vincent pried Lily off of him.

He thought he had won and even though he was punished to the highest degree, he was smug. In addition to taking all of Lily's task assignments for the next six months, he was forbidden from leaving the coven for the same time period. That really pissed him off. Still, when he wasn't tormenting Lily or Erica, he was often away from the coven, wreaking havoc in other places where Vincent wouldn't catch him.

The main place he would go was the Underground. He had a high rank among the fighters in the most prestigious fight club and most everyone knew him down there. The Atlanta Underground was very similar to the Nashville one. Atlanta's was much bigger and housed a thousand more vampires but the rules were the same. Homeless or traveling vampires stayed in the Underground tunnels to conceal their identity from the rest of the world. The occasional human police officer would sometimes venture into the tunnels chasing someone. They didn't often make it to the congregation areas, but when they did it wasn't a good thing. Other human officers that were aware of the tunnels and the vampires that lived there would take over the case if one where to arise from the tunnels. It would soon be swept under the rug and forgotten.

On one particular day, Eric had just finished a fight when Lily and Onyx walked in. Lily fought there occasionally but she and Eric never fought each other. Vincent made sure of that. The odds of them killing each other was too great. But the bets for their fight alone would bring in enough revenue to run the place for months. Ellen, the woman that ran the place, named affectionately, Ellen's, often poked and prodded Eric to fight Lily. He was all for it, of course. But Vincent was a strong motivator and Ellen didn't want to cross him.

Lily went to Ellen and she walked back to the where the fighting rings were. Onyx stood in the doorway and waited. There were only two rings in this fight club and between them was a small table with a computer on it. Ellen tapped a few keys and a list of names came up. The computer was new and Ellen was having trouble getting the "ranks" board to open. Even vampires have to learn new technology, and Ellen hated it. She jabbed at the keyboard and finally the screen changed.

"What was wrong with the paper lists? Hard copies can't get glitches," she complained.

"You'll get used to it, Ellen," said a man from the back of the room.

"Pft!" Ellen spat.

Lily looked at the floor and tried not to laugh.

"OK Lily," Ellen finally said. "You're fighting Taylor today."

"Yeeeessss!" Taylor shouted from beside ring one. "Been waiting for this day."

"This will be a ranks fight, the winner will increase in rank, but only if it's a fair fight," Ellen announced.

Lily climbed into the ring with Taylor. Eric sat down against the wall beside Onyx and watched. He wished it was him in the ring with Lily. Onyx sat down beside him and waited.

A referee climbed into the ring and soon a buzzer sounded. Taylor didn't wait around. He came at Lily with teeth and claws bared. He jumped at her and came down swinging. Lily ducked and slid sideways. She took a swipe at Taylor's leg but barely made contact. He was on his feet and jumping backwards before Lily could swing again. Taylor turned around and came back with a roundhouse to Lily's cheek. She went down but was back up in an instant. She took a swing with her left then her right and made contact. Taylor went flying backwards into the ropes. He rushed Lily and tackled her at the waist. She landed on her back hard then kicked her opponent off. She was on her feet before he was. She swung with all five claws and made solid contact across Taylor's face. Blood sprayed across the wall closest to the ring. He shook his head and staggered backward.

The referee held up his arm and went to Taylor. His face lay open with five deep gashes. The ref examined the wounds. When they were nearly healed, Taylor was coming back at Lily as soon as the referee dropped his arm. Lily ducked, turned then landed a hard kick to Taylor's chest. He gasped for air and stepped back three steps. He made an angry face at Lily as he grabbed his chest. After about 15 seconds, and he had caught his breath, he lowered his head and came running at Lily. Lily simply stepped aside and pushed him away using his own momentum. He bounced off the ropes and came at her again. This time Lily swung at his head and it was lights out. Taylor went down, face first.

The referee raised his arm again and the buzzer went off.

"Fight goes to Lily," the ref said.

After a few seconds, Taylor came to. He sat up and looked at Lily.

"Hell of a right hook," Taylor said rubbing his jaw.

Lily walked over to Taylor and put her hand out. Taylor shook it and then Lily helped him to his feet.

"Next time," she said to him.

"Yeah," he sighed.

"Do you want to fight again," Ellen asked the both of them.

"Yes," Taylor answered.

"Not today," said Lily.

Lily walked to the door and Eric was standing in it. She stopped in front of him and waited for him to move. After a few seconds, Onyx growled.

"Shut up," Eric snapped.

"Move Eric," Lily replied.

"Or what?" Eric smirked.

Lily shifted her weight and crossed her arms. Onyx stood up and walked over to stand beside Lily. Lily just tilted her head and stared at Eric. Finally, Ellen walked over to the door to leave and Eric moved. Lily stepped through the door and Eric punched her in the arm. Without any warning, Lily took a swipe at Eric's face and made contact with three claws. Onyx jumped on Eric and knocked him down before he had a chance to hit Lily again.

"Break it up!" Ellen yelled as she ran over to them. "Eric! Out!"

Eric flung Onyx off of him and stood up.

"You know better, Onyx. Just wait until I tell Vincent," Eric said as he walked out.

"I can revoke his membership permanently," Ellen said to Lily.

"Wouldn't do any good," Lily said. "He'd still be an ass hole."

Ellen didn't say anything.

Lily went to the club every other day for nearly two weeks. She was beginning to get bored with the fighting. She was faster than the vampires and that gave her the advantage. She won every fight. She had never lost a fight in the ring. The only fight she had ever lost was against Eric. He knew her moves and could anticipate what she'd do next. She did after all learn most of her fighting skills from fighting him.

One day after the fights, Lily got a call on her cell from Vincent. He wanted to speak to her. So when she got home she rode the elevator to the seventy fifth floor, the penthouse, of the Crown Building to see Vincent.

"I spoke to Ellen today," he began.

"About?" Lily questioned.

"About fighting Eric in the ring," he said.

Lily was shocked. She never thought Vincent would ever allow that. It was just too risky to put them together in the ring. Eric has always been out for blood and could possibly get it if they were to fight.

"What?" Lily said nearly choking.

"She didn't ask if you two could fight, but she did ask what she was going to do when you both reach the top rank."

"I'm not fighting him in the ring. Not that I'm afraid I'd lose. I'm not. I'm afraid I'd kill him. He knows I'm faster than him and in a fair fight I can beat him.

But Eric would never play fair. You know that, Vincent. It would end badly and you know it."

"Yes, Lily, I know."

LASHAY

E ric had caused the coven to have to leave Atlanta. The only coven that they could move into was in New York City. The most prestigious building in the whole city was the home to a large coven. It was empty at the time because the coven that was there was forced to leave because their numbers had gotten too low to stay at such a large estate.

The vampire coven had only been in New York for a couple of months. The first time Lily saw Shay, the person that would forever change her life, Shay was on the balcony outside of her apartment. It rarely got above 75°F just about anywhere, especially this far north, but on that day the temperature was pushing 90°F. A layer of perspiration covered her from head to toe. The tight outfit she was wearing left very little to the imagination. She was beautiful, absolutely breathtaking actually. She was exercising on a stationary bicycle and bobbing her head rhythmically as she mumbled breathy words.

Lily crouched behind the stairwell door of the building across from Shay's. It was a home for the elderly and she often used the roof access to get to the New York rooftops when she didn't want Eric to know where she was going. The rooftops had a much better view than the streets below and now, it had quite possibly the best view that Lily had ever seen. Since she never had to worry about being surprised by any visitors up here, she stayed hidden in the shadows and just watched.

In her whole existence Lily had 'fallen in love' with three people. Two vampires and one human and they were all males. And although it was a vampire she had fallen in love with, well, *thought* she had fallen in love with, she had never connected like most vampires do. She had always heard the stories of vampires and their loves and how strong the bond was. When a vampire falls in love, it is eternal. It's literally 'until death do you part'. You never want to leave the one you've fallen in love with and that's just the way it is. Lily had never felt that way, though. She thought that what she felt was love, but obviously it wasn't. Maybe it was just the longing for companionship, or just a desire to have what others had; forever with the one they loved. It sounded cheesy and romantic at the same time and she had wished for a century and a half that she would find her soul mate. She had heard stories of vampires literally dying because they couldn't be with the one they loved. Vampires that would have an elder end their lives because either their love had passed or something had permanently kept them apart.

She was starting to realize that her past loves were all a joke, at least that's what Vincent had thought, and now Lily understood why.

She was turning all this over in her head as she watched this beautiful woman bobbing her head and to the rhythms coming from the tiny speakers in her ears as she forced the wheel on the bike to spin. Lily could hear the music. It was muffled slightly, but she recognized the song and singer. It was a song she liked, too.

As the song came to an end, the new mystery woman slowed her peddling then stopped. The sun reflected off of her eyes and Lily's heart skipped a beat. She had never in her one hundred and sixty two years seen eyes as incredible as hers. They were hazel, a rainbow of color against her tanned skin. Black on the outermost edge, then into dark blue, which faded through a lighter blue to a forest green and then a deep brown against the pupil. Lily was mesmerized. Then the woman hopped off of the bike and leaned against the railing as she looked around the rooftops and then the alleyway and street below. She looked in Lily's direction and Lily froze. It was like she was looking directly at her, but there was no way she could see her in the shadows.

She had dark brown hair, with hints of a deep, reddish brown at the tips and where the sun hit it. Her face was a perfect oval shape, her eyebrows perfectly arched on high brows. Her lips were full and pink and the top lip had a tiny upturn just under her perfect nose.

She was a vision, as if a master painter had combined every perfect feature into one, breathtaking woman. She had to have been in her mid-thirties and Lily, at that moment, decided that she wanted her. But how? Lily was half vampire, this woman was human. Although vampires didn't usually fall in love with humans, it did happen. Lily had thought she had fallen in love with a human before. A twenty-four year old guy that Lily had met on a ski trip. Vincent had actually thought at the time, that it may have been the real thing. That maybe it was a human that she needed. But the relationship fell apart in a matter of months. Luckily, Lily had not yet told Kyle that she was a vampire. Vincent was happy for that fact. Vampires were once forbidden from telling a human about what they were or where they came from, but if you're truly in love with someone, eventually they're going to know everything, especially if you planned on spending the rest of your lives together. They would eventually figure out that something just wasn't right. I mean humans aren't stupid, well, not that stupid. They would definitely notice little things and over time would put the pieces together. Vampires never age, rarely got sick or even got hurt and eventually a human would notice that eating out at restaurants wasn't ever on the agenda. So, over time the rules changed.

But how would Vincent react? Lily knew that he would doubt the connection and probably forbid Lily from seeing her. Lily shook her head and laughed at herself.

"I don't even know her name," she said to herself.

Question after question raced through her head. *How will I approach her? How will she react? Would she think I was crazy? Probably. Does she even like women?* Which was a very big if.

The world had changed so much since Lily was born. Women with women and men with men was once completely forbidden, even among the vampires. She never understood why anyone would forbid anyone from loving someone else. What difference did it make? Wasn't love still love no matter who it was with? She had never been with a woman but it didn't matter, this woman before her was the one. The one person that she wanted to spend eternity with. It was her lips that she wanted to kiss forever. She just had to figure out how to make it happen.

Lily watched her for weeks. She learned her routines, her habits and even her favorite songs. LaShay Black was her name and her father owned several television stations across the US and Britain and as near as she could tell, Shay was given an allowance from her father and spoke to him almost daily. Lily wasn't sure about her mother as she had never heard Shay say anything about her. She still had to find out if she even stood a chance at all. *Was she even gay? Was she dating anyone? Was she even interested in anyone?* After a week she got her answer.

Shay was standing on the balcony when a man joined her. They talked about their weekend plans and then he kissed her. After he left, Shay pulled her phone out of her pocket and made a call.

"Hello, Shay," said the voice on the other end.

"Hey Shane," she answered.

"Did you do it?" he asked.

"No, of course not," Shay said. "I'm supposed to meet him at the bar on Lex at 8 o'clock."

Lily didn't need to hear the rest of conversation. She frowned to herself and let her back slide down the wall until she was sitting. Shay didn't like girls. Wow, a huge weight had just landed on Lily's shoulders. She didn't stand a snowball's chance... but she wasn't just going to give up. Lily still had to talk to her. But how? Why? Was there even a point now?

Lily shook her head and stood up in the shadows. Shay was still on the phone on the balcony.

"I have to try," Lily said out loud as she walked down the stairs.

She walked the twelve blocks back to the coven. A seventy five story high rise in Manhattan. When she arrived, she went straight to the seventy second floor to see Erica. She knocked on the door, waited for Erica and then walked in, head down.

"Ok, what's wrong? You've been practically floating on air for the past week. What happened?" Erica asked as she followed Lily down the hall to the dining room.

"Erica, what do you do if you're love with someone that you know you can never have?" Lily asked as she sat down in one of the high backed chairs at the table.

"So, you're in love. Again," Erica asked in a flat tone.

"Nevermind," Lily answered. She stood up from the table just as Erica sat down.

"Lily, wait."

"I knew that I'd get shit from Vincent, but I thought *you'd* at least listen to me."

"Sit down," Erica said, smiling. "I'm just giving you grief. So tell me about him. Where did you meet him?"

Lily took a deep breath and exhaled slowly.

"Her," Lily said softly. "It's a her, not a him."

"Oh! Her. So when did this happen?" Erica asked.

"About a week ago," Lily replied, slowly.

"OK, so what's wrong?"

"Well, for one, she's straight. Two, she's seeing someone. Three, she's human. And four... I haven't even spoken to her."

"Hummm," Erica said, trying not to laugh. "And you know you're in love... How?"

"I just know," Lily huffed.

Erica sat and just looked at Lily across the table. She could tell that Lily was really serious about this.

"So, tell me about her," Erica smiled and reached across the table for Lily's hand.

Lily took Erica's hand and looked up..

"Her name is LaShay and she lives across from the nursing home where I get roof access."

"I suppose you know her routine?" Erica asked.

"Yeah, she works at NY26 as a graphics director. She usually leaves about 6:00 AM and is usually home by 4:30 PM Monday through Thursday."

"Well, since you know her routine, meet her at the grocery store one day or somewhere else public."

"Grocery store, huh?" Lily smiled at Erica.

"You have to start somewhere," she smiled back and brushed her fingers across Lily's hand.

"She's supposed to meet her boyfriend at a bar on Lex tonight."

"Well, that's as good a place as any to start. But what about the whole 'she's straight' part?" Erica asked.

Lily just shrugged her shoulders. "I have to at least meet her. Maybe we could be friends at some point."

"What about the love part?"

Lily shrugged her shoulders again.

"Haven't thought this through very much, have you?" Erica joked.

"Uh, not really," Lily said, smiling weakly.

"Well, go play a few games of pool, or something. Maybe you'll find out it wasn't love after all," Erica said.

LILY MEETS SHAY

Lily knew that she wanted to meet Shay. Regardless. So she went home, put on some make up, a pair of jeans without holes in them and headed over to Baldwin's on Lex. She had never been there but apparently Erica had, because there were indeed pool tables. Lily arrived at about 7:30, ordered a shot from the bar, drank it down then went to the pool tables. A few guys came over from the bar and offered to play. Lily agreed politely and she went to rerack the pool balls. She was glad she had learned to play pool so many years ago and was happy that it hadn't changed at all. Except for the tables which were now made of a man-made stone and not natural slate.

Lily broke and called 'stripes'. They had each taken a few shots and none of them were doing very well. Soon they were all laughing at themselves at the easy shots they were missing. One of the guys, Derek, took a shot and the que ball went flying off the table. Lily ran after it, laughing. She bent down to pick up the ball and when she stood up she bumped into someone.

"Sorry," Lily laughed, reaching out an arm to steady the person she had bumped.

When Lily stood up she was looking directly into those beautiful hazel eyes that she had been dreaming about all week. Lily was going over all the scenarios in her head when she literally bumped onto Shay. She looked down at her hand, trying to think of something to say but nothing came.

Shay put her hand on Lily's arm, steadying herself even more. Then she looked into Lily's crystal blue eyes. She let out an auditable gasp when their eyes met.

"So sorry," Lily mumbled.

Lily wondered if she had scared Shay, because she didn't say a word. She just stared at her. Lily squeezed her arm slightly to get Shay's attention.

"Are you ok?" Lily asked.

"Uh, yeah," she finally answered after a few seconds. "Yeah, I'm sorry, I wasn't watching where I was going."

There was a big smile on her face now and Lily couldn't help but smile back.

"Me either," Lily said. "Maybe, next time we should plan on bumping into each other."

Lily wondered to herself if that was too much of a hint.

"Ha, maybe," Shay answered with a blank stare.

No, she didn't get it. Or did she?

"Shay, come on, there are seats at the bar," Josh said from behind Shay.

Lily watched as Shay walked away then Shay turned around and caught Lily staring. Lily smiled and Shay smiled back before disappearing into the crowd.

At the bar, Shay looked toward the pool tables but couldn't see it.

"Did you see her eyes?" Shay asked Josh.

"Who's eyes?" Josh asked before throwing back a shot.

"Her eyes..." Shay began but was interrupted by Josh asking the bartender for another round of drinks.

Every chance Lily got, she looked toward the bar. She searched every face for Shay's and when she finally saw her, their eyes locked.

It was only a split second but they had seen each other.

"Your shot, blue eyes," Derek said to Lily from across the pool table.

Lily turned around and took her shot. When she looked back to where Shay was sitting, Josh and Shay were gone.

Lily raced out of the bar and hurried back to the nursing home across from Shay's. They were just getting out of the cab when Lily peeked over the edge of the roof. Josh and Shay kissed and then he got back into the cab. Lily waited as Shay rode the elevator up to the twelfth floor. She heard her remotes drop on the kitchen counter and then she heard Shane's voice. He had apparently gotten there earlier and let himself in.

"So did you break up with him?" Shane asked as soon as Shay walked back into the living room.

"No," Shay said quietly.

"Why not?" he asked.

"Just didn't seem like the right time."

"The right time? He's a drunk, Shay."

"But if I break up with him, my dad will be on my case again about being single and I'd rather just keep seeing Josh for the time being than to deal with my Dad."

"Why are you so worried about what your father thinks? He's not the one kissing these losers."

"He's not a loser! He's a senior partner at his law firm and he's handsome at that."

"But you don't love him," Shane pleaded.

"Well... Maybe I do..." Shay began.

"Well? Is the sex *that* good?" Shane laughed.

"Very funny," LaShay said.

"Well, you are sleeping with him, right? I know you are, so don't lie."

"I saw this girl at the bar," Shay said, abruptly changing the subject. "She had the most amazing blue eyes."

"Humph," Shane snorted.

"You're right. But you should have seen her eyes," Shay said.

Lily decided that she'd be at the bar every Saturday night from now on and was hoping Shay would be, too.

The week seemed to pass so slowly. By the time Saturday came around again, Lily was aching to see Shay again. She had stayed away from her apartment all week and was really missing seeing her, if only in passing.

Lily was hoping Shay would be at the bar again so much so, that Lily went to the bar to play pool three times during the week. Shay never showed, but Lily made a couple of new friends. When Saturday finally arrived, Lily was playing pool with her friends, Derek and his girlfriend, Ann, when Lily caught a glimpse of LaShay through the heavy crowd. Lily leaned her pool stick against the table and told her friends that she'd be right back.

She walked over to Shay slowly, turning over in her head what she was going to say.

"I was hoping you'd be here," Lily said before Shay could speak.

Lily wondered if she should play it cool and act like she wasn't there for Shay, or totally cave and confess that she was.

"So now that I'm here, what are..." Lily was interrupted by Shane stepping in front of Shay like he was Shay's bodyguard.

Shane had shaggy brown hair, brown eyes, was a lanky five foot ten and weighed all of one hundred and thirty pounds soaking wet.

Lily was too focused on Shay to see him at first. She stopped and gave him a quick up and down glance before returning her attention to the absolutely gorgeous woman behind him.

But instead of being polite and moving aside, Shane stopped right in front of Lily. She was just going to step around him but he blocked her path, again. Now, Lily was getting angry. The woman that she was madly in love with was less than three feet away and her friend decides he wants to play keep away.

Lily's first inkling was to push his protective ass out of the way, but that may reflect badly on her so early in the courting game. So she decided to play nice.

"Uh, excuse me," Lily said with as little sarcasm as possible. "You're really cute and all, but I would really like to talk to your friend."

"Well, she's taken," he said rudely.

"By you?" Lily asked, still keeping her temper in check, but knowing the answer.

She looked around him at Shay and the look on her face was priceless. It was a mix of astonished disbelief and curiosity. Shay was thinking, *What in the world did he think he was doing? What is he going to say?*

"Maybe," he said, flustered.

Lily crossed her arms and took a step back. *This should be good.* She knew he was gay and she knew Shay was seeing someone else, so what could he possibly say?

"Not me," he said, trying to make it up on the fly. "But she's with someone else."

"Really?" Lily and Shay said in unison.

Lily grinned at Shay's expression and returned her attention to the one digging himself deeper by the minute.

"So what is this person like?" Lily asked Shane. "The one that she's with?"

"Rich," he said suddenly.

Lily nodded.

"And?" she prodded.

"Dark hair," he added.

At this point, Shay had had about all she was going to take of this.

"Shane," she said as she put her hand on his shoulder. "What *are* you doing?"

"What would Josh think?" Shane added. "You came here to see *her?*"

"Maybe!" Shay snapped. "But if you don't shut up..." She gave him an angry look as she pushed him to the side.

When she was finally standing directly in front of Lily, she put her hand out.

"I'm LaShay."

"Hi LaShay, I'm Lily."

Lily took her hand and stared into her eyes.

"It's a pleasure," was the only thing Lily could say.

Lily kept staring, trying to think of something casual to say but the only thing going through her head was a future with her. She could see them together at her apartment, curled up on her couch together, laughing at the television. Then she pictured them together walking hand in hand in the country in Tennessee. *Has she ever been outside the city? Has she ever ridden a horse or shot an arrow from a bow? Would she even want to?* Lily could see Shay in her arms, her hair blowing across her cheek and shoulder as they looked out over the waves from a pier overlooking the ocean.

Every part of Lily's being wanted nothing more than to take Shay into her arms and kiss her but Lily knew she couldn't do that. She had to be casual. After all they weren't even friends. Yet. Lily couldn't tell her what she had already learned about her. She could only imagine what Shane would say if he knew how much Lily had been around.

"So would you like to play pool?" Lily finally asked.

"No," Shane answered abruptly.

Shay slowly looked over at him and mouthed her objection. He only crossed his arms and stood his ground. Lily laughed to herself as she thought how quickly she could end him.

"Then go to the bar," Lily said to Shane just as politely as she possibly could.

"Shane, do you want to play pool?" Shay asked him, under her breath. "If not, go to the bar."

"Fine," Shane huffed and gave Lily a smug look and then he walked away.

Shane walked to the bar by himself. He was wondering what Shay was up to. She had never been very interested in making friends outside where she worked, so why was she here? He could see why she was so enamored with Lily's blue eyes, but that didn't explain why Shay had come back to the bar. He wondered if Lily was here every night or just the weekend.

He sat down at the bar and ordered a fruity mixed drink. No shots for him. It was fru fru drinks for him all the way. He glanced up through the crowd and saw Shay at the pool table. He didn't know if she had even played pool, much less if she was any good at it.

He had only a few sips of his drink before curiosity got the better of him.

Shay was bending over the pool table taking the last shot at the eight ball. She lined up the shot and tapped the que ball into the eight ball and it dropped into the side pocket.

"We win," Lily shouted.

Derek grumbled something under his breath.

"Play again?" Ann asked as she hit Derek in the arm.

Shane walked over to Shay and whispered in her ear.

"Do you even know how to play pool?" he asked.

"Sort of," she answered in a normal voice. "Josh taught me while we were here one night. Why?"

"Just wondering. I forgot that the drunk was here all the time," Shane said snidely.

"He's not a drunk!" Shay mumbled. "Do you want to play? You can be on our team."

"What are you doing?" Shane asked so no one could hear him.

"What do you mean?" Shay asked softly.

"What are you doing *here*?" He asked. "You don't play pool. You don't go out and meet strangers in bars."

Shay gave him an incredulous look.

"Well maybe it's about time I did!" Shay smirked.

"Everything alright?" Lily shouted from the other side of the table.

"Yeah," Shay answered, looking at Shane. "Who's breaking?"

Shay walked away from Shane and to the other side of the table to where Lily was standing.

"Is everything OK?" Lily asked when she was standing beside her.

Shay just nodded.

Shane walked back to the bar with his drink.

"I'll be at the bar," Shane shouted as he was walking away.

No one heard him.

COURTING LASHAY

ily and LaShay played pool for about half an hour when Shay decided that she had left Shane waiting long enough.

"Will I see you again?" Lily asked as Shay walked away.

"Pool? Tomorrow night?" Shay replied.

"Wouldn't miss it," Lily answered with a big smile.

Sunday night Shay showed up without Shane and Lily was grateful. She finally got to talk to Shay without feeling watched. They sat at the bar and talked about general things like favorite songs, favorite restaurants and the like. Lily wanted to ask about Shay's boyfriend, but was afraid to pry.

Shay was really beginning to like Lily. They quickly became friends and for Shay, was like having a new best friend. Someone new to hang out with and to talk to. Shay rarely had time with her schedule to do things before but was making time and enjoying it.

Shane was against the friendship from the beginning. Not that Lily had done anything wrong, he was just jealous that Shay had another best friend and wasn't always available for him anymore.

After talking for nearly two hours the two decided that they'd play pool.

Shay wasn't a bad pool player, but Lily still had to let her win. Around midnight Shay finally told Lily she needed to go.

"Would you like to go see a movie sometime?" Lily asked shakily.

"Sure," Shay answered.

They met the next weekend at the movie theater and went to see and action movie. Lily was afraid to take Shay to a love story. Thinking that she might get all romantic and tell Shay how she really felt. Sappy love stories always had that effect on her and she figured it was a safe bet that Shay didn't feel the same.

Shay had never felt so close to someone so quickly. She was really beginning to like Lily, a lot. She found herself thinking about Lily all the time. After spending most of her weekends hanging out with Lily, she finally broke it off with

Josh. She felt like she owed Josh more since they were dating and she was having so much more fun hanging out with Lily. The breakup went smoothly, he wasn't upset at all and had actually known it was coming. She did love him, but it wasn't the head over heels 'in-love' that she hears others talk about. The two had been dating for nearly two years and they got along great. The sex was great, the conversation was great and Shay had even introduced him to her father. Her father approved. Of course he did. Josh was a corporate lawyer and had an annual income of over a million dollars. But Shay just wasn't in love with him. They could talk about anything together. Even Lily. And Shay found herself talking about her a lot.

Lily had been playing it cool and trying not to let her emotions show... too much. After three weeks, Lily was dying to tell her. It was driving her insane but she was not going to screw this up. She couldn't, because she couldn't even imagine a life without Shay now.

Shay was beginning to look forward to her time with Lily, too. She had even invited Lily over during the week for dinner and drinks on more than one occasion. A month into the friendship Shay had a stray thought one evening when Lily was over for drinks. Shay wondered what it would be like to kiss Lily. It was just a passing thought and Shay just let it go. A few days passed and Shay began thinking about it again. She could picture her fingers in Lily's hair and the soft warm feel of her lips. Shay had never fantasized about being with someone before. She had never felt the way she feels about Lily. Could she be attracted to Lily? Could she possibly be falling for her? The two were getting increasingly closer and Shay was feeling uncertain about the way she felt. She surely didn't want to stop seeing her, but should she? *Did Lily feel the same?* Shay wondered.

The next night Shane was over to watch television and to just catch up with Shay. He immediately asked about Lily.

He sat down on the couch with a margarita that Shay handed him when he walked in the door.

"So how's your new best friend?"

"She's good," she answered almost too quickly.

"She coming over tonight, too?" He asked.

"No, do you want her to?" Shay shot back.

Shane just took another sip of his drink then sat it down on the coffee table.

"Shane, when did you know that you were gay?" Shay asked.

"What?" Shane answered, nearly spitting out his drink.

"How did you know?" She asked again standing in the doorway to the kitchen.

She just stared at the floor without saying anything else.

"Lily? Really?" Shane assumed.

"I really like her," Shay said after a long pause.

Shane took a deep breath then said, "Is she gay?"

"I don't know," Shay answered quickly.

Shane took a deep breath, picked up his drink and leaned back on the couch.

"Talk to me girlfriend," he said then took a big swig of his margarita.

"I think about her all the time," Shay admitted.

Shay and Shane had been friends for almost ten years. He once worked at the television station with Shay but had gotten a better offer and gone on to work for an advertising firm. Shay knew she could talk to him although he wasn't crazy about Lily.

"For the first time ever, I catch myself thinking about her and smiling. I've never thought about guys like that. Not even guys I'm dating."

Shane sipped his drink and nodded.

"Could that be why I've never really been all that excited about sleeping with guys? Even when I should have been 'boy crazy' like all the other girls, I wasn't. I could care less. And I always hated kissing guys in public. "

Shane took another sip then said, "Sounds like you feel really strongly about her."

"I do," Shay sighed.

"So what do you want to do about that?" he asked.

"I don't know. I'm afraid I'll scare her off if I tell her how much I like her."

"Maybe she does feel the same. Maybe that's why you two are spending so much time together."

"But how do I know?"

"You just have to ask her, I guess," he smiled. "My girl is gay!"

Shay had been friends with Lily for almost a month and half and she was beginning to have strong feelings for her. Not just friendship feelings, but deeper feelings. She was thinking about Lily all the time and couldn't wait to talk to her next. The feelings had been growing since day one at the bar. And the more they were together, the stronger Shay felt. She had never had these feelings before and she wasn't quite sure how to process them. She knew Lily was important to her and couldn't imagine them not seeing each other. She wanted to be with her all the time and the feelings were only getting stronger.

Was she falling in love with Lily? She had loved guys before but not like this. Not like having butterflies in her stomach and smiling for no apparent reason. She had never even thought about being gay before. But if she were being truly honest, she had always been really close to her girlfriends. She would get more upset when a girlfriend would cancel their plans than when a boyfriend she was dating would cancel. She actually remembered being in tears once when Shelly, her best friend in high school, decided to go to her boyfriend's prom at another school instead of double dating to their own prom. Shay just thought she was being emotional and never really thought it through. Maybe she did care too much.

Was that the reason that intimacy with guys had always been awkward for her? Why she wasn't like her female friends in school and always talking about boys and kissing and sex? Was that the reason that when all her female friends were gawking over boys, she was busy with school work and studying? Then Shay remembered one time in particular when she was with a friend at the park. Shay was with her boyfriend, Daniel. Shelly was with her boyfriend and Shelly's sister was with her boyfriend. Shay remembered Shelly and her boyfriend rolling in the grass, play wrestling, and thinking that she wished it was her, wrestling with Shelly. At the time, Shay didn't think anything about it. It never occurred to her that she should've been wrestling with Daniel and not thinking about Shelly.

"How did *you* know," she asked again as she sat down at the opposite end of the couch.

"I just always knew," Shane answered casually.

"I mean, at what point was it clear that you liked boys and not girls?"

"Pre-school," Shane laughed then looked at Shay with a serious expression.

Shay just sat there, sipping on the margarita she had brought from the kitchen.

"You know I don't trust her, right," he finally said clearly, then took another drink. "You don't really even know her!"

"I know her enough," she said.

"Have you met any of her friends? Have you been to her apartment? What's her last name? How old is she?"

"No. No. Honeycutt. And I don't know," Shay answered in order.

"Honeycutt? What kind of name is that?" Shane laughed.

"A family name. She's adopted, her mother died during childbirth and she was raised in Tennessee."

"Have you ever even been out of the city," Shane snorted.

"Yes! So? What's that got to do with anything?"

"You're right," Shane said seriously. "Where does she live?"

"The Crown Building."

"No way! And she's never taken you there. I don't believe it. There's no way she lives in the Crown Building. People like us could never get a place in the Crown Building even *with* your father's money," Shane spewed. "It's the most elite address in New York and she's never taken you there? No way she really lives there!"

"Why would she lie?" Shay asked.

"I just don't trust her," Shane repeated. "I know you like her and all, but there's just something missing with her. Like she's hiding something."

Shay just shook her head and took another drink.

It was another Sunday night and Lily was at Shay's apartment, as usual. Lily had begun to realize that Shay was beginning to have deeper feelings for her. The hugs were longer, the touching was more often and not a day went by that they didn't talk. Lily had to get up the nerve to ask Shay how she really felt. She had to convince her that she was serious and that she wanted to be around for a long time. Of course Shay didn't know how *long* that would really be.

They had spent hours just talking. That night was one of the rare occasions that Lily was with her alone without Shane, so they'd spent the time talking about everything from their favorite movies and music to deeper conversations like growing up and dreams that they had. Shay was very intelligent and Lily was usually amazed at how much she actually knew. Had she figured out Lily wasn't completely human? If she had, she never let on like she knew.

During that night's particular conversation, they were also talking about likes and dislikes, and Shay revealed that she was a little old fashioned in some ways. She liked hand written letters on old textured paper and hand-made gifts. Even turn of the century art and music.

"What's your favorite classical music piece?" Lily asked.

Shay tilted her head and stared off into space for a brief moment.

"Classical piece? How classical?"

"*Really* classical," Lily smiled.

"Um, *Fir Elise*," Shay answered.

"Really? Mine, too!"

"What is your favorite piece of art? Say... more than 100 years old or more," Shay asked, grinning and thinking it would stump Lily.

"Umberto Boccioni," she answered almost instantly.

"No way!" Shay squealed.

"*Elasticity*," they both said in unison.

Lily dropped her head and smiled. She shook her head before looking back to Shay. How was she supposed to explain that she had that painting hanging in her living room? That two other Boccioni's paintings were hanging in her apartment as well. And how was she to explain how Vincent knew Umberto, an Italian artist that fought beside him in the First World War. Umberto had died during the war, but not before promising Vincent some of his paintings and two of his preliminary sculptures. The bronze precursor to Boccioni's *Futuristic Man* sits on the mantle in Vincent's penthouse apartment. Vincent also had original works by Picasso, Georgia O'Keefe and Andy Warhol. Lily smiled to herself thinking about all of the famous and historical artifacts that the Crown Building held. She couldn't wait to show them all to Shay. But not before she knew how to deal with Eric.

Lily's thoughts floated back to the present and their conversation continued. After arts and music the subject turned to their own childhoods.

"Where did you grow up?" Shay asked.

"Nashville, Tennessee mostly."

"A country girl," Shay teased.

"Mostly," Lily nodded and smiled. "Have you ever been out of the city?"

"No, not really," Shay said, shaking her head. "I've never gone to another city and went site seeing or anything. I've been on business trips with my dad to other cities, like Vancouver, British Columbia in Canada. Big cities like Seattle, Los Angeles, Chicago and Dallas and they look no different than here, really. Just roads, buildings and more concrete."

"But I'm sure you've read how much bigger those cities used to be," Lily added. "And how different the skyline was here in New York before the towers fell in oh one."

Lily remembered the day like it was just yesterday. She remembered hearing that the first plane had hit the tower and thought that some pilot had made a drastic mistake. But when the second plane hit the other tower was when the United States changed forever. The coven had been in Atlanta at that time and Lily could still hear the roar of the fighter jet engines as they all left Dobbins Air Force Base just minutes after the second plane hit. F-18 fighters, fully armed, circled the city for days protecting the CDC from any attacks. The powers that be knew that if the terrorists were able to bomb the Centers for Disease Control that it would be catastrophic. So they took no chances.

"Yeah, I remember reading about that in my history books," Shay said. "That was a very sad day. All those people in the towers and all the people who knew someone that were in the towers. It was the worst terrorist attack on US soil."

Lily nodded, and thought back to the long drive from Atlanta to New York City after the attack. Vincent and Alexa had known past feeders that worked there and were going to comfort their families and offer any help that was needed. Everyone that went ended up helping the search effort at ground zero.

"I remember," Lily said.

"You remember reading? Right," Shay asked jokingly.

"Uh, yes," Lily smiled. "I remember reading about it."

"So why did your family move to New York after so long in the south?" Shay asked.

That's a very good question, Lily thought. *Ask Eric.*

"Well," Lily began. "There's a number of reasons but I guess the best one would be that we outgrew our old home."

She lied. They had to leave the south because Eric had had a violent confrontation with an Atlanta police officer and Vincent did not want another lynch mob like the one Eric had ultimately caused in New Orleans in the late 1800's. Eric had killed the local New Orleans police chief and when the officer was asked who shot him as he lay dying, it was misunderstood as "Dogoes", a slur for Italians, instead of "Dagas" which was the name Eric used there. It resulted in the worst lynch mob in American history and Vincent did not want it repeated.

"So you and your family have only been here less than a year?" Shay asked.

"Yes."

"Which do you like better? The North or the South?"

"Humm..." Lily mumbled. "They each have their pros and cons," Lily smiled and looked directly into Shay's eyes.

"Like," Shay prodded.

"Like the country has horses and fresh air, but the city has entertainment and activities on every corner."

"Horses?" Shay said as her eyes lit up.

"Horses. Have you ever ridden one?" Lily asked.

"Ridden one?" Shay balked. "I've never even seen one up close!"

"Not even the ones in the park that pull the sleds in the winter?"

"Not even those," Shay admitted.

"We're going to have to change that."

"What are your parents like?" Shay asked. "My dad is opinionated, overbearing and a general pain in the ass."

"Well, I guess my adopted mom would be Erica. Which makes my dad, Steven. My grandmother would be Alexa and my grandfather would be Vincent," Lily answered, with a slight giggle. "Then there's Erica's twin brother, Eric. He and I hate each other. Literally. We fight all the time."

It just felt weird calling Vincent and Alexa her grandparents, although that's technically what they would be in a *normal* family. *But they looked so young,* she thought. Lily didn't elaborate at all on Eric but she told Shay about Erica and how close the two are.

"You're going to love Erica," Lily told her. "And she's going to love you."

They talked for a little while longer before Lily looked at her cell and then at Shay. It was late. It was almost midnight when Lily finally told Shay goodnight. She didn't want to leave, but it was Sunday and Shay had to be at work early the next day.

They gave each other a hug and for the first time, LaShay kissed Lily on the cheek.

Hand written letters on woven parchment paper, Lily thought as she walked home. It had been probably twenty years since Lily had even picked up a pen, much less put pen to paper. She had legible handwriting, but no one would call it pretty.

While she was telling Lily how much she loved letters, Lily was turning over in her head whether or not there was a calligraphy book in the library at home. Then she remembered the little wooden jewelry boxes she used to make out of Craft sticks. It was over 75 years ago and she had given one to Alexa and one to Erica. She wondered if they still had them. *Surely not, it was just some silly box.*

Lily was grinning from ear to ear when Eric surprised her outside the main entrance to the Crown Building.

"Where have you been? We missed you at the finals tonight," Eric said then he noticed Lily's mood. "What's gotten into you? You've been gone an awful lot lately and you've been really quiet, too."

"Just busy doing other things, that's all," she answered shortly and tried to push her way past him. She wasn't in the mood for fighting with Eric. She had completely forgotten about Underground Fight Finals that week. Of course she wasn't fighting Eric, but they were both in the top rank finals.

"No!" Eric said, pushing her away from the door. "Where have you been the past month and a half? It's like you have some new life or something."

Lily pushed him back. "Maybe I do, why do you care?" She snapped.

"I don't," he said curtly.

"Then get the fuck out of my way!"

He pushed her into the door, hard. "Fuck you! Go on and play off by yourself then, see if I care."

She didn't say anything else because she was trying so hard not to fight Eric. They hadn't fought in a long time and now was just not the time for him to start something. Then he pushed her into the door again.

Lily dropped her bag just as she landed a solid punch to Eric's nose. She heard the bones break in his face and he dropped to his knees. Lily gave him a hard kick to the chest and he fell backwards holding is hand over his face. The nose wouldn't stay broken and misshaped for long, but it sure as hell hurt when it happened. She quickly scanned her hand on the palm reader by the door, opened the door and walked inside. *Why was he talking to me, anyway?* She wondered. Then she remembered the little wooden boxes and ran upstairs to find Erica.

It took about two minutes for Eric's face to stop throbbing and heal.

"Dammit!" He said and punched the door.

Lily found Erica in her apartment, reading. Erica still had the book opened when she answered the door.

"Hi Erica, whatcha reading?" Lily asked, trying to be polite, but not really caring.

"Boring stuff you wouldn't like," she answered probably quite honestly.

"Yeah, I figured," Lily chuckled.

Steven poked his head out from the bedroom and smiled.

"Hello, Lily," he said.

"Hi Steve. Whatcha doin'?" Lily asked.

"Nothin' much, just going through some old junk."

"Well, have fun!" she told him then turned her attention back to Erica as he disappeared back into the room. "Do you remember the little wooden jewelry box I gave you? The one I made out of craft sticks a long, long time ago?" she asked.

"Yeah, I remember. Why?"

"Well..." Lily began but then realized that she hadn't even told Erica about what happened over the past weeks with Shay. She had been so caught up, she hadn't even talked to her again about Shay and she usually shared everything with Erica.

"Remember that I met someone?"

"I do? Same girl as before?" she asked.

"Yes," Lily said, remembering the short conversation she had had with Erica about Shay. "She's so beautiful and smart and she has a great sense of humor and..." Lily began rambling.

"Whoa! Slow down. Take a breath," she said laughing as she closed her book. "Do you know her name yet?"

"LaShay Black."

"Black? As in Martin Black? As in Midnight Entertainment?"

"Yeah, that's her dad. He owns it."

"So she's human, huh. Why do you want to know about the box?" She asked. "I still have it."

"What?! You still have it? Why?"

"Because you made it with your own two hands and that makes it very special to me."

"Wow, I can't believe you still have it. I want to make Shay one. Do you think she'll like it?"

"I wouldn't see why not. Especially if she knows you made it yourself. No one does much woodworking anymore."

Erica walked into her bedroom and returned with the box Lily had made. It was just like she remembered it. An oval box with decorative ends sticking up through grooves on each side of the carved lid. The handle had a smooth wavy design on each side of a wooden ball shape. There was a small, decoratively carved peg protruding from the side that went through the upright on the side. That was the piece that held the lid on.

Erica handed her the box and she pulled out the peg that was still attached to the lid with a braided piece of thread. Inside, the bottom of the lid and the bottom of the box were a checkerboard pattern and the sides were made from matchsticks. Lily remembered making it like it was just yesterday. It took a week to glue, sand and carve the whole thing. It was over 75 years old but the stain and polyurethane coatings had kept it perfectly preserved. Erica even had an old matching necklace and earrings in it.

"Do you know if any of my craft stuff was saved?" Lily asked, still turning the box over in her hands.

"It was probably saved, but where it's stored is another question. I would start in the storage rooms downstairs. There should be a few trunks down there with your name on them. If you packed them, they should still be down there."

The thing was, she couldn't remember if they got packed or not. She knew she kept her stuff in crates and trunks in Tennessee, but did it get brought to the new coven or was it left to collect dust at the old coven? There was only one way to find out.

"Thanks Erica," Lily said as she handed her back the box. "I guess I'll be downstairs."

"Hold on young lady! You have to tell me about this LaShay person."

"She's incredible," Lily began, wide eyed.

Lily ended up talking about Shay until after 3 AM. She told Erica everything she knew about her. Where she lived, what she liked, what she didn't like. She told her about her job and how she worked all the time. She even told her about Shane and how much he was really getting on her nerves.

"I can understand that he's protective of her, but it's like he doesn't want me around," Lily told Erica. "It's almost like he's trying to keep me away."

"It sounds like he's just jealous. That's been his closest friend for years," Erica said. "And now that Shay is interested in someone else, he doesn't have her all to himself anymore. She is interested, right?"

"He's just going to have to get over it," Lily said.

"Yeah, just keep an eye out, love. And don't piss him off. Remember that she trusts him and his opinion does matter."

"Thanks, I'll definitely keep that in mind."

"Lily? She *is* interested isn't she?" Erica asked again.

"I'm not sure. I think so."

"Does she like women?"

Lily took a deep breath. "No. I don't think so, but we're getting along *sooo* well."

Erica decided that now was probably not a good time to try talking Lily out of falling any harder for Shay. So she just smiled and agreed.

"I hope it works out," Erica sighed.

She gave Lily a hug and she kissed her on the cheek.

"It's about time," she said.

"About time for what?" Lily asked.

"It's about time you fell in love." She smiled.

"I finally know what it feels like to live for someone else."

"Amazing, isn't it?" She said as she glanced over her shoulder toward the bedroom where Steve was still rummaging through closets and drawers.

"I just hope she feels the same way. I don't want to rush things. I want her to know how crazy I am about her."

"Does she know?"

"I'm still waiting for the right moment. It just hasn't been the right time, yet. I want her to know me a little first."

"Yeah, I can understand that. I have faith," she said smiling. "You're pretty amazing and there's no doubt she'll see that."

"Thank you," she told her and gave her a peck on the lips. "But you *are* biased."

"Yeah. Maybe a little," she said as she touched Lily's cheek.

It took two hours to find the trunk with Lily's old craft supplies in it. She dug through the contents and found an armload of supplies to make the box. She would have to go buy more wood and was hoping she could find craft sticks at some craft store but for now, it was time for bed.

She sent Shay a 'good morning' text, since it was already after 6AM, as she walked to her apartment. Ten minutes later Shay sent a message back and then Lily went to bed.

She was wide awake in four hours. Ever since she had met Shay, sleeping was a problem so she decided to start on the jewelry box.

That afternoon, Shay was sitting at her desk at work when her father walked in. He had a concerned look on his face and a stack of envelopes in his hands. The envelopes were large with dates printed in big black type on the front.

"What's going on with you?" Martin asked his daughter. "You've been late twice this week and you've even left early. Is everything OK?"

Shay wasn't expecting to have this conversation with her father so soon. *Never*, would have been preferred, but he was bound to find out at some point.

"I've met someone," she answered trying not to smile.

"Oh really," her father beamed. "So is it serious?"

"Maybe."

Shay wasn't sure how to answer. She really didn't want to tell him about Lily because she knew he would take it badly. He was very old fashioned and unlike most of the world's population, wasn't so keen on gays, especially if one happened to be his daughter. She had heard the way he would talk about his gay employees and knew that he would not be very accepting of her. It wasn't that he disliked gays, he just had made a lot of false assumptions and no one had ever corrected him.

"Can we talk about this later?" Shay asked.

"Hell no!" He said, taking a seat in one of the two chairs in front of her desk. "Tell me about this mystery man."

Shay swallowed hard and barely got out the words. "Her name is Lily."

Her father just stared at her for a moment.

"Her? It's a she?" He finally said. "Since when do you like women?"

"Dad, can we talk about this later?" Shay pleaded.

"My daughter is NOT gay," he said, raising his voice louder with every word.

"Dad," Shay said calmly. "Can we not get into this here?"

Lily dumped the box of wood and craft supplies on her dining room table. She sorted through what she had and decided on what she would need then headed to the craft store across town.

Once at the store, she went up and down every woodworking isle just to see what was available. She tossed a few things in her basket and then a few more. As she was looking at the tiny tiled inserts that were available, she noticed a row of music box inserts. They were bronze colored little machines that had a wheel with spikes sticking out and metal plate cut into slices that would flick and resonate sound when the spike on the wheel passed it. Lily searched for one that played *Fir Elise*. In the very back of the last hook, she found the only one they had. She grinned a big toothy grin at her find and headed for the door. Checkout was instant and her account was automatically charged as she left the store. The attendant at the door tore a small piece of paper from a small box in her hand.

"Receipt, ma'am," she said as she handed it to Lily.

"Thank you," Lily replied.

Lily worked on the box until it was time to meet Shay after work. As usual, Lily couldn't wait to see her. She had decided that this was the night that she would tell her how she felt.

She sprayed on a fair amount of sunscreen and headed to Shay's apartment.

LaShay's cheeks were already wet with tears before she even pressed the send button. She had to end the relationship with Lily before she fell any harder for her. But Shay was so crazy about her and Shane knew that.

"It's for the best sweetheart," Shane tried to soothe her. "You really *don't* want to piss off your father."

"Screw my father!" Shay cried.

Shane had met Shay at home after work and Shay told him about the conversation she had had with her dad. Shane convinced her that she should end things with Lily. If for no other reason than to appease her father.

"My dad doesn't even know her," Shay sobbed.

"She's just not right for you, hon. If she was gay, I would be able to tell. If she liked you, like that, wouldn't she have at least said *something*? She won't even take you to where she lives! And what about her parents," he said.

"She did tell me her mother died during her delivery," she sniffled.

"How old is she?" he asked.

"I don't know! Why does it matter?" She cried louder.

"Because she's hiding something," he said. "And if you ask me, it's something big. She knows too much about certain things, like the exact location of the extranet cameras and how to get around them and why doesn't she ever go out in the daytime without a hat or a hoodie? I'm telling you Shay, she's hiding something and I just don't want to see you get hurt. I know you really like her, but she's just not the one for you."

Lily was almost to LaShay's building when her phone buzzed. She was grinning when she began reading the message from Shay. But her pace slowed to a stop as she continued reading. The message said "Thank you for the time we've spent together, but I believe that it would be best if we didn't see each other anymore."

Lily's heart broke in two. *What is this happening? Surely there has to be some misunderstanding. There just had to be. What did I do wrong?*

Lily started walking again toward the apartment. She almost bumped into a man walking his dog because she was reading the text over and over. What had she done? She *had* to talk to her. She had to clear up the misunderstanding. There had to be one. There had to be a logical explanation. But what if there wasn't? *What if she didn't like me after all? What if she was just being polite and she was just waiting for the right moment to break it off? Please don't let that be the case*, she thought. She couldn't handle that. What would she do if Shay simply did not want to see her anymore?

Lily placed her hand on the palm scanner at the front door and the door opened with a clicking sound. She pressed the elevator button constantly until it finally opened. She pressed twelve and held her breath. When the door finally opened, she exhaled slowly and stepped out. She walked down the hall slowly and stopped at Shay's door. She stared for a moment and listened. She could hear Shane talking inside. She listened to him tell her that Lily wasn't interested in her. *What? Who the hell is he to...* She caught herself before she ripped the door off the hinges. She had to stay calm. Killing Shay's best friend would not be a good way of proving her feelings for her. Although it would directly reflect her feelings for him.

Lily stood silently outside the door until he stopped talking and she thought she heard Shay crying. *Did he put her up to this?*

Restraining herself to the fullest extent possible, she tapped lightly on the door. Suddenly the door flew open and Shane came barreling into the hallway.

Inside the apartment, Shane was talking but Shay wasn't listening. When it had been silent for a few minutes, Shay thought she heard a tap on the door but Shane was on his feet and across the living room before it completely registered. He swung open the door and stepped into the hallway, practically pushing Lily halfway across the hall.

"Didn't you get the text?" Shane shouted.

"Yes, I just want..." Lily began but Shane interrupted.

"What you want is to leave her alone, she doesn't want to talk to you anymore."

Shay stood up and walked toward the door. She saw Lily standing in front of Shane, her face was covered in tears and her eyes were puffy and red. Had she made a terrible mistake? Was she just in love with her and just taking it slow?

"I just want to talk..." Lily began again.

"She doesn't want to talk to you. What part of that don't you understand?" Shane interrupted again.

Lily looked around Shane and directly at Shay. She had been crying for some time. It was obvious by her puffy eyes, wet cheeks and crumpled tissues in her hand.

"Just talk to me," Lily pleaded. "Please!"

"Go home, Lily," Shane yelled over the two girls trying to talk.

Lily kept thinking *be calm Lily. Be calm. Do not kill her best friend,* she kept repeating this to herself as Shane yelled at her.

The only thing she heard was 'She doesn't want to talk to you'. The tears came harder now. She had to talk to her. She leaned around Shane and saw Shay.

"Just talk to me. Please," Lily begged from the hallway.

Then the door slammed in her face.

Lily lifted her hand to the door handle. She was shaking all over. The only thing she could think about was never seeing Shay's beautiful smile ever again. She grabbed the handle and began to push and then, somehow, she made herself stop. If Shay didn't want to see her anymore, what could she do? She couldn't make Shay see her. No matter how much Lily loved her, no matter how much she would sacrifice, it didn't matter if Shay didn't want to see her. But Lily wanted to hear Shay say it. She wanted the words to come from her lips. She wanted to hear her say goodbye.

She released the handle and staggered toward the elevator. She would give her time to calm down and try again.

Shane walked over and put his arms around Shay but she didn't want comforting. All she wanted to was to go after Lily and take back the message she had sent.

"It's for the best," Shane comforted.

Shay pushed him away, walked into the bedroom and collapsed onto the bed. It was done. Shay's best friend had just sent away what was quite possibly the love of her life. Maybe Lily *was* hiding something, maybe she just didn't think everything Shane had talked about was all that important. She had never asked about Shay's parents and honestly, what difference did it make. Maybe Lily's father was sentenced to die for a crime, maybe she doesn't talk to her father, maybe she just doesn't think it was important either.

Shay heard the front door open and close. Was she back? Shay jumped to her feet and ran to the door just as Shane was coming back in.

"Is she out there?" She managed to choke out.

"No. I was just making sure she left," he said snidely.

"Maybe she'll call"' Shay sniffed.

"No, she won't. I turned off your phone and hid it."

"You what? Why the hell did you do that? Where is it?"

"You need to sever all ties honey," he said coldly. "If you don't, she'll just be right back."

But how could she sever all ties? Shay was in love with her. She just couldn't imagine being without her now. But Shane was right. Was Lily hiding something? Why had she never invited Shay to her place? Was there something wrong with Lily? Did Shay fall for the wrong person?

Shane decided to sleep on the couch in case Lily tried to return. Shay tossed and turned, unable to sleep thinking about Lily and if she had just let Shane talk her into making a terrible mistake.

Lily walked over to the nursing home and went to the roof. Shane had closed the curtains and the windows so Lily couldn't even hear their conversation. Did he know something? Did he figure out that Lily wasn't entirely truthful? She tried texting Shay but got no response. Finally, around 8:30, she called. It went straight to voicemail.

Lily trudged home and went straight to her apartment. Luckily Eric wasn't lurking. The last thing she needed was to have him start a fight. Right now, she's kill him if she saw him.

She kept turning it over in her head. *She doesn't want to talk to you* was all she kept hearing. She paced the floor trying to figure out what she was going to do. After two hours of pacing and trying Shay's number and leaving message after message, she realized she had to leave New York. If she's going to have to live without Shay, she surly couldn't stay.

LEAVING NEW YORK

Lily packed a bag with clothes and toiletries. She stopped at Erica's door and knocked loudly.

"Lily? What's wrong?" Erica asked when she opened the door.

"She doesn't want to see me anymore," she managed to mumble through the tears.

"Why?" she asked.

"I don't know. I just know I can't stay here."

"Lily wait. Where will you go?"

"I'm going to the Nashville coven. I'll be safe there and maybe being outdoors will help to get her out of my head."

"But Lily," Erica pleaded.

"I have to go, Erica. I'm sorry."

Erica tried to stop her. At the elevator, Erica tried to talk to her.

"Lily, what happened?" Erica asked.

"She doesn't want to see me," Lily cried. "Shane had something to do with it."

Erica sighed and took Lily in her arms. Lily dropped her bag and put her arms around Erica. When the elevator finally dinged, Lily grabbed her bag and stepped across the hall and into the elevator. Erica knew that there was no stopping her. Maybe Lily had finally found love. Erica hoped that wasn't the case. Because if it was, Lily would love Shay forever.

Lily rode to the garage, walked to her car then fell to her knees. She couldn't believe that this was happening. She had finally found love and now it was over. She had to leave. She just couldn't stay. If she couldn't be with Shay, there was no reason for her to stay in New York.

She pulled herself up off the concrete, fumbled through her bag and found the car remote, the remote to the Nissan TurboMax then thought better of it. She put that one back in her bag and fumbled for the one to the Mercedes 1025i. She leaned down and unhooked the cloth cover that was over the car. She flung it to the side and let it drift to the floor beside the TurboMax.

Without LaShay, she no longer belonged in New York. She began to cry harder. She drove through the streets of the city to the interstate. Once on the interstate, she only stopped for gas and restroom breaks. Her thoughts would drift back to LaShay and her eyes would well up. *Dammit Lily! Stop it!* She would tell herself. She wasn't sure exactly how to get to Nashville from New York City, but she didn't care. She didn't even use the auto-drive system. She would just drive south as fast as she could until she reached the Carolinas, then she'd travel west.

After about five hours of driving she just didn't want to drive any longer. She exited the interstate and found a decent hotel. As long as it was clean and had inside access. She parked the car as close to the front door as she could, grabbed her bag and checked in. Once in the room, she locked all the locks, checked the window locks and fell across the bed. She was asleep before she felt the bed beneath her.

Her dreams were jagged and fractured. Glimpses of alternate futures, futures that seemed not only distant, but impossible now that LaShay was no longer in her life. She felt as if part of her had been stripped away.

She tossed and turned for what seemed like days. When she woke, it didn't feel like she had slept at all. The clock on the table said it was just after eight PM. Her whole body would shake occasionally, like an arctic wind whipped up her spine for only a brief moment. She was hungry, famished even, and remembered that she had been so caught up in Shay that although she had had food, she hadn't had any blood in days.

She was in a wickedly ill mood. She wanted to find Shane and find out how many swipes of her claws she could take at him before he hit the ground. And she wouldn't care if it resulted in her immediate death. He had taken away an unknown future that she knew was supposed to be with Shay.

She pulled a pillow to her chest and wrapped her arms around it. A low growl brewed in the back of her throat as the angered vampire began to stir. She wiped her face across the pillow to wipe away the tears as she felt her eyes begin to burn, then out of rage ripped the pillow in half. In the next instant she had slammed the bed into the far wall and was on the balls of her feet, crouched on the floor where the bed had been not two seconds before. A low, terrifying growl escaped her lips and her hands curled into claws that punctured the carpet then the concrete floor. Her hands pulverized the chunks into powder then she dug her claws down again.

How could this happen? she thought

Lily was furious..She wanted so badly to be in Shay's arms that it hurt.

Why hadn't she shown her how she felt? *Why didn't I tell her how in love with her I really was? Could she also feel the lingering sensations that my touch left on her skin every time we made contact. Just one time, why didn't I tell her I loved her?*

But she didn't tell her, and now she was gone.

She took a deep breath then another and another until she finally began to calm down. There was really nothing she could do. She had no idea why Shay had rejected her and there was no reason that she should think that she'd change her mind.

She looked down at her hands and at the light gray powder that covered them both. She turned them over to inspect the damage. Her human skin had torn when she hit the floor. She walked to the bathroom to wash the pulverized concrete and blood from her hands. According to the amount of blood, her knuckles had been pretty chewed up from the concrete and like many times before, her claws had punctured her palms. It didn't even hurt anymore when she did it.

After almost an hour, she had calmed down enough, to leave the room. She walked down to the front desk and asked about the nearest place to get a steak. She kept her hands in her pockets, just in case.

"Well, I don't know if they're still open but you can try the restaurant about two miles that way," the boy at the front desk told her, pointing out the window toward the opposite direction of the interstate.

"Thank you, I'll try there," Lily smiled and strolled out the double glass doors.

She drove down the street about two miles and saw a little diner that looked like no one ever visited. The glass windows across the front were caked with dirt and dead bugs. It still had a neon sign that read "OPEN". *It doesn't look open.* She searched for the reader board that hung on almost every other business in the U.S. It listed the type of place it was, if it were open or closed and the hours of operation. There was no board and no signs.

She parked the car in the empty, dusty parking lot than was still dirt and small rocks. Lily could remember when that was the norm. Everywhere else there was white concrete. She grabbed the rusty bar that was across the door and it flew open, almost hitting the glass behind it. *That is lighter than I thought it would be* she thought, looking at her hand to make sure there were no claws. She grabbed the door and walked in. There were a few couples finishing up their meals. *Where are their cars?* Lily wondered.The waitress looked her way and smiled.

"What time do you close?" Lily asked the waitress as she walked toward me.

"Five minutes ago," she smiled. "But I'm sure we can get you a meal to go if you'd like."

It was five minutes after nine.

"Yes, thank you," Lily said gratefully. "Steak, rare, please," she said, questioningly.

"How rare?" the waitress asked.

"The rarer the better," she said.

She paused a momentas if waiting for Lily to say something else.

"Oh, French fries?"

Then the waitress smiled and said, "One rare steak and fries, coming right up."

Lily sat down at the closest table to where she was standing, then looked around the restaurant. Five out of the six people in there, were looking at her but she just ignored them.

It wasn't five minutes before the waitress came out with a Styrofoam container. *Styrofoam?* Lily though. *Where in the world did they get* Styrofoam? *They stopped making that stuff over forty years ago.*

"What would you like to drink, hon?" she asked.

"Soda is fine, whatever you have," Lily answered.

She stood up and walked to the cash register where the waitress had placed the container of food before disappearing back into the kitchen. Lily opened the container and saw that the steak was barely even browned. She smiled. The waitress returned with a covered Styrofoam cup and sat it on the counter.

"Thirty eight dollars and thirty one cents," the waitress said.

Lily placed three bright blue twenties on the counter. "Keep it," she said nodding at the waitress.

"Oh," she said startled by the gesture, "but I really didn't do anything."

"It is after nine though," she smiled and picked the food up off the counter. "Thank you."

"Uh, no problem," she said as Lily walked out the door.

She took the food back to the hotel and ate in the room. The allow knife and fork wasn't quite up to the task so she ate the steak with her fingers. Not exactly lady like, but hey, she was hungry. Very hungry. The steak wasn't a great substitute for blood, but it had to do for now.

When she was done, she did her best to conceal the holes in the floor before she placed the bed back in its proper place. She clicked on the TV and started flipping through channels. She wasn't really looking for anything, She was just trying not to think about Shay. Or Shane for that matter. She found some cheesy chick flick and settled in against a stack of pillows. It didn't take long for her to doze off.

Shay wiped the tears from her face again and rolled over in her bed. She couldn't stop thinking about Lily and what Shane had convinced her to do. She decided that she had to talk to her. She got out of bed and went to the living room to get her phone off of the charger. Shane had finally gone home and given her phone back to her. She had promised that she wouldn't try to call Lily, but Shane still would not bring her phone to the bedroom.

Shay pressed the icon for phone and then tapped Lily's picture. The phone rang on the other end. After four rings someone answered but it wasn't Lily.

"Hello?" Erica repeated into the phone.

"Hello? Is Li... Lily there?" Shay asked. Her voice still cracking from crying.

"Is this LaShay?" Erica asked.

"Ye... Yes," Shay answered, shakily.

"Lily isn't here, hon."

"Do you know when she'll be back?"

"No, dear, I really don't," Erica answered honestly.

Erica wanted to question Shay about what happeded but decided that it wasn't her place. "I'll tell Lily you called if I talk to her."

"Thank you," Shay said, sniffling a little harder.

It was dark and the air was moist. Lily was crawling around on her hands and knees in the dark. She felt something soft but cold and wet. Then she focused in the faint light and could make out the shape of a face. She looked down at her hands and they were covered in blood and as she looked past her hands she could make out a body. The stomach area was a black, empty hole. She turned her face away only to feel a cold hand on her arm. When she turned, it was LaShay's face she saw.

Lily sat straight up in the bed, wide awake. Her heart pounded in her chest, sweat beads dotted her forehead and her hair stuck to the back of her neck.

"How am I going to make it through this?" She asked herself, hiding her face in her hands.

She turned off the TV, took a quick shower, got dressed and checked out. It was about four AM when she pulled onto the interstate. She put her foot on the gas and accelerated to over one hundred miles an hour. The needle crept to one hundred and twenty and she set the cruise control. She cranked up the stereo until it felt like her ears would explode.

She stopped only to fill up with gas. She wondered if she should stop and eat again. She couldn't allow hunger to let her temper flare again. She decided that since she was confined to the car, that she would be fine.

She slowed only when she feared a state trooper was over the next hill or around the next turn. Three times, she was right and waved at them as she passed them driving with auto drive turned on. As soon as she was out of laser range she resumed driving with cruise control.

She buzzed past cars that were in the auto-drive lanes. She drove for a few more hours before she began to see familiar signs.

It was about midnight when she turned off of the interstate and onto a familiar road. The road twisted and turned through the dark. She fought the urge to accelerate, there were too many deer in this area and she really liked this car. An old twelve cylinder Mercedes SL65 AMG.

When she reached an overgrown driveway, she slowly plowed through the weeds and underbrush. Gravel cracked and popped as the car drove over them. She cringed as saplings growing in the driveway scrapped down the sides and bottom with a high pitched squeal. It didn't look like anyone had been there in years. Vincent had left a trust fund to cover the yearly property taxes, as he did with the other coven locations. The trusts were also supposed to cover general maintenance, like lawn care and property upkeep. She had to make some phone calls to Vincent. Then she thought that she probably needed to get a phone since she left hers on her kitchen counter up north.

The driveways that lead to the houses were a good two hundred yards from the paved road. She made a few turns and saw a few rabbits in the headlights as she rolled slowly through the overgrown weeds and grass. When she reached the house she once lived in, she angled the car so the headlights were shining through the windows then dug through her bag for the keys.

She climbed out of the car, stretched for a moment and then walked up onto porch. It was cool outside, but not cold. Crickets and katydids chirped and sang. Frogs croaked from the banks of the creek on the other side of the driveway. The air was dry for this time of year. Lily unlocked the door and it creaked and squeaked all the way open. The house smelled empty. Like no one and nothing had been there in years. All the windows seemed to be intact, the door was still locked and the driveways were definitely not used regularly.

She made her way in the dark to the basement door, walked down the rickety wooden steps and searched for the fuse box. The squeak was way louder than she expected when she opened the metal door. It was so loud her ears rang for a second. She threw the main breaker lever up and an illuminated buzz came to life over her head. She walked back upstairs and out to the car to turn off the headlights and engine. She swung her bag over her shoulder and walked back to the porch. She stopped and listened to the sounds around her. Oh, how she had missed this place.

She thought about Shay. She wondered if Shay would like this place, the country air, the open spaces, the breathtaking view of the night sky and all its constellations. She shook her head and held back the tears. Then she dropped the bag on the porch and broke into a full run toward the trees. She cleared the creek in a single stride and the frogs were silent for a moment, then one by one the harmonies began again. She ran on a small path through the thick brush and took in all the sounds and smells that she had missed so much. She ran past the pond that she would swim in during the summers. She passed the tree that had a deer stand in it about twenty feet up where she would hunt for deer. She and Onyx had managed to kill their fair share back then.

She ran over the hill to the clearing where the horses used to be and followed the tree line to the adjacent side of the clearing She stopped in front of the old horse barn. One of the support posts that held up the feeding trough overhang had collapsed and fallen, along with half of the overhang. She walked around to the other side and walked through the wide opening. It was dark inside but her eyes quickly adjusted. She walked across the dusty dirt floor to the ladder on the opposite wall. She climbed up into the hay loft and to her surprise, there was still hay up there. Far from edible for any grazer, but more than adequate for a bed. She walked to the opposite wall, the wall above the entrance door downstairs, unhooked the rope from a bent nail and swung open the loft doors. She sat down in the opened doorway, her legs hanging over the edge and looked out over the empty rolling meadow. The moon was full enough to illuminate the darkness and she thought how much Shay would like this place.

Would she like it here? Would she ever want to leave the city to live in a place like this?

She remembered the many times that she and Erica had spent in this loft. She missed laughing and playing and spending hours on end talking.

Her memories were suddenly interrupted by movement across the meadow. A light bay mare with one white sock walked slowly out of the trees. She stopped a few yards into the clearing, tore off a few long pieces of grass then continued walking slowly as she chewed.

Lily jumped down from the loft without a sound and made her way toward her. She approached slowly and cautiously in the dark. Her eyes followed Lily across the meadow as she was well aware of her approach. Lily tore off a couple of handfuls of grass and held them out in front of her as she walked toward the large animal. The horse bobbed her head and her nostrils flared as she sniffed the air. Lily laughed to herself because she could see the confusion in the mare's eyes. She could smell the faint hint of predator. Her head bobbed and jerked as she tried to decide to stay or to run.

Lily stopped a few yards from her and held out the grass. She assumed the offering was just too much to pass up and after a snort and another head bob, she took a few tentative steps toward the offered grass. She was definitely tame. Lily could tell by her eyes and the way she watched her and the way she moved, not to mention her condition. She was well taken care of and was apparently accustomed to having humans around.

She stopped about two feet from Lily's hand, her neck stretched as far as it would go toward the grass. Lily often wondered if grass in someone's hand tasted better than all of the acres of grass around her, because the horses would literally follow you around the meadow if you had grass or hay in your hand. She smiled and leaned closer to the mare so she could take the grass from her hand then turned to walk back to the barn.

Lily heard her footsteps behind her then felt the mare's nose nudge her back. Lily stopped and the horse head-butted her in the butt. Lily had nearly forgotten how strong they were. She neighed playfully and pushed against her back again. She took a few steps forward this time and the mare followed. She held out her hand as she walked and slowed so her neck was over Lily's shoulder then she stroked her neck as they walked back toward the barn. At the barn Lily rubbed the mare's neck and stroked her over the shoulders. She looked down and saw the one white sock, Lily laughed out loud.

"Sugarfoot," she said aloud and it startled the mare.

The horse lifted her head and pranced a few steps. Then settled and walked back to Lily.

Lily once loved sleeping in the barn. On cool summer nights her and Erica would talk and laugh for hours on end in the barn, then fall asleep there instead of making the short trek home. So Lily threw some of the bales of hay down from the loft and spread them out over the dry dirt floor of one of the inner stalls. The mare started eating some of the old hay and Lily figured that she probably wasn't going to stop her. She pushed the horse's head out of the way so she could lie down. It was late and Lily was tired. She had nowhere to be and since she was here, she might as well get some sleep. The sun would be coming up soon. Lily figured the mare would get tired soon enough and probably go to sleep too. So she pushed a bunch of hay into a bed, curled up in the corner and drifted off to sleep.

LaShay stared at her cell phone. She had been calling and leaving messages for two days, but Lily hadn't answered. Finally Shay decided to go to her. She threw on a sweatshirt and headed out. She walked the twelve blocks to the Crown Building. She remembered that Lily had told her that she had an apartment on the fifty sixth floor.

Shay walked into the immaculate building just after seven PM. The doorman gave her a once over and the giant wolf standing guard beside him took a whiff of air. He smelled a hint of Lily and let Shay pass without incident.

The building lobby was an incredible sight. Marble columns that stretched up four stories. Red carpet accented by grey, black and red marble lined the floors. Statues from the Renaissance era dotted the walls in recessed apertures. Antique couches and high backed chairs dotted the open room. In one portion of the lobby, there were Egyptian artifacts in the recesses of the walls. Twelve foot tall statues of queens and kings like Nefertiti and the gods like Horus and a number of others that Shay didn't recognize stood in the recesses. The outer part of the walls in the Egyptian area were covered in hieroglyphs and paintings of Egyptian rituals. Shay made a mental note to study them in detail someday.

Little did Shay know that she had just walked into a vampire coven. One of the largest covens on the east coast. But no one batted an eye. No one even looked at her twice.

Vampires, humans and guardian wolves made their way around the lobby. She remembered that Lily had told her about the wolves and that Lily had one of her own. A black one, if Shay recalled correctly.

The doors to one of the eight elevators opened as soon as Shay stepped up to them. It was always the door that opened when a stranger came in the building. She stepped in and was asked by a young dark haired man, "What floor?"

"Fifty Six," Shay answered politely.

When Shay got off the elevator, Onyx jumped to his feet at the end of the hallway. He was hoping it was Lily. Shay walked slowly down the hallway, admiring the carving and detail work around and over the elevators. She noticed the lattice work in the trim around Lily's door. She knocked on the door.

Onyx was running up the steps to the seventy second floor and then scratched on Erica's door. He motioned with his head for her to follow him and he led her to Lily's floor by way of the elevators.

"Can I help you?" Erica asked when she was about ten feet from LaShay.

"I'm looking for Lily?" Shay answered almost as a question.

"Lily has gone to the... Lily went out of town, to Nashville," Erica said, almost saying Lily went to the Nashville Coven. She wasn't accustomed to outside humans in the building.

"Do you know when she'll be back?" Shay asked almost in tears.

Erica knew that this had to be Shay. She wasn't sure what to tell her. Lily had left her phone in New York and the phone wouldn't be in service at Lily's home in Nashville. So there was no way to get in contact with Lily. Erica honestly didn't know if Lily was even coming back.

"I don't know, hon," Erica said sadly.

Onyx knew Shay's scent as he had smelled her on Lily for the past month and a half. He walked over and nudged Shay's hand. It startled her at first, to be so close to such a large wolf. But Onyx nudged her again and she lifted her hand to pet him.

"You must be Onyx," Shay said, not knowing whether she wanted to smile or cry.

Maybe it was a good sign that she left her wolf. Maybe that meant it was only a short trip. Shay could only hope.

"Well, thank you," Shay finally said after petting Onyx for a minute.

About halfway home the tears finally made an appearance. Shay couldn't help but think that Lily was gone forever.

When she arrived home she noticed a black stretched limo in front of her apartment. *Just Great* she thought. She knew that her father was in her apartment, waiting for her, probably sipping on a glass of scotch. Shay trudged to the elevator and contemplated just leaving. But her father would only wait until she got home. So she pushed the button for the twelfth floor. She found her remotes in her purse and went inside. Keys were a thing of the past. If your front door wasn't on a scanner, you carried a remote for it, not unlike the one for your car.

"What do you want, Dad?" Shay asked as she put her purse and remote on the coffee table. She was still crying.

"So who is she?" Her dad asked angrily.

"She's gone! Ok Dad!" Shay sobbed.

"What?"

"She's gone! Left. Out of my life!" Shay nearly yelled.

"Well, that's good," said Martin. "Because you're not gay."

"Yes Dad, I am gay! And Lily was everything I had ever wanted in another person."

"I doubt that," he father said snidely.

"I'm not in the mood to argue," Shay sniffed. "You can stay if you want but I'm going to bed."

"It's barely ten o'clock."

"Bye Dad."

Shay was almost asleep when she heard a knock on the front door. She shot out of bed and raced to the door. Could it be Lily?

She flung the door open and Josh was standing there. What was her ex-boyfriend doing at her apartment at eleven o'clock on a week night? Josh took one look at Shay and could tell she had been crying. Her eyes were bloodshot and puffy and her cheeks were still red.

"What's wrong?" Josh asked, reaching out to touch her face.

Shay broke into tears once again and Josh just put his arms around her. He held her for a few minutes, standing in the hallway while she cried on his shoulder. He nudged her gently and they walked into the apartment. They sat down on the couch together and Josh wiped tears from Shay's cheek.

"What's wrong?" He asked again.

"Everything," Shay sobbed.

"Anything in particular," he asked.

Shay looked into Josh eyes and tried to determine if she should tell him about Lily. He had been a good boyfriend as well as a friend so she decided it probably couldn't hurt. Besides, she really needed an unbiased party to talk to. Shane didn't like Lily and her father refused to believe that she was gay. Shay wiped her cheeks with both hands and then began.

"I met someone a couple of months ago."

"Ok, that's why we broke up right? It's ok if it is, I told you I still wanted to be friends, and I meant it," he said then paused a moment. "So what happened? Obviously it ended badly so do I need a shovel? Did he hurt you?"

She laughed. "No! No shovels."

"Ok good," he smiled. "So talk to me. What's wrong?"

Josh put his hand on her knee and looked her in the eye then waited.

Shay took a deep breath.

"Her name is Lily."

She figured she'd get right to the point. Just get it out there and go from there. She wasn't sure how Josh would take the news, being that he was just sleeping with her not two months before.

"Ok," Josh said without batting an eye.

"She's beautiful," Shay smiled and relaxed a bit. "I met her the last time we went to Baldwin's on Lex. She was playing pool and the que ball was knocked off the table. She bumped into me and when I saw her eyes... I don't know. I just felt something. She was so beautiful. Her eyes were just so blue and I couldn't help but stare."

Josh didn't say a word, just let Shay tell the story.

"I went back to the bar the next Saturday and she was there. We started hanging out playing pool a few nights a week. Then I invited her over one night and we talked for hours and hours. After a few weeks I realized that I was looking forward to seeing her. That I couldn't wait to get a text from her. That I was actually falling for this woman. It scared me at first. I didn't want to be falling for her but I was and hard. I have never felt like this before, Josh. I have never had butterflies in my stomach from just being around someone. But I get them when I'm with *her*."

"So... what seems to be the problem? Does she not feel the same?" Josh asked.

"I don't know! I never got a chance to ask her."

"So what happened?"

"Shane con..."

"Oh, it figures that he had something to do with it," Josh interrupted.

"Yeah. He convinced me that something was wrong with her. That she was hiding something. All because she had never invited me to her place at the Crown Building."

"The Crown Building? Wow! *The* Crown Building?" Josh repeated.

"Yes, 56A," Shay smiled. "And as of today, I know for a fact that she does live there because I went there myself. But she's gone. They told me that she went to Nashville and that they didn't know when or if she'd be back."

"She just left?"

"Yes. And she left her cell phone and there's no land lines working where she's going."

Josh took a deep breath. "Well. Umm did you try her reader? She has to at least have that..."

"Not responding," she said.

I'm not sure what I should tell you to do. If she's gone with no way to contact her..."

"I know," Shay replied, trying not to cry again. "Then my Dad finds out and he's not happy about it. He doesn't *want* me to be gay. So, Mister I own the world, shows up here thinking that... that... that he could talk me *out* of it or something."

"I'm sorry about your dad."

Shay shook her head and rested her head in her hands.

"Me, too," she said.

Lily was awakened by the soft muzzle of the mare against the side of her head. She opened her eyes wearily and she was curled up against the horse's side. Lily guessed the mare was ready to get up and didn't want to hurt her when she stood. Or maybe she was irritated that she had disturbed her by talking in her sleep or something, who knows. Once she was on her feet, the mare stood up and shook off the loose hay. She neighed softly and nudged Lily with her head.

"What is it girl?" She asked and stroked her neck.

Lily leaned against her and rested her head against her shoulder. She was a rather big horse, at least fifteen hands, she had a light bay coloration, which was a reddish brown coat, a black mane and tail and black on her legs. All of her legs except one, her hind right leg was about six inches of white at the bottom above the hoof. She was probably a Tennessee Walker. Lily wondered what she was doing here and how she got onto the property. There must be a fence down somewhere and figured at some point she'd check the property fence line.

She led the mare outside and stood beside her for a minute. The sun was hidden behind a large stray cloud but it wouldn't be there long.

"I'll be back, Sugarfoot."

Lily took off at a full run toward the house. She had to on sunscreen if she was going to be out today.

The mare just was grazing in the meadow when Lily returned. She walked up to the mare slowly and just stood close to her for a few minutes. She stroked the mares back to get her used to her. Then she walked Sugarfoot around the meadow for a while and sat down while the mare ate. She watched the clouds drift by overhead and tried to think about anything *except* LaShay. It didn't work.

Lily thought about all the times they had been together. The laughing and the horrible pool playing. She was better than Shay even though she usually let her win. Lily wondered what Shane had said to make Shay not want to see her anymore. Erica had been right, Lily did need to watch out for Shay's best friend.

After about fifteen minutes she decided it was time to test her luck. Lily was dying to ride. She stood, walked over to Sugarfoot and stroked her back again for a few minutes. Then gave her mane a quick tug to test her response. She lifted her head slightly but continued to graze. Then Lily pulled herself up and swung her leg over the horse's back. Sugarfoot raised her head and turned to look at her. She gave a short snort and started walking. Lily just let her walk wherever she wanted to go. It was way too soon to try to lead her anywhere.

Lily sat, perched on the mare's back, as she walked around the meadow. She made a couple of wide circles and finally stopped and started to graze again. She swung her legs back onto her rump and wrapped her arms around her neck. She hid her face in her mane and allowed herself to relax for a moment.

It had been so long since she had ridden, that she just had to try. Finally she decided it was time to really ride this horse. The mare was still grazing. She sat up and positioned herself just behind her shoulder. She made a clicking sound with her mouth. Sugarfoot's ears perked up and she took a few steps forward. Then Lily gently pressed her heels into her sides and leaned forward only slightly. Was it possible she was a dressage horse? Nah, Lily would never be so lucky. But the horse did acknowledge the shift in Lily's weight and she did walk a little faster. She made another clicking sound and leaned forward a little more. The horse's pace quickened. She let her trot along until the horse decided to stop. Lily wanted to go for a run so badly, but that was enough for today. As she didn't want to push it. She had no idea how long it had been since she had been ridden and didn't want her to associate her with work, especially if she had been forced to in the past. So she slid off of her back and started walking toward the pond.

It was over the hill about four hundred yards or so and the mare followed. Sugarfoot nudged her as she walked then walked ahead. Sugarfoot turned to face Lily and stopped. She bobbed her head and pawed the ground.

"What is it girl," Lily asked out loud.

She snorted and bobbed her head again then she relaxed the shoulder that was closest to her and Lily laughed with delight. She had seen only one other horse do that, the mare that she had loved so much when she lived there when she was young. She would drop her shoulder for Lily to climb on her back.

Lily laughed out loud and took a handful of her mane and with a quick leap, swung her leg over her back. Sugarfoot lifted her head high and pranced off toward the pond. She couldn't help the wide grin on her face, maybe this was one of the mare's offspring, or maybe she had the same trainer or rider. Lily really didn't care, the horse loved to be ridden and Lily loved to ride.

About one hundred yards from the pond, Lily squeezed her legs against the bay mare's sides and dug in her heels. She shifted her weight forward and gave a quick kick. The horse was off like a rocket. She was at a full run in only three strides. When they were close the pond, Lily shifted her weight back and pulled on the mane. Sugarfoot slowed to a stop just before stepping into the water then she turned right and trotted along the muddy edge.

Sugarfoot had taken her there as if she knew exactly where Lily wanted to go. Lily had only wanted to see the pond in the daylight, to see if it looked the same as it did years ago. On the right side of the pond there was a deep trench in the path where the pond water overflowed during heavy rains. The mare simply jumped over it like it was nothing at all. Lily was really beginning to love this horse. She stroked her neck when she stopped on the far side of the pond, a foot deep in the water and dropped her head to drink. Lily looked around. Everything was exactly the way it was. Albeit a little overgrown with bigger trees, but the same.

When Sugarfoot was finished drinking, she turned around, walked down the trail and back toward the house. Lily needed to go shopping. She figured she could pick up some horse feed and some fresh hay for the mare while she was out.

"Sugarfoot," Lily said aloud and her ears rotated back. "Thanks for the ride."

THE ATTACK

Lily had been in Nashville for over two weeks when she finally bought a cell phone and called home. She called Erica, of course and nearly hit the floor when Erica told her that Shay had come to the apartment only days after she had left. Lily quickly packed her things and headed home. If Shay had come to see her, maybe she had changed her mind about not seeing her.

When Lily made it back to the city, she as anxious to talk to Shay, but decided that she would give it a little time to find out what Shay was thinking. So Lily spent most of her time on the roof of the nursing home.

Lily had been back for about six days. It had been three weeks since Lily had last spoken to LaShay. Now she had resorted to being a stalker. Lily watched Shay from the roof next door to hopefully catch a glance of the one she loved. She also had hoped to hear that Shay was okay or explain why she had gone the Crown Building. But Lily never heard.

It was nearly time for Shay to get home from her job at NY26, New York's equivalent to any other local news station. Shay was a graphics programmer for their major newscasts. The local news broadcasts no longer required a human newscaster. All of the broadcasts were either robots or a computer made image. Shay was in charge of Stormy, the animated weather girl. She loved her job and since Lily had left, she had been spending most of her time at work.

Well on this particular day Lily had been detained by Erica at home and was running a little late to see Shay, something she had grown to look forward to everyday although she still hadn't attempted to talk to her again. She kissed Erica on the cheek, ran to her apartment, just grabbed a hoodie instead of putting on sun block and headed out.

When she got to the roof of the nursing home something just seemed off. Shay wasn't home yet so Lily waited in the shadows. Then she heard a crash from Shay's apartment. She heard the sound again and again. It sounded almost like someone hitting a wall, hard. *Shay!!* She thought. Lily could only think of Shay; not the sun, not the threat of being seen and not even of how she would explain any of it to Shay. Lily took a running start and jumped from the roof of the nursing home, over the street and onto the balcony of Shay's apartment. She crashed through the double glass doors and ran to Shay's bedroom. Shay was being pinned to the floor by a hooded man dressed in all black. At this point, Lily was in full kill mode. Her canines, her claws and her eyes had all transformed her into a full vampire. There was no going back now.

Lily grabbed the back of the intruder's neck, dug her claws deep and threw him through the opened bedroom door into the living room. LaShay's shirt had been ripped nearly completely off, her face was covered in blood and she was barely conscience. Lily heard the intruder run toward the front door but she beat him to it. She grabbed him by the throat and squeezed. Her claws slid through his skin like butter and had crushed his windpipe before he even had a chance to scream. Blood ran down her arm as the man gasped for his last breath. Seeing the blood reminded her that she was in Shay's apartment and that she was leaving proof of a crime, so she quickly carried the now dead man to the bathroom and dropped him in the bathtub.

She ran to Shay, knelt beside her and placed her clawed hand under her back to lift her up. Shay opened her eyes and although Lily's eyes were completely red behind the blue, she gave her a weak smile. Her lids were heavy but her eyes saw everything. Lily stared into her eyes for a moment and Shay stared into hers. She had thought her eyes were beautiful before, but now that Shay was here, inches from her, they took her breath away. Then her lids slowly closed and she began to lose consciousness.

"No, Shay! Hold on, OK! You are going to be fine, OK. Shay, stay with me. Just keep breathing, love. Keep breathing," Lily said softly.

Lily was shaking all over. She held LaShay in a seated position and was finally able to see just how bad she was hurt. It was a hell of a lot worse than she originally thought. Her lip was torn completely through and blood poured from the gash above her left eye. She probably had a concussion and she was fading fast. Lily panicked.

Lily pulled her closer and placed her mouth over hers. She cut her tongue purposefully against her teeth. Lily's blood spilled into her mouth and reflexively she swallowed. Then, she felt Shay's tongue against hers. She kissed her gently, knowing that her lip was torn and wasn't healed yet. Lily pulled away from her lips, cut her finger with her teeth and ran it slowly across her temple and then over her brow. Lily's blood mixed with Shay's and the healing began.

Lily felt her take a deep breath. She hadn't even realized that her claws were still out until she felt Shay's soft hand on the back of hers. She wrapped her fingers under her hand and pulled it in front of her face. The shiny, white claws still protruded from under Lily's fingernails. She looked down at Lily's hand then back into her eyes.

Damn, she was beautiful. Her eyes burned through her and at that moment Lily knew that nothing else in her life mattered. Shay was what she lived for now. And she would do anything and everything in her power to prove that to her. She would never leave her again. If they could only be friends, so be it. As long as Shay was in her life.

Lily recut her tongue and ran it slowly over Shay's lip. It was nearly healed. Again, Shay's tongue found hers and this time they kissed like they meant it. Shay's fingers ran through Lily's hair and she pulled herself closer. Shay was still getting weaker by the minute.

"Thank you," she whispered before she fell unconscious.

Lily wasn't sure what to do so she called Jack.

"McGoo?"

"Lily?" he asked. "Is everything alright? You sound upset."

"No, I'm not alright. Well, I'm fine, but I have someone here that's just been attacked in her apartment," she said. "I healed the wounds and she should be okay on a few minutes. But her attacker..."

"Is it LaShay?"

"Yes. How did...." Lily shook her head, she didn't care how he knew.

"Where is her attacker?" he asked solemnly.

"He's dead," Lily said.

"That's what I was afraid of. Where are you?" he asked.

"Her apartment."

"Where?"

"Across from the nursing home on West 70th," Lily told him.

"What apartment number?"

"1202, top floor," she told him.

"I'm on my way," he sighed.

While Lily was waiting, still holding Shay, she called Erica and filled her in on what was going on and told her that she was bringing LaShay home with her if Shay wanted to go. Erica told her that that was fine and she'd make a room for her. Then Lily turned all her attention back to Shay. She was coming to.

Lily held Shay in her arms on the floor of the apartment. The light beige carpet was streaked with blood. There was a trail of blood drops from the front door to the bathroom. The doors to the balcony lay shattered on the floor and the frame hung from a single top hinge on each. Lily was already making mental plans to have the carpet cleaned and replace the doors.

Shay's wounds were healed. She didn't speak, she just stared back at Lily as Lily stared at her. She was breathtaking. If she only knew how in love with her Lily really was. In love with everything. Her mesmerizing eyes, her full round lips, her soft, sultry voice, the birthmark on her neck and every perfect tiny flaw. All she knew was that she was the one. She looked into her eyes and she finally knew what all the other vampires were talking about when they spoke of their loves. How they weren't complete without them. How they would lose their appetite if they are away from their love for any amount of time. How they knew that they couldn't live without them. Lily once thought they were crazy for thinking they couldn't live without someone, to think that you had rather be dead than to never see another person. She thought it was impossible to exist for someone else, but for LaShay Black, she would risk anything; her possessions, her pride, her life. For her, Lily would do anything, be anything she wanted her to be. A friend, a lover, even a protector. She had never needed anyone else, since the day she was born she was perfectly content being alone. Lily had always been the one that was different, not a full vampire and definitely not human, she was used to being by herself. She had wanted so badly to fall in love, but there was just never anyone that she just couldn't live without. Until now. Now she knew why she had never connected to any male. It was a female that her heart was looking for all along. She had had crushes on girls, but had never felt like this about anyone. No one even came close.

But was it mutual? What if Shay didn't love her? What if she had only gone to Lily's apartment to tell Lily in person that the friendship was over? But why was she crying while she was there? But why did Shay kiss her? Was it possible that Shay felt the same way? All these questions ran through Lily's head as she held Shay.

Shay stared into her eyes which were still quite red. It was like she was looking into her, into her soul. Could she see how in love with her she was? Could she see that she would do anything for Shay. She had already decided two months ago that she wanted to spend eternity with her. Would she believe her? Would she be able to convince her that she was everything to her? Would Lily be able to convince Vincent that she was 'the one'? That she was her one true love? Only he could change her into a vampire. But what if she despises what Lily was? What if she wants nothing to do with Lily? What if she can't convince her that she loves her more than anything else?

Would Lily believe that the same things were running through Shay's head? Would Shay be able to convince Lily that she was crazy about her, too? Would Lily forgive her for sending her away? Would Lily try to kill Shane?

Lily pushed a strand of Shay's hair off of her forehead to behind her ear then continued to run her fingers through her dark hair. She placed her hand on Shay's cheek and she finally spoke.

"What are you?" Shay asked softly.

Shay ran her fingers across her lip then across her temple.

"I'm completely healed. No pain, it doesn't even feel like there's a scar. And where did you come from?"

Lily ran her fingers across Shay's bottom lip then across her cheek and under her neck. She lifted Shay up so that she was sitting again. Lily took a deep breath and looked at the floor. She was almost afraid to look at her. This was the moment that would make or break everything. This was the moment she had to tell Shay that she was a vampire. She wasn't going to lie or try to put off the inevitable any more. Shay would know everything from this point forward. She would know what Lily was and that she planned on Shay joining her someday. She would convince Vincent to change her but not before she was absolutely sure that she would survive the transformation.

Lily exhaled slowly and lifted her head to look into Shay's eyes. She stared for a moment then took another deep breath. She opened her mouth and pushed her canines into view. Then placed her hand in Shay's and exposed the claws. The gasp and rejection that Lily was expecting didn't come. Instead Shay only studied the hand in hers before running her fingertips lightly across Lily's claws. Shay reached for the other hand and placed her fingers on the fingertips. She looked up at Lily then back to their hands. Lily pushed her claws out slowly and watched Shay's fingers being pushed away. Shay looked at her and smiled.

"So you're a vampire," she said. "That's why you were being so careful. That's why you didn't take me to your apartment or tell me how old you are or tell me about your family. They're vampires, too, aren't they?"

Lily nodded.

"So how much of the movies are true?"

"Depends on which movie you're referring to," Lily answered.

"Well you can obviously heal others with your blood."

Lily nodded again and ran her finger down Shay's temple.

"Where did you come from? I mean today, how did you get in here?"

"Through the balcony doors." Lily chuckled. "Well, literally *through* the balcony doors."

"But the balcony it's the twelfth floor, and I'm pretty sure you can't fly," she said smiling.

"Would you believe I just happened to be next door?"

She looked at Lily for a moment. Lily did her best to keep a straight face and actually thought she had succeeded.

"Just happened to be next door? I find it a little hard to believe you would have relatives in an elder home," she said. "You never age, right?"

"Right, for the most part. But under the right circumstances, we can age."

She smiled and shook her head. Lily could tell she was trying to wrap her head around everything. And to Lily, was an incredible job. Not once had Shay acted surprised or scared. There was short period of silence as Shay just stared a Lily and ran her fingertips across Lily's claws.

"So you're really a vampire?" she asked.

"Well, I'm actually a hybrid. I'm half vampire and half human. I was born like this. I wasn't turned into a vampire."

"You were *born* a vampire? I didn't think it worked that way."

"No, it doesn't. Usually." Lily stated. "I was born in a cave in 1925."

"Ok. This should be interesting," Shay smiled.

"I was an experiment that wasn't supposed to work, but my mother got pregnant and carried me to term. She was only pregnant for about twelve weeks and she could tell that I would be coming soon. She knew what I was. She knew the risks and knew that the baby, I, would be killed by the coven as soon as they knew, too. She also knew that she wouldn't survive the birth. So she ran away from the coven trying to give me a better chance of living."

"She knew you were born going be born with fangs and claws?"

Lily nodded and Shay ran her hand across Lily's cheek.

"That has to be hard for you to deal with," she said.

Shay had figured out the outcome of the birth without having to hear the gory story. Lily was glad she didn't have to tell the story, especially to Shay. Then Shay looked at her as if for the first time.

"You have the most incredible blue eyes," she said. "They changed. They were really red, but now... wow!"

Shay moved closer, wrapped her hand around the back of Lily's neck then up into her hair. Lily's heart pounded in her chest and it felt like she was shaking all over. Their faces were inches apart.

"You are so beautiful," Shay whispered as she looked into Lily's crystal blue eyes.

She thinks I'm beautiful? Lily thought then wondered if vampires could blush because suddenly, her face felt hot. She leaned closer and pulled Shay toward her. Lily could feel her breath on her face, the heat of her hand on the back of her head and her soft skin still under her clawed hand. Shay closed her eyes and their lips touched. This was exactly were Lily wanted to be, forever.

Should I tell her now how I feel about her or wait? Shay thought. *How will I tell her that I'm in love with her? That I have been in love with her for weeks. When should I introduce her to my dad? How will he react to the news?*

Lily was thinking about a million other things, too. *Would Vincent accept her? I knew that Erica and Alexa would but what about Vincent? He had already been through this three times before. The others have only fallen in love with one person, but me, I've thought I was in love three times. And one was a human that Vincent changed. He will never believe that Shay is my one true love. I know she is because thinking about being without her now scares the hell out me. To never kiss her lips again, to never hold her in my arms... I had rather die.*

Lily pulled her body closer to hers and circled her tongue with her own as they kissed deeper. Then Lily pulled away and looked into her eyes, hoping that she could see just how she felt. Lily opened her mouth to speak but didn't know what to say except I love you, but she didn't want to scare her away so she said nothing.

"What?" Shay asked. "You want to say something. Please just say it."

"You're taking all of this awfully well, considering," Lily said smiling.

"Well, it's kind of hard to argue with what I've seen with my own eyes. Not to mention what I've felt. You're real, no matter what I *used* to believe. And no, I probably would not have believed you if this had not just happened. But there's no way to deny what I've just seen."

Lily leaned back, stood up and offered Shay a hand to help her up. She took it and stood up. The look on her face nearly broke Lily's heart.

"Shay, what's wrong?" Lily asked.

"Did I say something wrong?" she said.

Lily couldn't help but laugh a little.

"No," Lily whispered.

"Promise?" she whispered back, almost in tears.

Lily nodded then kissed her hand.

"What now?" Shay asked softly.

"I'd like to stay," Lily answered.

"But you barely know me. I could be a horrible person."

"But you're not a horrible person. You're quiet, you keep to yourself and you work too much. Where are your shirts? I'll get you a clean one."

Her pink dress shirt was covered in blood and most of the buttons had been ripped off.

Shay pointed to her dresser and Lily went to find her a clean shirt. Then Lily took her hand and led her to living room and sat down on the couch. After she sat down Lily took her hand, kissed it again and then held it.

"Why didn't you want to see anymore?" Lily asked.

"I was just afraid that... That you don't feel the same way about me as I feel about you."

"What?" Lily asked, confused, trying to wrap her head around what Shay just said.

"I'm just afraid that you don't like me as much as I like you."

"Why would you think that?" Lily asked.

It really didn't matter. Lily loved Shay and that's the only thing that mattered. If Shay loved her back...? Was it possible that Shay did feel the same way? Could that even be possible? She *was* taking the whole vampire thing in stride.

"I care about you. A lot," Lily told her.

Shay exhaled as if she had been holding her breath.

"Really?"

"Really," Lily affirmed.

Shay looked around the living room and after seeing the balcony doors hanging from hinges, remembered that she had been attacked. "You scared off my attacker?"

"No. He's dead," Lily confessed. "He saw the fangs and claws, I couldn't just let him leave. And I was pissed, I thought you were dead and he was the one that did it. Be thankful he's not in pieces all over your living room."

"You could do that?" she asked.

Lily nodded.

"We're very strong and our claws are very sharp," Lily told her.

AFTER THE ATTACK

McGoo knocked on the door. He brought everything he needed to dispose of the body in Shay's bathtub; from plastic to cover the carpet, to an electric saw to cut it into pieces.

First, Jack examined the scene and determined that they would dispose of the body without removing it from the apartment.

Lily left Shay to help Jack. They cut the body into small enough pieces that would fit down the disposal. Garbage had grown to be such a burden to the planet that science had to create an alternative to disposal trash. Garbage dumps were no longer in use and everything that could not be recycled was biodegradable and suitable for composting. Therefore, garbage disposals had been designed to pulverize or liquefy everything from mashed potatoes to steak bones in lieu of garbage pickup. The waste from the disposals was stored in containers that would be used as compost. Lily made trip after trip to the kitchen, stuffing pieces of flesh and bone down the kitchen sink disposal.

After nearly two and half hours, Lily and Jack were coming back from the bathroom with the last of the pieces when LaShay stopped them on the way to the kitchen.

"Is that what's left?" she asked, curling her nose.

Lily nodded.

"Are you ok?" Lily asked.

She lifted her hand to her head and gave a weak smile then nodded.

"We're almost finished," Lily said.

Shay stepped aside and allowed them to take the rest of the body to the kitchen. She followed. Jack shoved the last of the body into the disposal. Shay watched Lily closely, not really paying much attention to Jack, who in Lily's opinion was a stranger looking character than herself. With his sandy blond hair and mustache, he would seem to have been a lot more out of place in that day and age than Lily. But she watched her.

After they had shoved the last of the evidence down the drain, cleaned up all the blood and bleached everything, McGoo told Lily to go talk to Shay and he would clean the rest.

Lily thanked him and walked over to the couch to sit with LaShay.

"Would you like to stand or do you mind if we sit?" Lily asked.

"We can sit," Shay answered.

"Now, what would you like to know?" Lily asked.

Lily's feelings for Shay had only gotten stronger and there was no way she was going to walk away from her again. Shay deserved to know what she had done and how she had done it. Lily wasn't thinking of the safety or confidentiality of the coven.

She looked into LaShay's mesmerizing eyes, took a deep breath and blew it out slowly.

"Where do you want to start?" Lily began.

Shay smiled and leaned over to Lily. She put her hand on Lily's face and leaned in closer. Their lips met and Shay couldn't help but smile.

"Sorry," Shay mumbled.

"What?"

"Nothing."

Shay leaned in and they kissed deeply. It was a long, sultry, opened mouth kiss. Shay wrapped her hands around the sides of Lily's neck and pulled her even closer. Lily ran her hands through Shay's hair and across the back of her neck. They made out for about fifteen minutes until Jack came back into the living room. He had all the supplies in his arms.

"I'll have someone come to clean the carpet and replace the door," Jack told Shay.

"Uh, ok. Thank you," Shay replied.

Lily walked over and opened the door for Jack.

"Thank you." She told him as he left.

"Be home by midnight," Jack laughed.

"Uh, I doubt it," Lily smiled then looked at Shay. "He's kidding."

Lily walked back to Shay and sat down next to her.

"So what do you want to know?" Lily asked.

"Why the Crown Building?" Shay asked.

"It was built for the vampires and their feeders over a century ago."

"Feeders?"

"Yeah, feeders are humans that live with the vampires to give them blood. It sounds a lot worse than it is." Lily smiled and continued. "The feeders are given vampire blood periodically so they won't age but not enough that will change them to vampires. So the feeders stay with us. They are allowed to leave and work and do whatever they want outside the coven, as long as they are at their feeding times and they keep the vampire's secret. Most of our feeders are over ninety years old."

"So does every vampire have a feeder?"

"They have a few, but one main feeder."

"So you drink blood? But I've seen you eat. You've eaten *here* before."

"I'm not like the others," Lily said. "I'm half human. So I can live on blood or food."

"Which do you prefer?" Shay asked.

Lily shrugged.

"Blood is easier than cooking," Lily smiled.

Shay leaned her head sideways and looked at Lily for a moment. "Could you feed on me?"

"No," answered Lily. "We're not allowed to feed outside the coven and should never feed on..."

Lily wasn't sure how to tell Shay that they were not allowed to feed on their true love, even inside the coven. It's a rule that has been in effect for centuries. Lily didn't know the exact story, but it had something to do with a vampire killing their love by accident.

"We can't feed on boyfriends or girlfriends," Lily finally answered.

Shay smiled. "Boyfriends or girlfriends. So does that make me your girlfriend?"

"I guess that's up to you," Lily smiled back.

The time had come to tell each other how they really felt. Lily was under the impression that Shay was straight until only a few hours ago when Shay kissed her. Shay had no idea if Lily was gay or not. But she had kissed her back when they kissed.

"This is all really new to me," Shay began. "I've dated guys my whole life and it never occurred to me that I was gay, until I met you. I'm not quite sure what to do, or how to act or anything."

"Me either. I've never been with a woman before either. But I knew you were the one the first time I laid eyes on you. It wasn't a complete accident that we met at Baldwin's."

"How did you even know who I was?" Shay questioned.

Lily laughed. "Yeah, that would be a good question, wouldn't it? I hang out on the roof across the street from you."

"So today, you really were already close?"

"Yes, I was on the roof across the street, checking up on you, when the attack happened today. I saw you from the roof when you were cycling on the balcony one day. I knew then that I wanted to know you."

Shay wasn't sure what to say. "So this is new for both of us?"

"Yes. So we can learn together."

"Can we practice the kissing part some more?" Shay grinned as she ran the back of her fingers down Lily's cheek.

They kissed for a while and before Lily knew what was going on, Shay reached down to Lily's waist and lifted her shirt. Lily put her arms up and let her take it off. Shay's tee shirt was off next and they continued to kiss. Lily pushed Shay onto her back then Shay started to slide her pants off. Lily raised up and slid them the rest of the way off. Lily's pants came off next. After a few minutes they were both naked on the couch.

Lily kissed down Shay's cheek to her neck. Then kissed across her collar bone to her shoulder and then back. She kissed her neck and down her chest. Shay ran her hands through Lily's hair as Lily stopped at a breast. She took the nipple in her mouth and sucked until she got a response. Shay grabbed a handful of Lily's hair and pulled her into her chest. Lily sucked the erect nipple harder then went to the other. Shay moaned softly when Lily began to kiss down her stomach.

Lily put her hands between Shay's thighs and pushed them apart. Lily began kissing up Shay's thigh. Shay reached above her head and grabbed the arm of the couch when Lily reached the warm, wet spot. Lily slid a finger inside and placed her mouth over Shay's clit. Shay moaned louder as Lily sucked gently. Two fingers slid in next and Lily sucked harder as she slid her tongue over little bundle of nerves. It didn't take long before Shay was writhing on the couch. Lily wrapped her arms around Shay's legs and licked harder.

Shay's back arched up and she clutched the arm of the couch. She called out Lily's name as she climaxed but Lily didn't stop. She kept at it and after only a few minutes a second wave washed over Shay. After Shay calmed Lily kissed up Shay's stomach to a breast. She lingered there a minute then moved up to Shay's neck. Shay grabbed a handful of Lily's hair and pulled her to her lips. They kissed long and hard until Shay pushed Lily back.

"You're turn," Shay grinned.

They made love for hours.

Afterward, they were spooning on the couch. Shay was laying behind Lily. Shay ran her fingers over the tear shaped scars on Lily's shoulder and the half-moon scars on Lily's side.

"I didn't think vampires would be able to get scars," Shay asked softly.

"I was really young when I was attacked. Eric had set me up. He sent me into town with one of the feeders and had tried to have me killed. He very nearly succeeded. He's hated me since the very beginning and tried to have me killed only a few days after I arrived at the coven. I'm not even sure who saved me that night. It might have been Vincent, I don't know, I was too busy running away to notice. Only another vampire's claws can cut through our skin. So can the Guardian Wolves. And in my case, it took longer to heal since I was still growing causing the scars to form."

"Eric? Eric is Erica's twin brother, right?" Shay questioned. "Erica is the one that raised you?"

"Correct," Lily said and turned over to face Shay.

"And Vincent is your grandfather and runs the Crown Building, right?"

"Right," Lily answered.

Lily ran her fingertips down Shay's arm and she felt goosebumps rise.

"Ah, the response you cannot hide," Lily smiled and kissed Shay.

After finally making it to the bedroom, they fell asleep in each other's arms. They woke a few hours later to a knock on the front door. Shay wrapped a robe around herself and answered.

"I'm here to replace the door," said a man in blue button up shirt and khakis.

"Already?" Shay asked under her breath.

She let the man in and pointed to the balcony where the doors still hung on the top hinges and glass covered the floor.

"Thank you," she said before going back to her room and closing the door. "You're awake."

"Barely," Lily grinned.

"The repair man is already here to fix the door," Shay told Lily.

"Yeah, McGoo probably sent the super for the Crown. He can fix anything."

"Ma'am?" he called from the living room. "I'll be back."

He had taken the measurements of the doors as was going to get the replacements.

"I really need to go into work. It is after all, Wednesday," Shay whined. "I don't want to go in, but my father will come here to check on me if I don't show up."

"That's fine," Lily said. "I need to go home and tell Erica what happened. I'm sure she's worried about me."

"OK."

"I can meet you here or you... can... come to my place," Lily said hesitantly.

"Your place? Will I get to meet Erica and Steven and Vincent and Alexa?"

"If you want," Lily answered.

Shay smiled, bent down and kissed her. Lily grabbed her, rolled her over onto her back and kissed her back.

"This is not helping me get to work," Shay laughed. "Ten more minutes."

Lily kissed Shay goodbye and the elevator door closed. Lily stood there for a minute, staring at the metal door.

Shay ran her fingers across her lips and smiled all the way to the lobby.

Hiding his face behind a magazine, Eric sat in a chair against the wall. Shay paid no attention at all. Not that she would recognize him if she did see him. Eric stood and followed Shay out of the building. He watched as she stepped into a cab.

Eric was long gone when Lily left Shay's building. She had waited for the doors to be fixed and the carpets to be cleaned. Lily walked into the Crown Building and waved at the doorman. The scanner was turned off since the doorman was there watching with his wolf. She rode the elevator to the seventy second floor to see Erica.

"Are you ok?" Erica asked as soon as she opened the door and saw Lily.

"I'm great!" Lily grinned from ear to ear.

"Come in. Tell me what happened."

Lily sat on the Victorian couch in Erica's living room. Erica went to the liquor cabinet and poured them each a glass of scotch. Erica sat down across from Lily in the chair that matched the couch. The furniture was probably one hundred and twenty years old, but well taken care of. Erica took a sip of scotch and sat the glass on the table between them.

"She was attacked Erica. Someone broke into her apartment and tried to kill her. Why would someone want to hurt Shay? She doesn't bother anyone. She goes to work and then goes home."

"Has anyone at the bar been acting strange lately? I know you two go there on the weekends a lot."

Lily thought as hard as she could about anyone out of place at the bar but couldn't think of any.

"No, I don't remember seeing any new faces and all the familiar faces seemed to be minding their own business. Not interested in Shay or me."

"Or you?" Erica said almost too low to hear. "Could Eric have done this?"

"No!" Lily gasped, dismissing the idea. "Do you think he was that mad that I missed finals at Ellen's?"

"I wouldn't put it past him, sweetheart. Look out for him from now on. You know what he's capable of."

"Yeah I do."

Lily finished telling Erica the story about what happened the day before.

"She likes me, too!" Lily practically yelled. "She kissed me then the clothes came off and..."

"Whoa," laughed Erica. "I don't need details."

Lily laughed. She told Erica all about the day's events and how much she loved LaShay. Erica believed that Lily was in love, but only time would tell if it were her one true love. Vincent was going to need a lot more than Lily's word. He was going to need proof. Lots of it.

Erica told Vincent about the incident and he called for Parker, the coven's computer genius. Vincent told him to search the cameras for any clue that Eric was at Shay's apartment. Parker searched through hours of video before he finally found what Vincent was afraid of. Eric had been at Shay's apartment today. The video clearly showed him walking in and walking out behind, who Vince assumed was Shay. He thanked Parker for his time and went to Alexa.

"What are you going to do about your son?" Vincent asked sternly.

"What has he done now?" she answered, looking up from the papers she was shuffling through.

"He attacked a human. Lily's human. And from what I hear from Jack, would have been fatal if Lily had not been close by."

"LaShay?"

"Yes," Vince confirmed.

"What am I going to do with that boy?" Alexa asked rhetorically.

"I have a few ideas," Vince said under his breath.

"Well, he hasn't been at the coven in weeks. Maybe he has found another place to live? If he gets in trouble again, I will personally turn him over to the Guardians."

"If you can catch him," Vince spat.

Alexa took a deep breath and stood up.

"Does Lily know that it was Eric?" Alexa asked him.

Vincent shook his head.

"And she is not to be told, yet," he told her.

"She deserves to know, Vince!"

"To what end? You know she'll go after him if she knows."

"So let them fight," Alexa suggested. "At the Underground fights. It's a controlled environment and it might teach Eric a lesson. Lily is faster and stronger and under the right circumstances, maybe she'll kick his ass."

"Even if she does, it won't stop him from going after LaShay again. And, to be honest, it would probably make matters worse if Lily beat him in the ring. He'd never live that down," Vincent confessed.

"You're right," Alexa admitted.

They stared at each other for a moment and thought.

"We can bring LaShay here," Alexa suggested. "Just take her in and make sure she's always surrounded by vampires and people that we trust. Let *me* talk to Lily."

Alexa called Lily and asked that she come to the penthouse. Lily didn't even ask why, she just left her apartment immediately, and went to the seventy fifth floor.

"Lily," Alexa began. "We have reason to believe that LaShay may be in danger."

"From what?" Lily questioned. "Was it Eric?"

"We believe that it is a possibility."

"That son-of..." Lily stopped there. "Why would he do that?"

"Why does he do anything that he does?" Alexa replied.

"Why don't you turn him over the Guardians?" Lily asked.

Alexa dropped her head and then looked back at Lily, "Because they'll kill him."

"Maybe that's what he needs! He's never going to play by the rules. We had to leave Nashville and Atlanta because of him. That means that another coven had to move to some hole in the wall coven just because Vincent is an Elder. Whatever he says goes. So what does Vince have to say about Eric?"

"You know how Vince feels about Eric."

"Yeah, it's mutual," Lily mumbled.

"Would you talk to LaShay about moving into the coven?" Alexa asked.

"Move here?" Lily asked.

"That's the only solution we could come to that was safe for you both."

"Yeah, sure. Anything to keep Eric a free vampire," Lily spat.

Shay wouldn't be home from work for another two hours. Lily left early and this time she took Onyx. If Shay didn't want to move to the coven, she would leave Onyx with her when she couldn't be with there to protect her. That is if Shay would allow Onyx to stay. Lily had only taken Onyx to LaShay's a few times. He liked her, which was unusual for him. Everyone thought that the only person, or vampire, he liked was Lily.

When Lily got to Shay's building she scanned her hand and the door clicked open. She went to the elevator and waited. Onyx went over to the chair by the wall and sniffed the seat. He could smell Eric's scent on the cloth chair. He made a mental note. But should he tell Lily? If Lily was sure that it was Eric that had Shay attacked, Lily would surely not take it well. She would do everything in her power to make sure Eric never hurt Shay again. Lily would kill him without hesitation. Or at least she'd give it her best shot, every chance she got. But Eric would retaliate, too. What would he stoop to to hurt Lily or Shay? There was no limit to his cruelty and it wouldn't be beyond him to have Lily attacked by his Underground friends.

Onyx decided that he wasn't going to be the one to break the news to Lily. He'd let Vincent or Alexa tell her.

The elevator dinged and the two rode to the twelfth floor. Lily knew that Shay wasn't home but she had given Lily a remote to the apartment, just as Lily had programmed Shay into the scanner of her apartment. Shay could also scan into the front door of the Crown Building. Shay was all smiles when she told Shane that she had access. He pretended not to care.

Lily let herself and Onyx in and he walked through the apartment to check it for any intruders. It was after all his job to protect Lily, and now LaShay.

LILY VS ERIC

Lily sat in her living room staring at the television. Sarah was in the kitchen filling a cup for Lily's evening meal. She picked up the cup, her wrist still draped across it, and carried it to the living room. Lily cut her finger on her teeth, then wiped the blood gently across Sarah's wrist. Lily took the cup and sat it on the table then picked up her cell phone.

Sarah stayed for a minute and talked to Lily. Small talk about her wanting to leave the coven and experience life outside the protected walls. After Lily drank the blood Sarah walked to the front door.

Lily typed 'flower delivery' into a search screen on her phone then pressed the phone number for the closest florist.

Sarah lingered at the doorway, listening to where and when the flowers would be delivered. When Lily hung up, Sarah silently pulled the front door closed. She went straight to Eric and told him that Lily was sending flowers to Shay but more importantly, she gave him the exact time they would be delivered.

He smiled an evil grin.

"What are you going to do?" Sarah asked.

"Well, if Lily won't fight for rank anymore, let's see if she'll fight for the one she loves."

"Won't she know it's you?" Sarah asked.

"Who cares?" He said smugly.

Eric was waiting outside Shay's building when the florist arrived. He followed the florist into the building and up the elevator. Pretending to live across the hall, he fumbled around in his pocket for his remote in front of the door across from LaShay's.

The florist knocked on Shay's door, waited a few seconds, then sat the vase of two dozen red roses in front of the door.

After the florist was gone, Eric replaced the card. He went back downstairs, let in five of his vampire and werewolf friends and then went to the roof. Eric explained what he wanted them to do then they waited.

The new card read, "Meet me on the roof, L". Eric knew that LaShay wouldn't question the instructions.

Shay was all smiles when she stepped out of the taxi. Eric watched from the roof as Shay walked into the building. When she arrived at her door, she did just as Eric had hoped, she read the card, opened the door, sat her purse and remote inside and headed to the roof. She was still smiling when she stepped out the door. The sun blinded her as she opened the heavy metal door to the roof. It was still hours before sunset and the sun lingered high above the horizon. She let the door close behind her as she shielded her eyes and searched the empty rooftop. As the door clicked shut she felt a sting across her left cheek. Before she could turn to see what had hit her, she was hit again. Her vision became blurry for a moment as she tried to stay on her feet. She was hit once again across the cheek and she began to feel weak in the knees.

"Lily!" Shay screamed as loud as she could then yelled, "What do you want?!"

Her cheek throbbed. She looked around and saw two hooded men. One was holding a nine iron in his hand. A second later, everything went black.

Two sets of large, hairy hands grabbed each arm and pulled her toward the edge of the roof. They stood facing the door. Three vampires waited against the wall beside the roof door.

Eric had arranged for Lily to be late to see Shay and made sure Onyx stayed home. Sarah was late and stopped by to see Lily about half an hour before Lily usually left for Shay's. Eric had timed it perfectly. Sarah rambled on about how she was going to leave the coven for a while to experience life outside the sheltered walls of where she grew up. It was all lies, but Sarah made sure that Lily wouldn't be there to greet Shay when she got home. When Sarah finally stopped talking, Lily just grabbed an oversized hoodie and she didn't bother putting on sunscreen since she'd be mostly in the shadows of the buildings anyway. She ran downstairs and the twelve blocks to Shay's building. She let herself into the front door and waited for the elevator. She was surprised that she could still smell Onyx in the hallway. When she stepped into the elevator, the smell was even stronger. She wondered why a werewolf would be in Shay's building. When she stepped off the elevator and saw the roses still sitting outside, she wondered if Shay had worked late. She checked the door and it was unlocked. Then she heard Shay scream. Lily's teeth and claws were out before she even opened the door. She tripped over Shay's purse laying with her remote inside the door.

The lights are still out and her purse and remote are here. Did it come from the parking garage or roof? She thought as she stepped onto the balcony.

The fire escape was faster than waiting for the elevator so Lily ran to the bedroom window and out onto the fire escape.

Two sets of hands grabbed Shay and pulled her toward the edge of the roof. The two vampires holding her turned her around to face the door. Her face was red and bleeding and the bruising had already begun to show. Shay fought to stay on her feet. The fourth blow was four claws across the face. She felt the blood pour from the gashes but when she saw the werewolves, she realized that it was a set-up and was determined not to scream again. She had rather die than give anyone the satisfaction of luring Lily out into the sunlight.

Eric had counted on Lily rushing out without sun protection. He and two more vampires stood against the wall behind the roof door. He was betting on the fact that Lily would come to save Shay, but what he wasn't betting on was Lily coming up the fire escape.

Lily couldn't tell where the scream had come from, the street or the roof. She looked down toward the street then up. She saw movement at the edge of the roof and could smell Shay's blood.

Roof, Lily thought.

It only took Lily three strides and in a flash Lily was on the roof. The werewolves weren't expecting an attack from behind. With lightning speed Lily attacked one of the werewolves holding Shay. She lunged and as she came down he turned toward her. Claws ripped through his face and chest. A quick swipe with the other hand and he was down. He fell to the rooftop, holding the severed arteries in his neck. She took a step and attacked the second. He dodged the first blow but she connected on the second. As he fell he let go of Shay. She caught Shay's head just before it hit the ground.

"Shay!" Lily yelled as she gently shook her shoulders.

The first werewolf was about to climb down the fire escape when Onyx was climbing up. Still in his half human form, Onyx grabbed him and threw him to the landing. He jumped on top of him, changing as he was in the air and with one quick, powerful bite, the werewolf's head was detached from his body before he could even make a sound. But the loud thud onto the landing hadn't gone unnoticed.

The vampires ran over, grabbed Lily by the arms and dragged her to the center of the roof.

"Lily?" Shay said groggily. "What's hap..."

Lily continued to kick and twist but she refused to scream. She wouldn't give them the satisfaction.

Two vampires held Lily as she kicked and twisted to get free. Then Eric ripped the hoodie into shreds. His claws ripped through Lily's skin and shirt then through her legs and the light blue jeans. Lily was being held in the middle of the sun exposed roof with no protection.

Shay never even saw Lily, but knew that she was in trouble. She crawled to the fire escape ladder and climbed down just as fast as her swimming head would allow without falling. With her head spinning, Shay finally fell to her knees onto the fire escape landing. She looked down at her blood covered shirt and reached up to feel the gash in the back of her head. She felt her head get lighter and lighter then everything went black.

Lily was held in the middle of the roof, fully exposed to the afternoon sun for almost forty five minutes. The vampires, protected with hoodies and heavy sunscreen, cringed as they watched her skin burn. The skin peeled away in burnt cinders as the muscle beneath slowly began to burn, too.

"Go get Shay," Eric ordered. "She won't be far."

With her feet, Lily clawed at the legs of her attackers. She got one arm free and managed to get in a few good licks before she landed a lucky swipe across Eric's chest. He looked down at his ripped shirt then his accomplices held Lily as he stood and stared at her for what seemed forever as she struggled to get free. She was beginning to lose the battle with the sun. She forced the strength to swept the legs out from under one of the vampires holding her. Before he had time to regain his footing, Lily stomped down on his chest, crushing his sternum. He gasped for air but was able to roll out of the way of the second blow. He struggled to get to his feet.

The door to the roof swung open and Shay, fighting to stay conscious, fell into the sunlight.

Onyx leaped over her and landed squarely on the chest of the struggling vampire. Eric wrapped his claws around Onyx's neck and threw him off. Onyx had barely even hit the ground before he was coming back at Eric.

Lily was beginning to fade, fast. Her skin had begun to fall away as she was held, unprotected from the sun. Onyx tried to get to her but was pushed off of the roof. He bounced onto Shay's balcony and was quickly running back through Shay's apartment to get back upstairs.

Lily was burning now. Her hair was fizzling up into matted clumps on her head. She gave another jerk and a tug then swept her foot under her attacker's legs. He fell flat on his back and this time, Onyx was there to make sure he didn't get up. Onyx's front paws landed squarely on his chest and the crunch from inside stopped his heart. A well placed bite and the heart along with a few ribs, were no longer viable. Three down, two to go.

Lily had stopped struggling and had fallen to her knees, then onto her stomach. Onyx leaped at the remaining vampire but before he reached him the vampire darted out of the way. He ran for the door just as Erica was about to walk through. Without warning, the vampire entered the building just long enough for Onyx to pounce. Erica jumped to the side. The vampire crashed into the floor head first and soon, he too was dead.

Lily's eyes were clouded and distant as she still tried to fight Eric. Her charred skin had begun to peel from the muscle and the muscle was now burning. She still hadn't noticed that Shay was laying in the doorway to the roof. Lily mustered everything she had and made it to her feet.

"Shay!" Lily gasped but barely even made a sound.

Unable to stay on her feet, Lily crawled over to LaShay and rolled Shay over so her head was in Lily's lap. Right away Lily cut her already skinless wrist to heal Shay's wounds. Lily was fading in and out of consciousness and she thought she heard Erica.

"Erica?" she said weakly.

"Lily? Oh my god!" Erica said as she stepped onto the doorway.

Eric disappeared down the fire escape before Erica saw him. Erica scooped up Lily and carried her downstairs. Onyx, knowing he could hurt her more if he carried her as a wolf, changed into werewolf form, carefully picked up LaShay and carried her to her apartment.

Erica brought Lily down to Shay's apartment. Erica thought she was dead as she laid her gently onto the sofa. She didn't move or make a sound. She stood over her and stared as tears began to well in her eyes. Lily was in horrible shape. She was burned almost beyond recognition.

Onyx put Shay on her bed and then quickly changed back into a wolf. He was, after all, naked. Erica went to check on Shay. Shay's face was bloody and red. Her eye was swollen shut and her lip was deep red and swollen three times its size. Erica cut her finger with her teeth and spread the dark red liquid across her eye, then her lip and then her cheek. She cut her wrist and placed it over her open mouth. She jerked her head away and tried pushing Erica with her hands.

"Drink," she said softly as she lifted Shay's head.

In a matter of minutes the bruises began to fade. The gash in her cheek slowly closed and all of the swelling went down.

"Where's Lily," she asked as soon as she could talk again.

The look on Erica's face said it all.

"No!" Shay screamed.

"Shay, there was nothing you could've done," she soothed.

Tears streamed down her cheeks as she stumbled into the living room. She stood beside Lily for a moment before dropping to her knees and sobbing.

Meanwhile, at the Crown Building, Alexa was arguing with Vincent, again.

"Vincent, you have to let us change LaShay. You know damn well that Lily will leave us permanently for her," Alexa said for the fourth time that day. The 100th time that week. Lily had been staying out a lot more and Alexa and Erica were getting increasingly worried. It wasn't like Lily not to bring her love interests home. She knew that this was the safest place for both of them..

"She's only here long enough to feed and change clothes, Vince. She doesn't even call. We love LaShay and she knows that, so why is Lily avoiding the coven? Something's wrong and you know it as well as I do," she added.

"Would you feel better if I went to check on her?" Vincent asked Alexa.

"No, I know she's alright, I want to know why she's not coming home, Vince!" Alexa nearly yelled.   "Onyx would've come to us if anything had happened."

She was right and had every right to be worried, but Vince wasn't aware at the time what was going on in his own coven. He knew that Eric and Lily were always fighting and always at each other's throat, but he didn't know that Eric had finally gone off the deep end.

"Lex, she'll bring Shay home when she wants to, but I am not changing her," he said firmly.

But he still wanted to go and check on Lily and Shay. He thought there was no need to rush anything. Lily could take care of herself and he knew that. She had been perfectly capable of caring for herself since the moment she was born.

If he had known what was really going on, someone would've already been dead, and it wasn't Lily. He didn't find out until it was almost too late that Eric had threatened to kill Shay if Lily ever brought Shay to the coven, to Lily's own home.

Turning LaShay Black was just out of the question, though. He knew she could easily die if he tried.

He had been completely against turning her and not even Alexa could convince him to change his mind. Lily was just too prone to changing hers. It was her human half that he blamed for her indecisiveness. Vampires fall in love with one person and only one person. And that one person is who they love forever. The only way to stop loving them is death, either yours or theirs. Love wasn't something that they could turn on and off but Lily could and he had seen her do it too many times.

He liked LaShay and she did truly love Lily, but Lily had fallen "in love" with three others, two vampires and one human, before she fell in love with LaShay. Luckily the human she had fallen for before was able to change. Vincent had changed him, thinking that Lily had finally found her one true love. He wasn't about to chance putting anyone else through the agonizing process of changing for the sake of Lily. If LaShay even survived, Lily would simply change her mind and LaShay would be left still in love for an eternity with someone that had moved on to someone else. That would be a miserable existence, and he wouldn't do that to anyone, again.

He thought that Shay was just another crush that Lily had mistaken for love. It wasn't until Onyx came to get McGoo late that afternoon that convinced him otherwise.

Vincent was walking through the coven sub-basement when Onyx came barreling down the hallway on his way to get McGoo. Vince was just leaving the lab and was about to walk into the hallway just as Onyx was rounding the corner. Onyx plowed into him and nearly knocked him on his ass. When Vince regained his footing, Onyx tried to push past but Vince stopped him. Then Onyx did something no wolf had ever done, he snarled at Vincent. His head dropped and his pearly white teeth nearly glowed. Vince was in a mind to backhand him down the hallway, but when another deep, rumbling growl came from Onyx's throat and he bared his full canines, Vincent knew something was definitely wrong. Onyx pawed the floor and then quickly changed

The only thing he said was, "Its Lily."

Onyx grabbed McGoo by his shirt sleeve and nearly drug him down the hallway toward the exit. Vincent followed him and McGoo to LaShay's apartment.

When they arrived at the apartment, Shay was on her knees and half draped across Lily's torso. She was crying uncontrollably and mumbling.

"Why, Lily? You knew better".

She didn't even look up when Vince touched her shoulder.

"Please tell me that you can help her," she sobbed, still not looking up.

He bent down and picked Shay up from the floor and off of Lily. McGoo and Vince stood and stared at what was supposed to be Lily. She lay on the couch barely breathing and so badly burned she wasn't even recognizable. It looked as though Lily had literally been covered in petrol, lit on fire and left to burn. Her hair was a large, black matted clump and what was left of her face was like a scene from a horror movie. Lily lay bloody and charred so badly that part of her lower jaw bone and teeth were clearly visible. The skin above her left eye had been torn away. Her eyelids were nearly gone and her retinas and pupils had already begun to cloud. Her face, arms, legs and torso were covered in deep gouges from Eric's claws. Pieces of the pants she had been wearing did little to cover what little skin was left. Her shirt was the same, but the blood that soaked the once white sweatshirt, was much more noticeable than on the light jeans.

"Onyx!" Vince yelled. "What were..."

Shay interrupted, "He did, Vincent!" she yelled. "He did everything he could to fight them off and get her out of the sun. She was protecting me, Vincent! She's gonna die because of me!"

"Fight who off? Who did this?" He asked, trying to keep calm. "Who were they, Onyx?"

Onyx only dropped his head and shook it slowly. He would know any vampire's scent that he had ever encountered but yet he didn't recognize any of them except Eric.

Jack was on the phone to Alexa and giving her a list of what he needed for her to bring. Vince could hear the panic in her voice when Jack told her to bring feeders. Alexa knew that meant that Lily wasn't able to feed herself. He looked at Lily then back to Shay. He had to tell her that the odds didn't look good for Lily's survival. He had never seen anyone burned so badly and still breathing. Lily had less than a ten percent chance of surviving this. She was just too badly burned. In addition to the catastrophic burns, she had deep gashes across her chest and stomach that had drained her tissues of life sustaining blood. If they didn't get a substantial amount of blood into her very quickly, she wouldn't stand a chance.

Just as Erica walked through the door from the bedroom, Eric appeared on the fire escape. Onyx was on his feet before Eric had taken two steps into the living room. Vince saw the look on Shay's face as she quickly turned toward the kitchen and left the living room.

"Onyx! Don't!" Vince yelled before he reached Eric.

Onyx stopped in his tracks but he didn't turn away.

Eric entered the room and as soon as he saw Lily on the couch, his demeanor changed.

"She's alive?" Eric asked.

"Barely!" Erica answered.

"Damn, she stinks!" Eric huffed.

"Why are you here?" Vince asked Eric.

"I was headed home when I saw you running toward Shay's building."

"Figured something was up," Eric said.

"Did you have anything to do with this?"

"Would I *be here* if I had something to do with this?" he said smugly.

Vince grabbed Erica by her shoulder before she was able to get to Eric. If he had known it was Eric, he would've let her go. But he never thought that Eric would take the rivalry this far.

Eric smirked and went the same way out of the living room that Shay had gone.

Vincent heard Eric speaking softly then he began to whisper. A low rumble reverberated through Onyx's throat. His ears perked up and rotated to focus on the sounds from the kitchen.

"You're lucky she got here?" Eric said to Shay.

"Fuck you!" Shay spat.

"Next time I'll just kill you myself!" Eric whispered into Shay's ear.

Shay reached behind her and grabbed a knife from the drawer as Eric walked away. In a split second Eric had turned toward Shay, with his teeth bared, but Onyx was already airborne. He leaped through the door, knocking Eric into the refrigerator and leaving a clear path for Shay to get out of the kitchen. Onyx stood in front of Eric with his head hung low, his ears flat against his head and a snarl just below the surface. White canines and pink gums waited for Eric to make the slightest move.

When Eric tried to run after Shay again, Onyx went into full predator mode. It was Eric's fault that Lily was going to die and Onyx was bound and determined that Shay would not be next. He knew he could be put down for attacking any member of the coven but for him to attack a high member of the coven? Obviously Onyx knew something that Vince didn't. When Eric came for Shay a second time, he may as well have been coming after Lily. If Lily was no longer alive, the only thing Onyx knew to do was guarantee that LaShay was always safe, for Lily's sake. Onyx attacked Eric with the fury of a guardian wolf protecting his master. Before Eric even knew what had happened, he was pinned to the floor by a trembling 300 pound wolf. Onyx had both paws on Eric's chest and his nose was inches from Eric's. Two inch fangs and pink gums gleamed from beneath quivering, black lips.

"Onyx!" Vince called out.

But he only growled and snarled louder as the saliva from his mouth began to drip from his canines and onto Eric's face. Vince hadn't seen Onyx so fiercely protective since Lily's first day at the coven and he had never seen him attack anyone. Onyx had heard something that he hadn't and it was obviously something he felt was worth dying for if he was attacking Eric right in front of Vince.

"Did he do it?" Vince asked Shay, now wrapped around Lily as McGoo worked.

Shay nodded reluctantly.

Onyx lifted a paw long enough to grab Eric's shirt, and a little shoulder in his teeth, and ripped half of the shirt off. He then lifted the other paw and ripped off the other half.

That's when Vince finally put the pieces together.

"He threatened to hurt you, didn't he?" Vince asked LaShay.

"He said that he'd kill me and make Lily watch if Lily and I ever went back to the coven," Shay finally confessed.

Alexa walked into the apartment with the supplies and feeders Jack had requested. She let out an audible gasp when she saw Lily.

Onyx looked at Vince and the sounds that came from his throat were a combination of whines, pleas and rage.

"Not in here, Onyx," he said and before Eric even realized that the order had been given, Onyx had picked him up by the neck and shoulder and was dragging him toward the front door.

Eric struggled against Onyx's powerful jaws to no avail. Onyx had a vise-like grasp on Eric. He could even feel the enamel of Onyx's teeth grinding against his collar bone. Eric clawed at Onyx repeatedly and blood dripped from Onyx's coat, but he wasn't letting go.

"What?" Eric mumbled, turning over the situation in his head. "Wait! No! You can't do this, Dad! Mom won't allow it." He struggled harder against Onyx. "Mom will stop you! Mom!"

"Not this time, son," Alexa told him as Onyx dragged him through the doorway.

"Where are you... No! Dad! You can't do this!" Eric's muffled pleas continued all the way down the hall and into the stairwell to the roof. "You can't, Dad, it's against the Elder's Code?"

"And so is taking the life of one of a member of the coven," Vincent said loudly.

"Dad! What are you doing?" Eric's fading voice called from the stairs.

"What I should've done decades ago," Vince said under his breath.

His pleas grew softer then silenced when the roof door closed.

McGoo was busy trying to save Lily and was completely oblivious to what had just happened. It wasn't until Eric's screams from the roof above rang through the apartment that McGoo took his attention from Lily for a split second.

Vince walked out onto the balcony to listen. Onyx should have bitten clean through Eric's neck. It would serve him right but Vince saw Eric leap from the roof to the nursing home and heard Onyx bark and growl as he chased after Eric.

Ever since he had tried to kill Lily the first night she was brought to the coven in Nashville, he knew Eric and Lily would never get along, but threatening her love, and apparently her one true love, was inexcusable. Now Lily lay lifeless in the arms of the woman she risked everything to protect.

"The feeders just aren't cutting it."

Vince heard Jack mumble under his breath.

"Not enough umph to do any good," McGoo continued.

"Erica?" Jack said.

Erica sniffed, "Yeah?"

"Would you let me try something?" he asked.

"Anything," Erica answered.

"She's lost way too much blood and feeding isn't going to restore it fast enough to keep her alive for very much longer I'm afraid," Jack began. "I was thin..."

"Just fucking do it!" Erica yelled. "Whatever it is, just do it!"

"You have the closest blood to hers," Jack said as he lifted Erica's arm and with a scalpel, cut Erica's forearm nearly from elbow to wrist.

Erica cringed from the pain but remained silent as Jack placed her arm over the tear in Lily's abdomen. Jack placed his hand over Erica's arm and pulled the skin together on the back, opening the incision further and keeping it from healing as quickly.

"Lily," Shay whispered. "Baby, hang in there, ok."

Lily's eyes rolled toward Shay and she gave a tiny nod. Shay kissed Lily's forehead then took Lily's hand. No one spoke.

Everyone in the apartment would all agree that Eric had indeed set Lily on fire and left her to die. That is basically what he did. He knew that Lily would fight to protect Shay to the death.

A knock came from the door. Vincent looked out over the balcony at the street and saw that the police had shown up.

"Metro," Vince whispered.

"Shit!"

Erica let herself be nearly drained of blood before she lifted her arm away from Lily. The tissues around where Erica's arm had been had begun to show faint signs of healing.

Alexa walked to the door. Jack placed a wet towel over Lily's face.

"Who is it?" Alexa called.

Onyx barked.

"Metro Police, do you own a black canine?" the officer called back.

"Yes, sir," Alexa said as she opened the door.

The officer walked in and his nose wrinkled from the smell that permeated the apartment.

"An eye witness claims that this animal is responsible for attacking a man on the roof," the officer began. "I am..."

Before the officer went any further, LaShay lifted the towel from Lily's face.

"The man did this and the animal was protecting her. The man got away but if he shows up at any medical facilities with dog bites, would someone please be sure to arrest him," Shay said to the officer knowing that would never happen, but making it sound convincing.

Shay was crying by the time she finished speaking to the officer.

"Oh my!" the officer responded. "Is she alive?"

"No," Jack said.

LaShay placed the towel back over Lily's face and draped herself over Lily's torso. The officer walked over and was going to pick up Lily's wrist to check for a pulse but after seeing it, thought better of it.

"Can you show me where the attack occurred?" the officer asked.

"I can," Vince said.

He led the officer to the roof and let him look around to his content. He knew he wasn't going to find anything more than a few charred pieces clothing. He may even think that was where Lily had been burned. Luckily, the rooftop was considered a private residence and was not part of the extranet recordings. But it did have its own security surveillance. After he was sure that no one was on the roof, they walked back to the apartment.

"I'm sorry for your loss, ma'am," the officer said to LaShay then he looked around to everyone else, "I'm sorry for your loss, I truly am and I wish the canine had been able to save her."

The officer bowed his head and walked out the front door. Onyx walked over to LaShay and nudged her side. She scratched him behind the ears and then wrapped her arms around his neck.

Alexa motioned toward two feeders, Sam and Darrel, then pointed to Lily and Erica. Sam quickly made himself available to Erica and Darrel, without even the slightest prompting, cut his own wrist before laying it across Lily's mouth.

Shay looked up at Darrel and gave a weak smile.

Darrel stroked her hair gently and said, "She's going to be fine. She's just too damn stubborn to die, she loves you too much." Darrel smiled.

"Thank you," Shay said softly.

McGoo stood up from sitting on the coffee table to look at Lily's face and eyes. He took a deep breath and shook his head slowly. Then he looked over to Vincent.

"Vincent," he said reluctantly. "She needs vampire blood. Stronger vampire blood. Your blood"

"What are the risks?" Vince asked.

No vampire had ever been given the blood of an elder, and no one knew exactly what it would do. Would it kill Lily or heal her. Or heal her just long enough to kill her. Lily had never had vampire blood again after the night she drank from Erica.

"Maybe Lily's blood is the same as the elders. Maybe that's why she's still alive," McGoo rambled. "She does have spikes and I don't think I've ever seen a vampire quite as crispy as our girl here. It could be what's kept her alive this long. And maybe she is just too in love and stubborn, but even the most bull headed vampire would've succumbed to burns so bad that there is no longer a term for it. I'd say deep tissue burns, but some of the burns go all the way to bone. I've never seen anything still breathe after their skin and muscle have been barbequed fallin'-off-the-bone well done. She does..."

"Jack, would you get to the point already?" Vince asked impatiently. "Will it save her or kill her?"

"Don't know." Jack shrugged his shoulders. "Could do neither. Could do both. I don't know how strong her blood is. I know it isn't like anyone else's but I've never compared it to an elder's. Would you be willing to try?"

Jack knew that he was asking to break all kinds of coven laws and quite possibly have them brought up on charges by the Guardians if they were so inclined. Elder blood was as sacred as anything vampire related could be. Only an elder's blood could change a human in less than two weeks. Any other vampire's blood was just too diluted to cause the change to occur in anything under a month, which was just an unreasonable amount of time. It could even change a human in less than ten days, if the human were strong enough to survive the excruciating transformation. Elder blood could tame a wild wolf or send a stallion racing so hard his heart would explode. But what would it do to another vampire? Make them stronger? Make them heal faster? Or would it be seen as an invader, like a virus, causing an immune response so strong that it killed the recipient?

No one had ever given Elder blood to another vampire. But why would they? All vampires were created with an Elder's blood. But Lily wasn't created, she was born a vampire.

Vince looked at Lily for a long moment, then to Erica and finally to Alexa.

"If we do nothing, I'm afraid she won't survive," Jack added with a hint of urgency.

Vince walked over to the coffee table and sat down behind LaShay who was draped across Lily's chest. He placed his hand on her shoulder and spoke.

"LaShay?" he said. "It's your call."

She raised herself slowly from Lily and turned toward Vince.

"I don't know," she answered, nearly crying.

She looked at Alexa then Erica. "What do you think? Lily has told me enough about vampires to know that giving her Elder blood is risky. But McGoo is right, Lily isn't just any vampire. She has Elder traits and giving her their blood may be exactly what she needs, since she lost..."

Shay began to cry and her voice cracked as she tried to continue. "Since she lost so much blood. What would you do, Erica?"

"Personally, I had much rather lose her because we tried to save her and not because we did nothing," Erica answered.

Vince walked over to McGoo who was standing over Lily and staring at Vince for an answer.

"What are the odds it will work?" Vince asked him.

"Well since she's still breathing, as bad as she is, I'd say she had a fifty fifty chance with or without your blood. But with your blood." McGoo scratched his head. "I'd say that she would have a better chance with it. Her blood is strong, that's why she's not dead yet, but your blood is stronger. I think."

"You think?" Vince questioned.

"Yeah, I think. I've never actually tested them side by side. Never had a reason to. Hers *might be* stronger, but yours is definitely stronger than anything else she's been given. I'd say it would work if I was sure that it wasn't too strong. Only one way to find out."

Vince picked up the knife from the table, slit one wrist then the other, then placed one over Lily's mouth and the other over her stomach.

Lily swallowed slowly and then again. For almost a minute nothing happened. Within two minutes muscle tissue around her jaw and eyes began to heal very slowly. The color of her eyes began to return and the gashes across her torso and legs began to close.

"It's working too slowly," McGoo said.

"Let her feed on me", Shay said calmly.

"No, Shay, it's not allowed, and you know that." Vince told her.

"I don't care if it's allowed!" she countered. "She's dying because of me and if there's anything I can do, I'm going to do it."

Shay had put the knife on the coffee table and she grabbed it. Before Erica or Alexa could stop her, she had cut a four inch gash in her forearm. She parted Lily's teeth as carefully as possible and laid her bleeding arm across the exposed flesh and bone. For thirty agonizing seconds, Shay's blood flowed into Lily's mouth with no response what-so-ever. Everyone just knew it was too late. Then finally, Lily swallowed. Tears flowed down Shay's and Erica's face. Slowly the muscle on her face began to regenerate. Then her torso and then her arms and legs. It was slow at first, but after a minute or two began to heal faster.

The charred, exposed bones turned from black to white. Her color began to turn pink again. The muscles on her face began to cover the exposed jaw and teeth. Then the skin began to cover the muscle. The tendons holding her claws in the fingers began to turn from black to white. Muscle began to turn red as it filled with blood and seemed to inflate as it healed. Bluish looing nerves began winding their way through the muscles. Blood vessels split once then twice then spider-webbed out as the capillaries wove through the new vampire skin. Human skin then covered everything.

McGoo looked on in awe as this normal human's blood healed Lily.

"What are you?" Jack asked her. "How did you know this would work?"

"I didn't," Shay answered, shaking her head.

McGoo looked at Vincent questionably. He was trying to figure out why Shay's blood had healed Lily. An elder's blood wasn't strong enough, but this seemingly normal human being's did?

"I love you," Lily told Shay.

"And I really believe that," Alexa said.

Everyone cried happy, thankful tears as they watched Lily hold LaShay close.

"Why in the hell..." LaShay began.

"Shhhh," Lily said placing her finger over Shay lips.

"Because I love you," Lily said.

Shay took a deep breath and took Lily's head in both of her hands then kissed her gently.

"I love you, too," Shay said as she buried her face in Lily's neck.

"LaShay? Where is your Extranet?" Vince asked. "I want to see what happened."

The building had its own cameras in the hallways and this particular building had cameras on the roof. It wouldn't take much for the videos to mysteriously disappear.

Shay pointed to the desk against the wall next to the balcony doors. It was already on so Vince looked at his cell then entered the coordinates of LaShay's apartment and searched until he found when Eric arrived. He followed the florist delivery guy into the building. Vince didn't want to upset LaShay anymore so he didn't ask her for any other details. The security cameras would tell him what he needed to know. He didn't want to upset Erica anymore either, so he muted the volume.

"Do you have access to the roof cameras," Vince asked.

"I don't know, I've never tried," Shay said.

Vince pushed a couple buttons on his cell and called Parker, the coven's computer guru. He would be able to get into the files and make sure that they were never seen again.

It only took him ten minutes to get to the apartment from the coven. He must have ran the whole way. He asked Shay for her bio-password and reluctantly she left Lily's side to press her finger against the little black square in the bottom corner of the keyboard. The screen flashed green as light scanned Shay's eyes.

Parker typed for a few seconds and the next screen was the main screen of the building security system.

"They set up the security system so residents could review the footage if they wanted," Parker said to anyone that was listening as his fingers flew across the keys. "Here it is."

The first image of Eric in the building was him following the florist upstairs. He watched as he pretended to fumble for his remotes outside the door across the hall. He changed the card that came with the roses and walked back downstairs. He let in three men and two wolves and went straight to the roof. He told each of the wolves to hold LaShay so Lily could see her when she stepped outside. Then he told the vampires to wait behind the door and attack when the door closed. Then he told them to hold Lily on the roof.

"Then nature will take care of the rest," Eric had said.

McGoo walked over to the computer just as one of the vampires hit Shay in the face with the golf club. The second blow to the back of her head knocked her out. Blood leaked from the gash on her cheek. Then she was hit again in the ribs, the mouth and again to the face.

After Lily attacked the two werewolves, Erica turned away from the computer and went back to Lily. She couldn't watch anymore.

Vince fast forwarded the images through Onyx's attack and watched him change just long enough to get Shay into the apartment. Then he forwarded it to when Onyx took Eric to the roof. Eric clawed straight across Onyx's eye and Onyx let go for just a split second, but it was long enough for Eric to get away. Eric ran to the edge of the roof and jumped to the building across the street. Onyx jumped after him and chased him across the rooftops for about six blocks then Eric ran down a fire escape ladder to the ground. Onyx couldn't change to chase Eric. It was daytime and the cameras would catch the werewolf out in the streets. Most of the rooftops didn't have cameras, but some did and catching a wolf chasing a man wouldn't be all that suspicious. Onyx let Eric go, this time.

Vincent was furious.

"Eric is no longer a member of the Crown Coven," he announced.

Alexa gave no objection.

"I want you," Vince said, looking at LaShay, "I would like for you to come to live with us in the Crown Building."

"I'll give you your own place," Vince continued. "If you want that is. Otherwise you can live with Lily, she does have two bedrooms."

"What's wrong with here?" Shay asked.

"You're not safe here. And I don't want Lily to stay here either. Eric will only up his game from here on out. If he tried to kill Lily in broad daylight, there's no telling what he might do."

"You are more than welcome in our home," Alexa said to Shay.

"You can stay with us and we'll even escort you to work and back," Vincent added.

Shay looked at Lily, perplexed. *What if I don't want an escort to work? What if I don't want to live with a coven of vampires?* The thought scared her a little. She trusted Lily with all her heart but what would it be like surrounded by blood consuming vampires all the time? *Will I be nervous all the time? Would they accept me?*

"Can Lily stay here?" Shay asked Vincent.

"Not permanently," Vince answered. "She's not safe here. And neither are you."

"We have plenty of room at the cov... The Crown Building," Erica added.

"If Onyx is here...?" Lily began.

Vincent interrupted, "Even with Onyx, six against three isn't very good odds. And Eric will only try harder next time. And I'm sure there will be a next time. He's been beaten at his own game."

"Shay, I know you have martial arts training, but today, it didn't even matter, you were out before you even started. Eric just doesn't play fair," Erica added.

"It doesn't sound like I have a choice," said Shay.

Vincent shook his head. "Not really. Not if you want to be kept safe."

"OK," Shay shrugged looking at Lily. "When do I need to be packed?"

"We'll take care of all that," Alexa assured her. "We'll have you moved tomorrow. In the mean time you can stay with Lily. Or Erica if you prefer."

"I'll stay with Lily."

Jack examined Lily. He checked her heart rate, her blood pressure, her temperature and everything else he had tools for. She was healed. And as near as Jack could tell, completely. He had watched as Lily's body transformed from a burned piece of charred vampire, into a whole vampire. He had watched the bones that were exposed and black turn white. He saw the muscle regenerate from what was left. He saw the tendons around her claws stretch and connect to bone. Then the skin grew over it all. Not only had he not seen a vampire so injured and still be alive, but he had never in his thousands of years seen a vampire come back from that point.

"Shay, would you allow me to get a sample of your blood?" He asked.

"Sure."

She was sitting on the coffee table in front of Lily, getting in Jack's way as he examined Lily, but she didn't care, she wasn't moving. Jack got a needle and took a small sample. Hopefully he'd be able to figure out what was so special about her blood.

MCGOO'S EXPERIMENTS

McGoo looked through a microscope in his lab. He had to figure out what was so special about Shay's blood. And what had allowed Lily to live through such horrific injuries. Love is a powerful thing, but what brought Lily back from the brink was much more than that.

The blood on the slide looked like normal human blood. He compared it other human blood and it was very similar. There were more white blood cells in Shay's blood, but that could've been explained by her injuries that day and the blood she received from Erica. Vampire blood dissipated quickly in human blood. It had to, otherwise they would be detected by the humans if a simple blood test was given after a vampire healed a human. The next logical thing for the human to do after an injury is to go to the doctor.

"So have you figured anything out, yet?" Lily asked as she walked into his lab.

"Not yet," he said. "But it's only been two days."

"Whatcha looking at?" Lily asked as she nudged Jack aside.

"Shay's blood," he answered.

"Looks human," Lily told him.

"Where is LaShay?"

"She took the day off and right now she's supervising the move into her apartment across from mine. Fifty six B."

"She's across the hall!?" Jack laughed. "How did you manage that?"

"It was Vincent's doing. He thought that she'd be more comfortable living close to me. He basically evicted Brian and Sarah."

If Lily had known that it had been Sarah that had eavesdropped on her conversation to get information for Eric, there would've been a lot more than an eviction. But luckily for Sarah, no one expected her and Brian were spying for Eric. If they were to be caught now, there would be dire consequences for the both of them. They could only hope that if they were found out, that it wasn't Lily or Erica that learned the truth.

"I bet Brian and Sarah weren't very happy about it," Jack said.

"Eh, they didn't have to do anything. Vincent had the movers pack, move and unpack for them. They just have to go to another floor now. I think Vince put them in 52B. Eric's lucky that he didn't put them in 68A! His apartment. Guess there just wasn't time to pack up his stuff."

"So Eric is officially out of the coven?" McGoo asked.

"Yup. Alexa even agreed this time," she said.

"Well, it's been a long time coming. That boy should've been put down a long time ago," he agreed.

After a few minutes of silence, Lily finally asked, "So why did you want to know where Shay is?"

"I want to get some more of her blood."

"More?"

"Yes, and let me get a sample of your blood, while you're here."

"Why do you need my blood?"

"It never occurred to me before that your blood may be stronger than Vincent's."

The importance of that statement hit home with Lily.

"You mean I may be able to change vampires? Then the numbers would rise again and we can come of the endangered species list." Lily laughed hard. "We could fill the covens again."

"Very funny. We're not on the endangered species list, threatened maybe, endangered, no," Jack snorted a laugh.

"Well, since Vincent can only change the very strongest of humans, the vampire numbers are declining. He can't change enough to keep up with vampires that are killed. Isn't that right?"

"Yes, Lily, that is correct. But don't you worry about..."

"What about Shay!" Lily interrupted. "If Vincent won't change her, she doesn't stand a chance against Eric. She can't be a human forever, she'll die!"

"Lily, calm down," Jack reassured, "We'll figure it out. Don't worry about Shay, she's safe here."

"But she goes to work, she can't stay here forever. She likes going to work. She would never work from home like most people."

Lily was getting irritated and decided that she should probably leave.

"Your blood," Jack reminded her.

"Right."

"If you want Shay's blood, call her," Lily said.

Lily took a pen and small notepad out of the front coat pocket of Jack's lab coat. She wrote down Shay's cell number, handed the pen and pad back to Jack and turned to leave.

"You're not going to see Shay?" McGoo questioned.

"No, I'm going to blow off some steam."

McGoo took her blood then Lily left the Crown Building and went to Ellen's Fight House. Eric had made her so mad that she just felt like she had to hit something. She needed to blow off some steam and knew that she could always find a fight at the club.

"Well look what the wolf dragged in!" Ellen nearly yelled when she saw Lily walk into her fight club. "Where have you been?"

"Around," Lily smiled.

"Well welcome back. I hate you missed the finals this year. It was a lot of fun," Ellen told her.

"Yeah, I'm sorry, it just totally slipped my mind."

"No worries, hon. So, are you here to fight?" Ellen asked.

"Yes ma'am."

"OK. Come with me," Ellen said and walked toward the back.

She tapped on the computer keyboard and a screen full of names and ranks came up. Ellen scanned the screen and pushed a few more buttons. Lily took off her jacket and shoes and walked toward the ring.

"OK Miss Lily... Jenkins is here, so how about him? He's your rank but a lot bigger than you. Will that work for you?"

"Perfect," Lily nodded.

"Jenkins! Get in here, you have a fight," Ellen yelled toward the back wall.

Jenkins walked in from one of the back rooms.

"Lily? Hell yeah!" He yelled. "Let's do this!"

Jenkins held the top rope up as Lily stepped through. He stepped through himself and waited until Lily was across the ring. He stretched his arms and his claws on his hands came out. Then the claws on his feet and last he pushed his canines into view. Lily did the same. The referee climbed into the ring and the doctor sat in a chair by the wall.

The buzzer sounded and they both headed toward the center. Lily took a swipe with her left hand then a hook with the right. She was surprised when the hook connected. *That almost hurt me!* Lily thought. She kicked at his head and their shins met in the air as he kicked back. There was an audible pop when they hit. Lily then turned, jumped and kicked a perfect round house right into Jenkins right jaw. Lily turned again but this time her feet were swept out from under her and she hit the concrete hard. It took a moment for her to refocus. She rolled out of the way of a foot stomp from her opponent then jumped to her feet. He took a swipe with each hand and connected the second across Lily's chest and shoulder.

"Yeah!" Jenkins yelled out. "Blood! Smells like human blood, Lily!"

Jenkins licked the blood from his claws.

"It even tastes human," he smiled.

Lily didn't say a word and went straight at Jenkins. When she was within reach, she started swinging. First he ducked but Lily kept swinging. She connected three consecutive swings across each side of Jenkin's head when he stood up. He put his arms around his head and ducked again. Lily kept coming.

"Time out!" The referee yelled.

Lily stopped and took three steps back.

"You OK Jenkins," the ref asked.

"Yeah," Jenkins said shaking his head and rubbing his jaw.

Blood dripped onto his shirt and floor from the many gashes. He shook his head and waited a moment while he healed.

"Fight!" The ref called out.

This time Lily stood her ground and let him come to her. He took a running start, jumped and came down with a right punch. Lily stepped out of the way then swung her leg to meet his. He went down with a thud flat on his back. Lily was on him before he could clear his head. She straddled him and began punching, left then right then left again. All Jenkins could do was cover his face with his hands. Lily kept swinging.

"OK," Jenkins mumbled from under his forearms.

The buzzer went off just as the referee yelled, "Fight goes to Lily."

Lily stood up and offered her hand to Jenkins. He took it and she pulled him to his feet. He brushed himself off and looked toward Lily.

"Next time, human," he joked.

McGoo took the elevator from the basement below the garage to the fifty sixth floor. He was carrying an old black medical bag. He walked to LaShay's apartment and knocked on the half open door.

"Hello?" He shouted as he stuck his head inside.

"Coming," Shay called from the back bedroom.

"It's Jack," he called back.

The movers walked out of the back room in front of Shay.

"What can I do for you, Doc," Shay asked.

"I came to get another sample of your blood, if that's alright," he told her.

"Sure, why not," she said. "Can I sit?"

"Of course," he said. "I'm trying to figure out why your blood healed Lily. And why she survived such a horrendous attack. I've ran tests on your blood but they all come back normal. If you would be so kind, could I get a couple vials from you today so I won't have to ask you again any time soon."

Shay sat on the arm of her couch and lifted her arm, palm up to McGoo.

"Oh, thank you," he said.

He took the blood quickly, thanked her again, told her the apartment looked nice and was on his way back to his lab.

He removed the three glass vials from his bag and placed them in a holder with LaShay's other blood sample. He poked a needle through the rubber end on one of the new vials. He placed a drop on a slide, covered it and put it under the microscope. He saw plasma, red blood cells, white blood cells and platelets. Nothing unusual.

Then he took a sample of Lily's blood and placed it on a slide. Lily's blood was very similar to Shay's. But in addition, it had stem cells floating around in the sea of red blood cells. The stem cells were larger than the other cells in the blood and had a visible nucleus. There were also more white blood cells in Lily's sample. Although it couldn't be seen here, McGoo knew there was also the virus that had created the vampires in the beginning. The virus had been mistaken for influenza ever since human scientists has first seen it in the 1930's with the invention of the electron microscope. McGoo had an electron microscope built from his own schematic almost fifteen years before the humans.

Under an electron microscope, the virus looked almost exactly like influenza, a ball with spikes all over it. At the ends of about half of the spikes there were clusters of small oval shapes. But in the vampire virus, about three of those spikes ended in a single long, oval shape. It was a detail so small that human scientists had never realized that the virus they were seeing would create an entirely different species. Luckily, vampire scientists in the virology field had kept the vampire virus from being confused with the influenza one during flu research.

This vampire virus could replicate itself so rapidly in human blood that it literally took over. Quickly, if the volume of vampire blood was equal to or more than five parts human blood to one part vampire blood. When enough of the virus is introduced to human blood, the virus begins to create stem cells that make *more* stem cells that take the place of every cell in the entire human body. That's why the transformation is so painful. It literally rewrites the entire DNA code in a week. The human that is changing feels the dying of the old cells and the replacement with new cells. It's like the equivalent of recovering from major surgery of your entire body. Everything inside has been cut on or moved and the body fights to heal it. It once was a process that only took a couple of days. Now, the human has to endure ten to fifteen days of agonizing pain. Most did not make it through the change.

McGoo never thought that Lily's blood was special so he never had a reason to study it. Now he did. This whole time he just believed that her blood was just a mix of human and vampire blood. He made more slides of Lily's blood and studied each of them. He did notice that there was less plasma in Lily's blood. Which meant that her blood consisted of a higher concentration of all the other components. And after examining the sample under an electron microscope, the blood also had more of the virus. As near as he could tell, Lily had about one third more virus in her blood than vampires.

"Humm," he thought out loud.

He got up and rummaged through a rack of blood samples in his refrigerator. He found Vincent's blood sample and made a couple of slides. Over the centuries, Vincent's blood had weakened, but Jack could never figure out why. Now he knew. It had simply thinned. There was more plasma than Lily's sample and nearly half as many platelets. Lily's blood *was* stronger.

One could only pump so much blood into a human's body. The average body can only hold about five liters of blood. And with less virus and less stem cells, it takes longer for the change to happen. It took longer for the virus to affect every cell because there was less virus. At least that was Jack's theory. The only way to test it was to change a human with Lily's blood.

Jack went straight to Vincent.

"Absolutely not!" Vincent nearly yelled.

"But Vince, if her blood..."

"No!" Vincent said sternly.

"Vince, you're not listening!" Jack yelled back. "Lily's blood may be the answer to changing vampires like we did centuries ago. Look how empty this building is. At one time a coven would fill every room in this building and then some. You know our numbers are declining. They have been for decades, Vince. Lily may be able to raise our numbers again and be as strong as we once were."

"Our numbers are fine," Vincent countered.

"The Nashville coven is empty. The Houston coven is at less than half its capacity. The Seattle coven lost over thirty vamps just last year. Our coven has let feeders go into the free world and live their lives there because they just weren't needed. We've kicked out feeders, Vince. Our numbers *are* dwindling. And you know it. When was the last time you successfully changed a human?"

Jack waited for an answer. After a moment of silence, he continued.

"If Lily's blood could even cut the time in half that could mean that twice as many survive."

Vincent shook his head and looked over at Alexa who had entered the room shortly after Vincent and Jack began yelling. She heard the conversation.

"What do you think, Lex?" Vince asked.

"What could it hurt?" She answered.

Jack crossed his arms and looked at Vincent.

"Well? What do you say?" Jack asked.

"Fine, as long as it's not Shay," Vincent finally answered after a moment of silence.

"Lily wouldn't allow that anyway," Jack shot back.

Vincent just shook his head and continued what he had been doing when McGoo arrived, reading reports from the other coven leaders. Jack smiled at Alexa and mouthed *Thank you.*

Lily returned to the coven and went directly to Shay's. Then she remembered the little box she had made. She had finished it and had written a short letter and decided to give it as a housewarming gift. She ran and grabbed the box with the letter inside. She knocked on the door and waited. After a minute, Shay answered, covered in sweat and breathing heavy.

"Why are you knocking?" Shay asked her.

Lily looked around the hallway and shrugged. "I don't have a remote yet."

"That's a good reason," Shay smiled and grabbed Lily's arm.

She pulled Lily into the living room and stopped.

"What do you think?" Shay laughed.

"Looks *just* like your apartment."

"Yup! Now come on and help me move the guest room around."

"Why didn't you have the moving guys move everything?" Lily wondered.

"They had already left when I decided I didn't like it."

"Wait, I have something for you," Lily said.

"For me?" Shay questioned.

"Yes. I made it."

"Aww. Really?"

Lily handed Shay the little box made out of craft sticks. The letter was inside. Shay took the box and looked it over. The box was an oval shape and had little diamond shapes on each side. On the outside there was a peg that held the lid on.

"Are those craft sticks? How did you get them to bow like that?"

Shay tried to open the lid but it wouldn't budge. Lily reached over and pointed to the little peg protruding from the side. Shay slid out the peg and opened the box. The tiny music apparatus came to life and played the first thirty notes of *Fir Elise* as she looked inside and pulled out a folded piece of paper. She looked at Lily as she opened it. She read the short, hand written letter that told her how much Lily loved her. She wrapped her arms around Lily's neck.

"Thank you. I love you, too," Shay told her.

Lily took a deep breath, hugged Shay tight then followed her into the back bedroom. When Shay turned to face Lily, she noticed a small drop of what looked like dried blood on Lily's neck.

"What happened? Is that blood?"

Lily had never told Shay about fight club. And really didn't want to now. But she didn't want any secrets between them either.

"It happened at a place called 'Ellen's Fight House'. It's place where vampires go to fight with other vampires."

"Fight?" Shay questioned. "Like as in claws and fangs fight?"

Lily only nodded.

"Why?" Shay asked.

"To blow off steam mostly. I started when I was young as a punishment by Vincent. I was young and bored and fighting with the other young vampires and feeders in the coven. I think Erica took me there just to scare me. But it backfired. I enjoyed fighting. I had been fighting with Eric my whole life. And it just came naturally to me."

Shay took a deep breath and stared at Lily for a moment.

"You enjoy fighting?" Shay asked slowly. "And I have Eric to thank for that?"

"I won't go anymore if you don't want me to."

"Can I go with you?" Shay asked.

"No, it's not a place that's safe for humans."

"I don't want to tell you that you can't go. But what if you got hurt?"

"I won't. Really," Lily reassured. "I've never been seriously hurt in the one hundred plus years I've been attending."

"Then I'm not going to stop you," Shay said.

"I don't have to go," Lily told her. "Today is the first time I've been in months. Well, since I met you,"

Shay wasn't sure what to say. She didn't want to tell Lily she couldn't go but she didn't want to tell her she could, either. She knew nothing about vampire fighting and was afraid to ask.

"I'm not going to tell you that you can't go, Lily. But you fighting scares the hell out of me."

Before Lily could respond, someone knocked on the front door and Shay went to answer. Lily was only a few feet behind her. She didn't know who could possibly be knocking on the door already.

"Hey Doc," she said when she opened the door. "Need more blood already?"

"Well yes, but not yours. I assumed Lily would be here."

"You assumed right," said Lily. "Why do you need more of my blood?"

"I actually need all of your blood," Jack told her.

"Huh?" Lily and Shay said at the same time.

"I would like for you to administer a blood transfusion to a human."

"You want me to change a human? I can't do that! What will Vincent say?"

"Vincent knows and I have his approval," McGoo reassured.

Lily looked at Shay and Shay looked at her. Lily shrugged and looked at Jack. About then, Alexa appeared behind Jack in the doorway.

"It's an experiment Lily," Alexa stated.

"An experiment to what? Watch me kill a human after a couple of weeks of agonizing pain? What are you thinking, McGoo?" Lily asked.

"I think your blood is stronger than Vincent's. Actually, I *know* it is."

"Then I assume this is not open to discussion," Lily smirked.

"Not really," McGoo confirmed.

"Well then Shay is coming to keep me company," Lily demanded.

"No arguments here," McGoo agreed. "Tomorrow at noon in my lab."

Lily nodded, watched Jack leave then went back to rearranging the back bedroom with Shay.

The next morning at around eleven thirty, the girls headed down to the lab to meet McGoo. Vincent was waiting in the lab when they arrived. Standing beside him was a rather large man. Muscular with a heavy build and broad shoulders. He was already wearing a hospital gown that was more paper than it was cloth.

"This is Mark," Vincent announced to everyone. "He wants to become a vampire and has ever since the day I met him, twenty-two years ago."

The man didn't seem to be that old. Lily didn't recognize him as a feeder, in fact she had never seen this man before.

"I met Mark at the Atlanta coven. He was only five years old at the time and he already knew that vampires existed. He would not take 'no' for an answer, because apparently, he had seen a vampire. He was an orphan that was found living on the street with a group of street kids. He had found his way to the coven by way of a doctor of psychiatry. Word of mouth throughout the community had brought him to me, as I was the so-called vampire expert. I made him a feeder at the Atlanta coven and although we rarely take in anyone not born into the coven, he was determined. He wanted to be a vampire. So I told him I would make him one as soon as I could find a way to guarantee his survival.

"That day is today," Vincent continued. "This is the only shot that there will be, Mark, you understand that, right?"

Mark only closed his eyes and nodded, as if for the hundredth time.

"If this works, the vampires may be 'off the endangered species list' as Lily so lovingly put it," Vincent added.

Lily could barely even smile at the joke. She was nervous. Her part would only take a few hours, but what if it didn't work. What if Mark was still writhing in pain after two weeks?

"Lily, if this doesn't work, it is not your fault. It's mine," McGoo told her. "There's only one way to see if it will work and that is to try."

McGoo motioned to the hospital bed that was facing the opposite direction of Mark's. Lily sat down and McGoo connected her to a blood transfusion machine. It was basically a modified bypass machine that took blood out of the human and replaced that blood with vampire blood. The vampire blood had to be warmed to 98.6°F because it was too cold to go directly into the human. It would've caused hypothermia if it weren't heated in the machine.

It was obvious that Lily was nervous. Alexa left and came back with a chair. She sat it next to Lily's hospital bed and motioned to Shay. Shay sat down and took Lily's hand.

Next, McGoo connected Mark to the machine. Only this time, there were four tubes instead of Lily's two. They connected to Mark's major arteries. The carotid in the neck, the brachial in the shoulder and the femoral artery in each leg. McGoo then connected blood bags to the machine. These would replace Lily's blood as hers was being drained. McGoo looked at Lily, took a deep breath then threw the switch. The machine whirred to life.

Shay squeezed Lily's hand and Lily remembered that she was there.

"This is not normal," she told Shay.

"She's going to be weak for a few days after this," Erica told Shay.

Lily didn't even realize that Erica had walked in.

"Is there anything I need to do?" Shay asked.

"No, she'll be fine, just no *marathons* for a few days," Erica smiled then winked at Shay.

"Oh," Shay nodded then smiled.

After about three hours, McGoo finally unhooked Lily from the machine. She was lightheaded when she stood up. Shay braced herself against Lily so she wouldn't fall.

"Take it easy," Erica told them.

Lily only nodded and walked out. She was afraid that she had just killed a man. She wasn't sure why Jack thought it would work but she had to assume that he had his reasons.

"Jack," Alexa said, "I'll be back tomorrow to see how things are going."

"When will we know something," Erica asked Jack.

"When he wakes up or when he stops breathing," Jack answered.

"That's kind of grim, isn't it," she asked.

Jack only shrugged his shoulders. That was the truth of it. There was no halfway from this point forward. Either Mark would wake up a vampire, or he would die trying to become one.

Three days passed and Mark was still changing. His fists would clutch and his body would tense every few minutes. The pain was excruciating. Every vampire knew what it felt like to change from a human into a vampire. Except, of course, Lily.

"Seems ironic that the one vampire that never had to make the change is the one vampire that may end up being the only one that can change them. It would save us from extinction," Vincent told Jack.

"For her sake, I hope you're right," Jack said.

Three hours into the fifth day Mark opened his eyes.

Jack called Lily immediately.

"Lily, it worked. Five days and three hours," was all he said.

Lily was nearly in tears when Shay noticed something was wrong.

"What is it?" Shay asked.

"Mark's awake."

"Now what," Shay asked.

"Now, he gets to learn how to be a vampire."

Lily, Shay and Onyx rode the elevator down to the lab where Mark was being kept. Mark was a big man and should he go into a rage, he could cause a lot of damage within the coven. So he would stay in the sub-basement behind heavy doors and large wolves until it was known that he could control his hunger and his temper. It was common practice for all new vampires. He would be there for a few days although it usually took three to four weeks for the new vamps to learn how to fully control their teeth and claws. Hunger and temper control depended on the individual.

When Lily walked into Mark's room he ran straight at her. Onyx and two wolves were on their feet in a flash and blocked his path. Mark stopped cold in his tracks and held up his hands, palms out.

"I just want to hug her, I promise," he said.

Raven and Venom walked back to their place on each side of the door. But Onyx wouldn't move from in front of Lily and Shay.

"It's OK, Onyx," Lily said and patted him on the shoulder.

He looked at Lily then Mark and then stepped aside. Mark gave Lily a hug so tight that it almost hurt.

"Mark, I can't breathe," Lily gasped.

"Oh, sorry," he said and let go. "Thank you, Lily."

Lily only smiled and looked over to Jack.

"What?" Jack asked when he realized Lily was looking at him.

"How did you know?" Lily asked.

"You have strong blood, Lily. Pure blood. But we still want to figure out how to make the transformation period shorter. Mark, here, is a young, strong man and had been told what the change was like all his life. He knew almost what to expect. Shay, for example, probably wouldn't last five days. The transformation used to take two to three days. That's what Vincent and Alexa experienced. I was a little weaker than them, older, and it took a little longer. But you never forget the pain of the change. No matter how long ago it happened. You're lucky, Lily, you'll never have to go through that," Jack rambled on as he was known for doing. "Your blood cut the time in half from what it had been. Shay I would like to test your blood some more. I still can't quite pin-point what is so special about it and why it healed Lily."

"OK, Doc," Shay said, trying to interrupt his rant. "Do you want it now?"

"Sure," he said smiling. "Let's go to my lab."

Lily, Shay and Onyx followed McGoo down the hall. He took some more of Shay's blood and took more of Lily's since she was already there.

On the other side of the city, the sun was setting low in the sky. Long shadows and bright sun made it hard to see toward the west. But Titian, Rader and Arius were on Eric's trail. The three vampire trackers were told by Vincent to find Eric and bring him back to the coven. Vincent was serious this time and Alexa wasn't stopping him. He was done with Eric's games. The trackers had seen Eric duck into an alleyway up ahead wearing a black hoodie and black pants. When the trackers reached the alley, Eric was ready for them.

Five vampire friends of Eric's, all wearing the same clothes as Eric, came out of the shadows cast by the tall buildings. Eric gave a signal and his friends attacked the trackers. Steel rebar and chains swung in every direction. They were outnumbered, so the only thing the trackers could do, was run. But Eric had one more trick up his sleeve. He sent two wolves after the trackers. Two of them were able to escape the much faster wolves, but Arius was caught. The wolves ripped him to pieces before Rader and Titian had a chance to get back to him.

The trackers phoned the news to Vincent. He was furious.

"If you get the chance, kill him," Vincent told them.

Eric listened to the phone call hidden between two parked cars. He knew he was on the assassins' list now.

Back at the coven, Jack was back in the lab testing blood. He was looking at a sample of Shay's blood when he had decided to walk away for a day and let his mind clear. He had been looking at these same samples for hours. He was at a loss. Under the electron microscope, he had thought he caught a glimpse of the virus in Shay's blood. He searched the image again but saw no virus. He gathered up the samples to throw them in the trash when one of the corners pricked his finger. The surprise caused him to drop all of them on the counter. The tiny glass slides broke as they landed and the blood mixed together.

"Shit," Jack spat.

He almost just swept the mess into the trash can when he wondered what they would look like under the microscope. He took a dropper from the drawer, plunged a little of the mixed samples then dabbed it onto a few slides then slid them into the electron microscope. He had to look twice at what he was seeing. The blood wasn't attacking each other. He knew this couldn't be right. But maybe the blood didn't mix after all.

Normally, when human blood and vampire blood are mixed, the vampire blood will quickly begin to overtake the human blood. The virus begins to basically 'eat' the red blood cells of the human blood. Once fed, they begin to multiply into mostly stem cells. It's the stem cells that immediately begin to heal humans that have been given blood, but not enough to overtake their own and start the change. But this wasn't happening. He pulled another couple of slides out of the drawer and went to get fresh samples. He put a drop of Shay's blood then three drops of Lily's blood. In the electron microscope, he saw the same thing. They weren't fighting one another. He couldn't understand why. What was so different about Shay's blood? Lily's blood should be attacking.

Jack had another idea. He went to his refrigerator and searched through his samples until he found human blood. Not feeder blood, but blood from a regular human. He put a drop on a slide and looked. It looked like Shay's blood. Except for the extra white blood cells. He removed the slide and placed a drop of Lily's blood with it. Under the microscope is was doing what it should, only faster than McGoo was used to seeing.

Then he had a thought. He took a fresh slide, put a drop of human blood then a drop of Shay's blood. Nothing. He thought for a moment. He took the slide with human and Shay's blood and dropped on a sample of Lily's blood.

Jack looked at the slide, then looked at the slide again. Under the microscope he could see the virus begin to consume the human blood. But in this sample, the vampire blood also began to merge with the white blood cells.

"What the hell?" Jack mumbled.

He made another sample. Human blood, Shay's blood, Lily's blood. Same result. Then he dropped each onto the slide but left them separated. Once under the microscope he used a needle to combine Shay's blood with the human blood. Nothing. Then he added in Lily's blood.

McGoo watched as the vampire blood began eat the red blood cells of the human blood. Which was normal. But he also watched as the vampire blood merged with the white blood cells, but it appeared to only be happening on the end with

Shay's blood. He watched as the merged white blood cells split. They were never consumed by the vampire blood.

"Holy shit!" McGoo yelled. "Her blood is already at the halfway point! No need to be remade into completely new cells. It simply picks up where it left off."

Jack thought about the gravity of his discovery. He determined that with Shay's blood added first, it would cause the change to happen faster. The added white blood cells in Shay's blood had a special purpose. To initiate the change and speed the process. He tested the three blood types again and again. If Shay's blood was added to human blood, it skipped a step in the process. He couldn't wait to test it on a human.

Jack went directly to Vincent and told him what he had found.

"This is it, Vince! This is the answer we didn't even know we were looking for," Jack began. "Shay's blood is the catalyst we've needed all along. I didn't even know it existed! But her blood is like a missing piece in the bloodlines. It's not completely human but it's not vampire. It's like pre-vampire blood. It's almost like it prepares the human blood for transformation."

"How?" Vince asked.

"How what?"

"How is Shay's blood different? What is she?"

"She's a regular human, Vince. Her blood is just special."

"How do you know that?" Vince questioned.

"I've examined her from head to toe. She's human," Jack continued. "Lily's blood cuts the change down to just over five days. With Shay's blood, we may be able to get that down to two to three days. Almost any human could survive that."

"But what about Shay?" Vince asked. "What happens when Lily wants to change Shay? You know that day is coming."

Jack took a deep breath and thought for a moment. "Well, we can't change Shay. If she becomes a vampire she loses the special blood. Then what? Maybe... Maybe I can synthesize her blood. Maybe I can replicate the special white blood cells. But they look the same. Maybe they're all the special cell."

Jack continued to ramble on, "If I could isolate the special cells maybe I can get them to divide on their own. Create a synthetic plasma and use white blood cells from humans or even feeders."

He continued talking as he left Vincent's apartment. He was still talking, to himself, when he rode the elevator all the way from the penthouse to the sub-basement. Brian, the feeder and Eric's personal lackey, got on the elevator at the fifty second floor. McGoo acknowledged that he gotten on but didn't stop talking. Brian listened as they rode.

"What makes Shay's blood special?" Jack asked rhetorically. "The white blood cells. The white blood cells could be harvested and made to replicate themselves maybe with the help of an outside source, like the vampire virus. If I can isolate the white blood cells, introduce the virus and let the virus reproduce the cells. But would the new cells contain DNA from the virus? Probably. Would that interfere with the changing process? Would it still shorten the process to less than five days?"

The elevator door opened at the lobby level and Brian stepped out. He immediately called Eric.

"What?" Eric snapped.

"Eric, I just heard that Shay's blood is special. It will change humans to vampires in less than five days," Brian told him.

"How do you know that?"

"I just heard Jack talking in the elevator."

"Talking to who," Eric asked.

"Whom," Brian corrected.

"Whatever," Eric quipped.

"He was talking to himself."

"Shay huh? Find out more and get back to me," Eric told then hung up before Brian could say anything else.

Brian forgot about what he was doing and went to the sub-basement. He and Jack had always gotten along in the past, maybe he could get McGoo to tell him more. He rode the elevator down to the sub-basement and walked through the white tiled hallways. It was bright and reminded Brian of an old hospital. He walked past the lab that Mark was in and stopped. The doors were open and Mark was sitting on a hospital bed. He was looking at his hands with stern concentration. Veins protruded from Mark's forehead as he tried to expose his claws. Brian also saw the two wolves inside the door. Brian figured out quickly that Mark was being guarded because he was a new vampire. Brian also knew that there hadn't been a new vampire in the coven in over twenty years. The last was in Atlanta and it had been a miracle he even survived.

Brian walked into McGoo's lab and knocked on the opened door to get his attention.

"Hello, McGoo," he said.

"Hi Brian, what can I do for you?"

"Just wondering what was going on down here. Rumor has it there's a new vampire."

"Yes, that's true," Jack replied but offered no more information.

"Is there anything I can help you with down here?" Brian asked.

"No, but thank you," McGoo said, looking back into his microscope.

Brian figured that he wouldn't press the issue. So he decided he'd go talk to the new vampire. He walked to Mark's room and knocked on the open door. Mark looked up from his hand and smiled.

"You're human," Mark said smiling, "I can smell that you're human."

The wolves stood when Mark stood.

Venom walked over to Brian and sniffed. He then turned around and went to his spot beside the opened door.

"How are you adjusting to being a vampire?" Brian asked.

Mark looked down at his hand and the vein in his forehead popped out again. The tips of his claws protruded from under his fingernails then disappeared.

"I'm getting there," Mark smiled. "It's a lot harder than I thought it would be."

"I bet," Brain said halfheartedly. "When did Vincent change you?"

"He didn't," Mark answered.

Brian was confused. The only vampire that had ever changed anyone into a vampire in his lifetime, was Vincent. Brian had been with the coven for over a century, and he only knew of a few humans that had been changed. He also knew a lot that had died trying.

"It wasn't Vincent's blood that changed you?" Brian asked.

"No," Mark said without offering anything else.

"Whose blood was used? Dr. McGregor's?"

"Nope."

"Whose blood did they use?"

"Lily's," Mark said without looking up from his hands. He had put both in his lap and was still trying to expose his claws.

Brian was shocked. Lily's blood was strong enough to make vampires. He thought of all of the possibilities for Eric. He would rule the Underground. Being able to make vampires would make Eric a god in the circles he ran in. Mark pulled his phone out of his pocket and was calling Eric before he was even out the door but there was no signal in the basement. So when he reached the lobby he tried again.

"What now, Brian?" Eric groaned.

"Eric, Lily's blood can make vampires. There's a new vampire in McGoo's lab right now and he's not even a few days old. And there's no way it could've taken more than six days to change him, because I was down here a week ago."

"Wait slow down," Eric said. "It sounded like you said Lily can make vampires."

"That's right," Brian nearly yelled, then looked around to make sure no one was listening.

Eric didn't need to hear anymore. Lily could make vampires. Which meant that if he had Lily, *he* could make vampires. He could raise the numbers of the vampire population in the Underground. No longer would it depend on an Elder. He could make anyone a vampire. He was rolling around the enormity of this discovery.

Eric went straight to the Underground from his new apartment in the city. On the way, he made a number of phone calls to his vampire friends. He found a storefront that led him down. When he arrived at Ellen's Fight House, some of his friends were already waiting for him.

"Gather around boys!" He announced. "How would you like to rule the vampires?"

THE UNDERGROUND VS THE COVEN

McGoo was busy trying to recreate Shay's blood in his lab. He had isolated the white blood cells from Shay's blood and was scanning them with an electron microscope to see what, if anything, was different from normal human white blood cells. At a magnification of one thousand times, he finally noticed the tiny red dots on Shay's cells. The normal white blood cell usually looks a little like a bumpy white snowball. On Shay's, there were the occasional tiny red dots on the surface of the cell.

After days of studying the blood, McGoo finally figured out that the specialized white blood cells didn't attack the vampire virus. It was as if the virus had already turned off the search and destroy order for the cell. It was only the vampire virus that the cell ignored. It acted normal toward all other contaminants that McGoo introduced.

So was Shay exposed to the vampire virus? How? And how did she manage to rid her body of it? McGoo wondered.

How was Shay's blood already prepared to be turned into a vampire? She wasn't a vampire nor had she any traits of a vampire. It was as if someone attempted to change her and then somehow stopped. She's not a vampire and she's not dead. So how did this happen? McGoo had to talk to Shay.

He rode the elevator to the fifty sixth floor and knocked on Shay's door. Lily's door opened.

"McGoo?" Lily called from behind him.

"Lily," he said as he turned to face her.

"Is LaShay here?"

"Yes, come in."

Jack entered the apartment and Shay was sitting on the couch. There were two glasses of scotch on the table and it appeared that that wasn't their first glass.

"Have a seat," Lily offered him a seat in the chair across from the couch.

"Thank you," he said as he sat.

"Shay, may I talk to you about your family?" He asked.

"Sure," she said.

"What were your parents like?"

"Well my dad is Martin Black and..." she began but was interrupted.

"Your father owns Midnight Entertainment?" McGoo asked.

Shay only nodded.

"Well, we're pretty sure that he's not a vampire," McGoo thought out loud.

"A vampire?" Shay laughed. "Uh, no."

"What about your mother?"

"My mother died during childbirth. I never knew her."

"Was it possible that she was a vampire? Or *turning into* a vampire when you were born?"

"Not that I'm aware of," Shay said seriously. "I didn't know her, but what my dad has told me, she wasn't a vampire she couldn't have been. He told me they went to Hawaii for their anniversary. And he never mentioned sunscreen."

Jack took a deep breath. "Well, I don't even know if a changing vampire could even deliver a child. I've never heard of it happening but I suppose it's possible."

"Why?" Lily asked.

"Because Shay's blood is the, how can I put it...? Um, a missing link in our bloodline. Her blood speeds up the changing process even more when used with your blood," he said to Lily.

"It's like a catalyst that the human blood needs to make the change in less than three days. It's only a theory that it would take three days, but I'm sure that's what it would cut the duration to. I've run countless tests and that's the working theory. Vincent is looking for another candidate to be changed as we speak."

"It's only been four days since we changed Mark," Lily reminded him.

"No time like the present," McGoo said. "When he finds someone, I'm going to need you *and* LaShay to do the transfusion."

"Jack, Shay has to work. Her father is already furious that she just up and moved without asking him. If she misses too much more work, he'll show up here to make sure she's OK." Lily informed him.

"Well, he's bound to show up at some point," McGoo said. "Just so you know, LaShay, he *will* be able to get into the building. Alexa made sure of that. The last thing this coven needs is a powerful man like him looking into us."

"Agreed," Shay sighed.

"Well, I guess we'll just have to wait until Shay gets home from work to do the change. McGoo began his trademark rambling again. "Granted, Vincent finds someone. He has someone in mind, he's just trying to get all his ducks in a row, you know. It's not every day that you're asked if you want to become immortal. I would assume there would be a lot you'd need to do if you were about to become the new member of a vampire coven. Like forwarding your mail and..."

"We get it, McGoo," Lily interrupted.

"OK," McGoo said. "I guess that's all."

He stood up and walked toward the door. "Oh, by the way, Shay, do you know if your father owns a private jet?"

"He does, why?"

"Always wanted to ride in a private jet."

Shay laughed. She wasn't sure where in the world that had come from, and she wasn't about to ask. He would have an hour explanation and Shay knew that.

When he left, Lily poured a little more scotch into their glasses and sat on the couch beside Shay.

"So my father is welcome in the Crown Building, huh?" Shay reiterated.

Lily shrugged her shoulders. "I guess so. It's probably for the best though. From what I know of him, could you imagine him not being able to get in to see his daughter?"

"No," Shay said flatly. "He would have been here already if he weren't out of the country."

"Oh, that's why," Lily smirked.

"Yeah."

"So do you miss your old place?" Lily asked.

"Are you kidding? I live in the Crown Building," Shay laughed.

The two looked at each other for a long moment then Shay grabbed a handful of Lily's shirt and pulled her toward her. They kissed. Lily ran her fingers through Shay's hair and pushed her back onto the couch. Shay lifted Lily's shirt over her head and unhooked her bra. She slid the bra over Lily's shoulders and let the bra fall to the floor. Shay sat upright and took off her shirt and bra then pulled Lily close. Lily kissed down Shay's neck and lowered her back down onto the couch. She unbuttoned and unzipped Shay's pants and slid them off along with her panties. Then Lily undressed and laid on top of Shay. They kissed deeply and Shay ran her hands down Lily's back and back up through her hair. Lily kissed down Shay's chest to her breast and took it into her mouth. Shay moaned softly and grabbed a handful of Lily's hair. Onyx just whined and tried to cover his ears.

I can't believe I live in the Crown building now, Shay thought. *My girlfriend is a vampire and here I am, completely in love with a species the rest of the world thought went extinct fifty thousand years ago.* Her thoughts rambled. *What is my dad going to think about me living in the Crown Building? Has he ever tried to live here? What did they tell him? How did they tell my dad 'no'?*

Lily continued to suckle Shay's breast then moved to the other. She kissed down her stomach and down between her legs. Lily kissed the inside of Shay's thighs then kissed closer and closer to the center. Shay moaned when Lily found the warm wetness. Lily slid her tongue inside and rolled it around then slid up to Shay's clit where she pressed her lips against her and sucked gently. Shay's back arched off the couch. Lily wrapped one arm around Shay's leg and held tight. She spread Shay open and pressed her tongue into Shay's clit then rolled it around under her tongue. Lily slid two fingers into Shay then out again then back in. She twisted her fingers and licked harder as she sucked.

"Oh god!" Shay cried out.

She took a handful of the sofa and gripped it as hard as she could. Her legs began to shake and she draped one over the back of the couch. Offering more access to Lily. Lily slid her fingers in and out and pressed her lips against Shay. Shay was so wet. Lily's fingers were covered in lubricant and slid in and out so easily. She slid in three fingers and sucked Shay clit into her mouth again. This time, Lily didn't let go. She sucked hard and flicked her tongue over the warm pink bundle of nerves. Shay's legs shook harder and she grabbed a bigger handful of the couch cushion and squeezed as a wave of pleasure washed over her. She moaned Lily's name and her back arched again. Lily kept at it until Shay calmed and the climax was over.

Lily slowly kissed up Shay's body, stopping again at a breast. Shay ran both hands through Lily's hair. Lily rested her head on Shay's chest. The sound of Shay's beating heart was so relaxing to Lily. Shay played with Lily's hair and in a few minutes they started again.

McGoo went back to his lab and worked on the blood samples some more. Like McGoo had said, Vincent was looking for another candidate to change. It had been decades since there was a list to go by. Back when it was common to change humans to vampires, there was a running list of would-be vampires. The majority were humans that worked for the vampires outside the coven. If a vampire had fallen in love with a human, they were first on the list. Police officers and government officials that helped cover the existence of the coven and the Underground were second, if they chose to be. There was still a strict criteria for becoming a vampire. Secrecy was the priority and all would be vampires were told the rules. Basically it was 'keep your mouth shut', do not let your teeth or claws show in public and absolutely no fighting with humans. Because it always ended badly.

Two hours passed and McGoo was hungry. Or thirsty, in his case. He took the elevator to the thirteenth floor. There was no '13' on the elevator panel. It required a hand and eye scan to get there. This floor existed for one purpose only, to feed the vampires that either didn't have a feeder or who didn't want a feeder. Blood was always available to all the vampires in the coven. The only catch was, there was no blood allowed off the floor. Feeders were only allowed to give blood in the vampires' residence. McGoo was usually just too busy to stop for a feeder. They were on a schedule, he wasn't. So he used the blood bank more often than not.

McGoo walked into the first door on the floor and a young woman greeted him.

"Hello Dr. McGregor, what can I get for you?" she asked.

"I'll have a bourbon on the rocks," he joked.

"Funny. How many bags do you need?"

"Give me three B's, please."

"Yes sir."

She walked to the nearest refrigerator and pulled out three bags of B+ blood. She handed them to him and he walked down the hall to a room that looked like someone's living room. A large screen TV, a sectional couch and a couple of recliners were in the room. The full length of the wall to the left was covered in book cases and was packed full of books and magazines. McGoo walked about halfway down the wall, took a book from the third shelf and went to sit in a recliner. He bent the plastic on the top of the blood bag and it broke off with a snap.

He opened the book, reclined back and took a drink. He read and drank casually for about an hour then decided he should get back to work.

As he walked back into his lab, he caught someone going through his blood samples.

"Hey!" McGoo yelled.

The person just froze in place. He slowly turned and faced Jack. It was Brian.

"What the hell are you fucking doing?" McGoo cursed.

Brian was trying to come up with an excuse for being there. But he was coming up empty. He had never been very good at thinking on his feet. Eric had sent him there to get all of Lily's blood from McGoo. He just couldn't have the good doctor go and ruin his fun by synthesizing the blood.

"There you are, Dr. McGregor. I was looking for you," Brian finally said.

"What are you doing in here?" McGoo asked.

"I was waiting for you and I was just being nosey," Brian was making it up as he went. "You have all kinds of samples here, don't you?"

"What do you want, Brian?"

"Nothing really. I was just curious about the new vampire."

"There's nothing to tell."

"I know that there's a new vampire down here. I spoke to him. He said that Lily changed him."

"You are not to share that information with anyone, do you understand, Brian?" McGoo said sternly.

"Uh, OK. My lips are sealed. Not a word," Brian told him.

"Now get out!" McGoo yelled.

"Yes, sir."

Brian looked at the floor all the way out of the lab. He had failed to get any of Lily's blood.

Sarah went to Lily's apartment for her scheduled feeding. Shay let her in and she walked to the kitchen like she always did. Onyx watched her closely. The wolf had never been very fond of Sarah, but then again, he didn't really like anyone.

"Sarah?" Lily called from the bedroom.

"Yes Lily," she yelled back.

"Not today," Lily said.

"Lily, it's ok. It's been four days since you've had blood and I know that you need it," Shay said to Lily in the bedroom.

"Sarah," Lily called again.

"I heard," Sarah replied. *Whew.*

Sarah got a glass from the cabinet and placed it on the white marble counter. She looked around to make sure that no one was watching. She took a vial out her pocket and poured a white powder into the glass. She took a knife out of the knife rack on the counter and cut her wrist. She filled the glass about two thirds full and then stirred the liquid to mix in the tranquilizer. Eric had sent it with her to drug Lily. Tonight was the night he was planning on taking Lily and killing Shay.

Sarah met Lily in the living room with the glass of fresh blood. She had a towel around her wrist. Lily slid her thumb across her teeth and waited for Sarah to remove the bloody towel. She then wiped the blood on Sarah's cut. After a moment the gash was healed.

Sarah wiped away the blood that remained with the towel and smiled at Lily, "Is that all?"

"Yes, Sarah, thank you," Lily replied.

Sarah left the apartment with a big grin.

Lily drank the blood and held up the glass to offer Shay a drink. She wasn't serious, she just wanted a reaction from Shay. Shay wrinkled her nose and shook her head. Lily shrugged and drank the rest of the blood. It only took a few minutes for the tranquilizer to take effect. Lily's head began to spin and her vision became blurry. Shay noticed immediately that something was wrong. Lily managed to get to the couch before she passed out.

"Lily?" Shay yelled. "Lily!"

Shay grabbed her phone and called Erica.

"Hel..."

"Erica! Something's wrong! Lily has passed out on the couch."

"Passed out? Is she that drunk," Erica laughed.

"No! She just had her feeding and she passed out almost immediately after."

Erica was up and out the door. She ran to the elevator and pressed the down button repeatedly.

"Come on! Come on!" She mumbled as she tapped her foot on the carpet.

Eric and his vampire friends had already entered the building and made it to Lily's floor before Erica could even get on the elevator.

Eric, six vampires and a wolf walked down Lily's hallway. He got to the door first and simply kicked it down. Onyx was on his feet and practically flying over the couch when Eric entered the room. He landed square on Eric's chest and knocked him to the floor. Shay froze.

Onyx's teeth chomped loudly as he took bites at Eric's face. Eric held him at arm's length by the neck. Two of the other vampires threw Onyx off and helped Eric up but Onyx was on them again immediately. He managed to bite around the neck of one of the other vampires. He chomped hard and bit all the way through. *One down*, he thought.

Two vampires went to Lily and one to Shay as the other two stayed guard in the hallway.

The elevator opened down the hall and Erica came running out. She had called Steven and Vincent on the way down.

The two vampires in the hall went after Erica. She took two swipes to the chest and one of the vampires went down. The other took a few steps back and steeled his stance. Erica bent down swept his legs out from under him and stomped on his chest once, then twice and finally a third time, crushing his heart. She plunged her clawed hand into the vampire's chest and pulled out his damaged heart.

This one isn't getting up, she thought. *Now where the hell is Eric?*

Downstairs, Jack got a call from Vincent that Eric was in the building, but he didn't know where. He could only assume he was going after Lily and Shay. He didn't know that Eric knew about Lily changing a human to a vampire. Vincent had also called building security to converge on Lily's floor.

Down in the building's lobby, twelve more vampire friends from the Underground began firing guns into the air and then at anyone in the lobby. Eric had discovered bullets that would kill vampires. The armor piercing and exploding bullets would penetrate a vampire's skin, and if it hit the heart directly, the explosion would explode their heart, killing them. Feeders and vampires alike took cover. Some vampires covered feeders and others just ran. These bullets may not always kill the vampires, but they still hurt like hell.

The special elevator dinged and the attendant came out with guns blazing. He was the second line of defense after the doorman that had been dragged down the street by two other vampires. The elevator attendant rained bullets across the lobby.

He was hit several times with the exploding bullets before he had to reload. He ducked back into the elevator and replaced the magazines in his large caliber guns. Two guardian wolves were busy attacking the intruders when the vampires turned their fire to them. The wolves didn't turn tail and run until one was hit in the head with an exploding bullet. It killed him so the other one ran to the elevator. The elevator attendant fired off the rest of his clip and hit the button for the fifty sixth floor.

Upstairs, Vincent and Steven joined the fight. When Erica walked in, Eric was in Lily's living room with a knife to Shay's throat.

"Let her go, Eric!" Erica said sternly.

"Not a chance."

Two of the vampires in the apartment attacked Erica. She threw one off and made a solid right hook to the others face. Before the first one had time to get back to her, Steven stepped in between them. In one quick blow, Steven jammed his fingers in between the ribs of the vampire. He had just enough time to look down and see Steve's arm sticking out of his chest. On the inside, Steven squeezed his claws through the heart. The vampire fell at Steven's feet. Steven pulled out the destroyed heart and dropped it on the dead vampire.

"You OK?" Steven asked Erica.

Erica nodded and the third vampire in the apartment went after Steven. Vincent and Jack walked in in time to see the third vampire fall to the floor in front of Steven. The vampires in the hallway were all dead. Onyx was standing beside Eric, teeth bared and just waiting for an opportunity. Eric was still holding a twelve inch blade to Shay's throat.

"Eric! What the fuck are you doing?" Vincent asked.

"I'm taking Lily to the Underground. If she can change humans to vampires, I'm going to rule this city. With an army of vampires that can protect me from you."

"You need Shay to make the transformation, too," McGoo told him.

"What do you mean?" Eric asked.

"Shay's blood is just as important as Lily's," McGoo added.

"How?" Eric questioned.

"That isn't important," McGoo said. "Just let Shay go. You know you're not going to get out of here with either one of them."

Onyx growled and took a step toward Eric. Eric pressed the blade harder against Shay's throat. Erica took a step closer and Eric pressed the blade slightly through Shay's skin. Blood trickled down her neck and Erica took a step back.

"Eric!" Alexa yelled from the doorway. "What the hell are you thinking?"

"I was wondering when you were going to show up," Eric smirked. "But you're too late, Mom. I'm taking Lily and Shay."

"No you're not," Erica told him.

The attendant and wolf raced down the hall to the only open door on the floor. When they saw that Vincent and Alexa were present, they turned and stood their ground.

More of Eric's vampires were on their way to Lily's floor. Security personnel stepped off three of the elevators just as the other opened. The stairwell door flew open and more security ran out. The fifth elevator opened and Eric's friends poured out. There was a battle in the hallway and bullets flew everywhere. More vampires and more security crowded the hallway. Chunks of drywall and ceiling fell to the floor as bodies hit the wall and claws swung everywhere. Blood splattered everything. Bodies from both sides littered the floor. A few of Eric's vampires ran down the stairwell in retreat.

Everyone took a step closer to Eric.

"Back off," he said and blood ran thicker down Shay's neck.

All at once, Erica, Vincent and McGoo rushed Eric. He barely had time to press the blade into Shay's throat and push her toward Erica. He fell backwards over the couch and rushed to his feet but Vincent was already on him. Onyx was there, too. Vincent had his hand around Eric's neck when the bullet ripped through Vincent's leg. It was just a distraction long enough for Eric to slip free. He hurdled the couch but Onyx caught him by the waist mid-jump. Eric hit the ground hard and the full momentum of the huge wolf landed on his chest, knocking the wind out of him. Eric gasped for a moment then threw Onyx off of him.

Erica grabbed LaShay. She was gasping and holding her neck. Erica held her and quickly healed her neck.

A new wave of vampires entered the apartment. Vincent's leg was nearly healed and he walked toward the door. Two of the Underground's vampires blocked his path. Jack joined Vincent and fought off the two vampires. In the process Eric ran out the door. Erica chased him.

The battle in the hallway had left a littering of vampire bodies. Eric jumped over the heaps and almost made it the elevator before Erica caught him by the back of his neck. She pulled hard and he fell onto his back. Onyx was on him just as he hit the floor. Four vampires and a wolf came running out of the stairwell. They attacked Erica and held her off long enough for Eric to escape down the stairs. Once Eric was gone, the other Underground vampires and wolves retreated. But Onyx followed.

Erica ran back to the apartment to check on Lily and Shay. Shay was on her knees beside the couch. She was holding Lily's hand and crying.

"It's alright, Shay," Erica comforted.

"No, Erica, it's not!" She cried. "Look at this apartment. Look at Lily! I almost died today!"

"Uh, no. I would not have let that happen, Shay. I promise you," Erica said.

"No Shay, we would not have let anything happen to you," Alexa reaffirmed. "Eric caught us off guard. We have no idea how he even got into the building. It wasn't through any entrance on the ground floor. And there are no fire escape stairs or ladders."

"The only way he could've gotten in was through the old tunnels in the sub-basement," McGoo added. "There are countless tunnels under there, and he could've found one that we didn't know about. It wouldn't take much to knock down a wall or to dig through."

Shay looked down at Lily. She placed her fingertips on Lily's neck and checked for a pulse, for the fifth time.

"It was Sarah," Shay said. "Lily passed out just after she drank the blood. And it was my fault she even drank it."

"How is it your fault, hon," Erica asked.

"Lily had told Sarah that she didn't need her today. And I convinced Lily that it was OK. I should've just kept my mouth shut," Shay said.

"You couldn't have known, Shay," Alexa said.

Onyx chased Eric and his vampires down all fifty six floors plus the additional three floors of the garage and sub-basement. He chased them down a dimly lit hallway to a literal hole in the wall. It was nearly pitch black in the tunnel. The floor and walls were rock and dirt supported by old and rotting four by four posts. After a short run, it led to another set of stairs. They were old wooden stairs and the weight of all those bodies caused them to collapse. Onyx heard the crack of the breaking steps just before he stepped onto them. He stopped and waited for the footfalls to stop. When he was sure Eric was gone, he turned around and retraced his steps.

It took almost two hours for Lily to wake up. Workman were busy repairing the door and cleaning the apartment when she came to. Shay was sitting on the couch with Lily's head in her lap. Erica was sitting in the chair across from the couch. McGoo and Vincent had left to go rally the troops against Eric.

"What the h... hell happened," Lily slurred.

"Lily! You're awake," Shay said as she stroked Lily hair.

"Eric," was all Erica said.

"The blood," Lily said. "It was the blood."

"Yes, Sarah spiked your drink," Erica told her. "Probably a horse tranquilizer. It would have had to be something that was very strong to knock you out for over two hours."

Lily sat up on the couch and Shay immediately kissed her.

"I had no idea what to do," Shay told Lily. "It was just so fast. If Onyx hadn't been here, Eric would've killed me and taken you. That was his plan."

Lily wrapped her arms around Shay and pulled her close. Lily kissed her neck.

"I am so sorry," she whispered.

Lily looked at Alexa.

"What are we supposed to do now?" Lily snapped. "Eric has proved that not even an entire coven will stop him."

"He did this because he thinks that if he has the person that can again change humans to vampires, that he'll rule the Underground." Erica said.

"Well! He's probably right!" Lily said loudly. "What is Vincent going to do now to make sure that Shay is safe?"

Alexa sighed, "I don't know, but I'm sure he has a plan."

"First, he'll put wolves on your floor permanently. Onyx will be with you at all times and there will be guards at all the entrances to this floor." Erica said. "If I have to stay here with you myself, I promise you that Eric will never get that close again."

"What kind of life is that going to be?" Lily asked.

"I promise you, Lily, Eric will never get that close again," Alexa reassured.

"Can you leave us alone?" Lily asked. "I need to talk to Shay."

"Of course," Erica and Alexa replied.

When they had left, Lily turned to Shay and took both of her hands in hers.

"Shay, I cannot tell you how sorry I am," Lily began.

"Lily..."

"Let me finish, please. I am so sorry. But Eric will not stop until one of us is dead. There is one way to help ensure that doesn't happen."

"How?"

"I can change you into a vampire."

"But what about my blood?"

Lily sighed. "I know. That does create a problem. Vincent won't allow me to change you if your blood actually speeds up the process even more. They haven't tested it yet, though."

"McGoo seems pretty sure of his theory," Shay said.

"Do you want to be a vampire?" Lily asked seriously.

"Of course, but you know what Vincent is going to say. If my blood actually speeds the process, he'll never let you change me."

"Then we leave!" Lily told her.

"And go where?"

"The Nashville coven. It's empty and it's out of the way and it's a place that Eric would never think to go, he hated Nashville."

"Let's talk to Vincent first," Shay said. "Maybe he has a plan. Maybe we won't have to leave. I like it here in New York, it's the only place I've ever known. And where in the world would we be safer? I mean Eric surprised everyone this time. But no one is going to let that happen again. Erica and Alexa said so themselves. And I'm sure Vincent already has a plan of action."

"Do you not want to go to Nashville?" Lily asked.

"It's not that I don't want to go, I'm afraid to go. I'd rather be here with a building full of vampires than out there where Eric could show up at any moment."

"But he..."

"I know he could show up here again, but the likelihood of that is slim to none."

They heard someone knock on Shay's door across the hall. Lily and Shay looked at each other.

"Who could that be?' Shay whispered as if the person across the hall could hear her.

Lily shrugged and stood up. She walked to the door and looked through the peep hole then turned to Shay. Standing at Shay's door was medium built man with salt and pepper hair, cropped short and wearing what appeared to be a black pinstriped suit.

"I think it's your dad," Lily said.

"Oh shit! Get me a clean shirt!"

Lily nodded and ran to her room. She came back with a white blouse. Shay had already taken of the bloody one and was waiting for Lily. She grabbed the clean one and put it on as she walked to the door. Lily was right behind her.

"Dad."

Martin turned around and smiled but it was short lived.

"The address they gave me is Fifty Six B. Not A," he said matter-of-factly.

"This is my apartment," Lily said pointing to the 'A' on her door.

"So is this her?" he asked.

"Yes Dad. This is my girlfriend, Lily."

Martin looked around at all the workers on the floor repairing the walls, ceiling and carpet.

"Did a bomb go off here?" He asked.

"Long time coming," Lily said. "Been in need of repair for some time and they finally got around to it today."

"Humph," Martin snorted.

Luckily the repairmen had made good progress on the repairs and they had cleaned all the blood off the walls and ceiling first. It could have been a lot worse. They were still working on cleaning up Lily's apartment.

"Shall we go in?" Shay asked her father as she walked toward her apartment door.

"Sure," Martin answered reluctantly.

They stepped into the apartment and Martin looked around in awe.

"You're already moved in and unpacked? That was fast. It's only been a week."

"I had help," Shay smiled looking at Lily. "Would you like a tour, Dad?"

"OK," he said.

Shay showed her father around her new apartment. First they went into the kitchen, with the white marble counters and sinks to the brushed aluminum refrigerator and stove. Then she walked him through the living room to the master bedroom that looked basically the same with the furniture from her other apartment. Then she showed him the back guest bedroom that had new furniture courtesy of the coven. She didn't mention that part. He just assumed that she had bought the new bedroom suit.

They walked back to the living room with the intricately detailed cherry crown moldings and the recessed lighting. They sat on Shay's sectional couch. Lily was in the kitchen pouring them all a drink. She brought them from the kitchen, sat them on the coffee table in front of Martin and Shay then took a sip of hers.

This may not be a pleasant experience, Lily thought. *I'll just drink and pretend I'm not here.*

Shay looked at her dad and waited. She knew it was coming.

"So why didn't you ask if it was alright for you to move?" He asked.

And there it is, Shay thought.

"Dad," she took a deep breath, "I am thirty four years old. I do not need to ask your permission to move."

"Well at least you called and told me you had moved. Although it was after I got a phone call from the building security guy to give me instructions on visiting." He paused. "And how in the hell did you get an apartment in the Crown Building? There's never anything available here! I was just under the impression that all the apartments were previously owned and passed down to the next generation. How did you manage to get in here?"

"Lily's grandfather owns the building," Shay said.

Lily looked at Shay and tilted her head. She raised her eyebrows and gave a tiny shrug. Shay just gave her a reassuring look and continued.

"Yeah, there just happened to be an open apartment across from Lily. I just got lucky, Dad."

Got lucky, my ass, he thought. *No one could get that lucky.*

"He owns the Crown Building?" Martin asked Lily, voice full of skepticism.

"Yes sir," Lily just played along.

Lily guessed that technically, Vincent did own the building. He was the leader of the vampires here, and the building belonged to the vampires. Vincent was responsible for letting people and vampires move in and out and the residents were responsible for taking care of their own apartments. The maintenance department took care of the repairs and maids took care of the cleaning, for most of the apartments, not all. She decided that she'd just play along with Shay. She figured that if Martin looked up who owns the building, it would probably come up under some corporation. All the covens were probably owned by the same company, probably out of Britain.

"The Crown Building, huh," Martin said.

Martin took a minute to let his head wrap around that. *Lily, my daughter's girlfriend's grandfather owns the most prestigious address in New York City.* He still didn't like the idea of his daughter having a girlfriend.

"Yes, the Crown Building," Shay said. "Why are you really here? I know it's not to find out who owns the building I live in or how I managed to get an apartment here."

"I just wanted to see you," he answered. "Didn't know I'd be meeting your girlfriend, too, but I guess that was inevitable since she lives right across the hall. That's really convenient."

Too convenient, he thought. *Way too convenient. What is really going on here? Does her granddad really own the building? That would make him about as rich as me, I guess. Well, at least the girl has family money. But where did the money come from? Real estate? Legal means? Drugs? Illegal means? I'm going to have to look into this more.*

He scanned the apartment once again. He couldn't believe he was actually sitting in an apartment in the Crown Building. He was still trying to wrap his head around that when his eyes caught sight of the painting on the wall above the fireplace. He stood up to get a closer look.

"This is the original! Holy shit!" He nearly yelled. "How in the hell did you afford an original O'Keeffe? And *Blue and Green Music* at that!"

"It was a gift from Lily's grandparents," Shay said.

"A gift? Her grandparents are giving you eighty million dollar paintings?" He asked in disbelief.

"You should see Lily's apartment," Shay said.

Lily just looked at her wide-eyed, as if to say, "Be quiet, Shay."

"And does Lily have a Picasso? Perhaps a Warhol or Germotta?" He said sarcastically.

"Actually, yes," Shay grinned. "She has *Elasticity*, two other Boccioni's, a couple of Germotta's and that's just hers. Her grandfather has a Boccioni sculpture that was his practice design for *Futuristic Man*."

"*Three* Boccioni's?" Martin asked in disbelief. "Figures that you're the one that owns *Elasticity*. I tried to buy that for you for your birthday years ago. But it was said to be in the possession of a private collector and wasn't for sell. What other two?"

Martin looked at Lily as if he was trying to stare a hole through her.

"Dynamism of a Cyclist and Composizione Spiralica," Lily answered proudly.

"And are we talking about the same Germotta? From the 2020's? She only painted like seven total. And you say you have two of them?" Martin asked.

"Yes, one is dated '23 and the other is dated '26," Lily said.

Lily remembered the 2010's and 2020's so well and how she followed Stefi around the country before the singer settled into motherhood and painted a handful of abstract paintings. Which was how Lily managed to get *The Monster* from 2023 and *The Perfect Illusion* from 2026. She just happened to be in the right place at the right time in 2027 when Stefani decided to auction off the paintings to benefit the Foundation she had begun about a decade and a half prior. Lily didn't care that she had spent millions on the paintings. She wanted to keep a reminder of the artist and in memory, Lily still gave to the Foundation every year.

Lily thought about how odd it was that she started funding a cause over seventy years ago that is now so very close to her heart. It made the investment mean even more to her.

Martin shook his head slowly and looked at the O'Keeffe painting again. He was having a hard time wrapping his head around the fact that all of these paintings that were two hundred and some over two hundred and fifty years old, all existed in this one building. *What other ones are here?* He wondered. *What is so special about this building? I know it's old, but how old is it really?* He made a mental note to investigate.

He still didn't understand the whole being gay thing, either. *How, after thirty four years, do you suddenly realize that you're gay?*

"Please explain the gay thing to me. Is it a phase you're going through? Is it something that is going to pass after its run its course?" He asked.

"No Dad. It's not a phase. It's not just going to go away. I'm gay and that's the way it's always going to be. I love Lily. And I would do anything for her, just like she'd do anything for me."

Shay wished she could tell her dad about the times that Lily has saved her life. The first time, Lily didn't even know her, but she risked everything to save her. The second time, Lily almost died.

A knock came from the front door. Lily and Shay looked at each other, eyes wide and took a deep breath. *Oh, please don't be McGoo!* Shay went to answer the door. It was Vincent.

"Vincent," Shay greeted nervously.

"Hello LaShay. I heard that your father was here."

Vincent heard right away when strangers came to the building and he was already expecting Martin to show up at some point.

Shay nodded to Vincent and turned around. She wasn't sure this was the best time for the two men to meet. Martin was already taking a lot in. Lily joined Shay at the door. She stepped into the hallway and motioned to Shay to close the door.

"Vincent, what are you doing here?" Lily asked. "This probably isn't the best time..."

"Nonsense, no time like the present," Vincent smiled and his fangs were clearly visible.

"Vincent!" Lily yelled then covered her mouth.

"I'm kidding, love," he said and retracted his teeth. "Lighten up, Lily. So why is this not a good time?"

"Because Martin is still working through the whole 'Shay being gay and living in the Crown Building' things. He's still trying to wrap his head around that and I think he'd feel a little intimidated by you right now. You're my grandfather, by the way, and you own the building."

"I'm your what!? Grandfather?" Vincent clarified. "Do I look old enough to be a grandfather?"

"Yes, you're my grandfather." Lily paused. "You're not going to go away are you? Not going to take 'no' for an answer either, are you?"

"Nope," Vincent chirped.

Lily took a deep breath and opened the door. Shay had gone back to sit on the couch beside her dad. Vincent followed Lily in. Vincent looked like he was in his forties, was six foot three and a very solid one hundred and ninety pounds. He had medium brown hair that was cut short. His eyes were emerald green and rimmed by long black lashes. His skin was only slightly darker than Lily's. He was wearing a black, button up shirt and black pants with black boots. He rolled up his sleeves as he followed Lily to the couch. When he was close to Martin, he put out his hand.

"Hello, I'm Vincent Sterling. I'm Lily's grandfather."

Martin stood up and shook Vince's hand.

Grandfather? Martin wondered. *He barely looks forty. I wonder what her grandmother looks like.*

"I'm Martin Black," he said a little bit too proudly.

Vincent only nodded and shook Martin's hand.

"May we sit?" Vincent asked.

"Sure," Martin said and sat back down.

Vincent sat on the perpendicular section of the couch and Lily sat down beside him. Shay was already sitting beside her dad.

"So, Vincent, what do you do?" Martin asked immediately.

"I'm in real estate."

Vincent looked at Lily, patted her knee and smiled.

"Real estate?" Martin questioned.

"Yes. This building was passed down to me. The family business is real estate. We own property in every major city."

"Impressive," Martin said.

"So you're in the broadcasting business. Isn't that correct?" Vincent asked before Martin could ask another question.

"Yes. I own several television stations in the US, Canada and Europe."

"Impressive," Vincent repeated.

"So how do you deal with your daughter being gay?" Martin finally asked.

"Umm, what do you mean?" Vince asked.

"She likes girls, right? How do you deal with that?"

"I don't *deal* with that. Lily loves who she loves and that's that. Why would that concern me? I'm not the one that's dating them. I'm not the one who wakes up next to them every morning. I don't have to argue with them over what's for dinner or what color should they paint the bathroom. Lily choses who Lily loves and I'm not going to question that."

"You are completely OK with all this?" Martin asked.

"I wouldn't have moved Shay into the building if I had doubts."

Vincent looked at Lily and she knew what he was thinking. That she had loved three others the same way and this, too, would probably pass. But Lily knew he was wrong this time.

"Well, it's getting late. I should probably go," Martin announced suddenly.

"Dad..."

Martin stood up and put his hand out to Vincent. Vincent stood and shook his hand.

"It was nice meeting you, Vincent."

Before anyone could say anything else, Martin walked to the door and left.

"Well, that went well," Shay said sarcastically.

"He'll come around, dear," Vincent reassured her. "He's your father and he loves you."

Shay took a big drink from her glass. Then another. Lily stood up and went to sit beside her. Lily took the glass from Shay just as she was about to take the last drink.

"Shay, you know how he is. He's old and set in his ways and who knows what is going through his head. He will come around," Lily told her.

"Shay, no matter what your father thinks, you have a home and a family here," Vincent said. "How are you doing, by the way? I mean from the whole attack. Are you OK."

"I should be used to it by now," Shay said.

"I am so sorry that...," Lily began.

"Shhh, I know, babe. It's not your fault," Shay interrupted.

"I promise you, Shay, that Eric will never step foot in this building again," Vincent assured her. "You are safe here. Wait. Where's Onyx?"

"We were surprised by Martin's visit, so he stayed at my apartment," said Lily. "One thing at time, you know. Didn't want to spring a three hundred pound wolf on Martin just yet."

"There will be guards and wolves on this floor at all times. Regardless of who visits."

"How are we going to explain that to Martin?" Lily asked.

"Bad neighbors?" Vincent joked. "We'll make sure the guards are in plain clothes with no visible weapons. As far as the wolves in the hallway, seriously, blame it on the neighbors. But Onyx is yours Lily. Martin should know that Onyx is part of the package."

"Understood," Lily said.

"OK," Vincent said." I'll leave the two of you alone. But Shay, when you get a chance, I would like to talk to you."

"Yes, sir," Shay answered.

Eric was planning his next attack. He was hoping that the first one would catch everyone off guard. Which it did, but they were able to rally faster than Eric thought they could. He had barely gotten away and had it not been for the collapsing staircase in the tunnels, Onyx may *still* be chasing him. He was sitting at a table outside Ellen's Fight Club surrounded by his vampires and other fighters. He had managed to get quite a following. With the news of being able to change humans to vampires once again, it seemed everyone was all ears. Most of the vampires gathered around Eric were fighters from the club. All of them knew Lily. None of them could be trusted.

The Underground was all a buzz about Lily having the ability to change humans without killing them. Some thought it was just a hoax made up by Eric to get help catching Lily. Everyone knew that he hated her and would do just about anything to get his hands on her.

"How do we know that she can really change humans?" Jenkins asked.

"Have you seen her change a human?" Taylor piped in.

"Yeah, how do we know that you're not just making this up to get help catching Lily?" Asked Maggie from the back of the crowd, one of the few female fighters.

"I have a very trusted source at the coven that has spoken to the new vampire that she created. He told my source who changed him and why would he lie?" Eric said.

"How is Lily able to change humans? She's not an Elder," Taylor asked.

"I don't know," Eric told him.

"Pft! What do you know?" Matt asked. "Do you have proof?"

"No."

Eric remembered what McGoo had said about Shay's blood being as important. *Shay's blood is just as important as Lily's*, McGoo had said at the apartment. Eric thought that he may be able to catch Shay on her way to or from work. It had almost worked twice. Then he remembered how badly Lily was burned. And she lived. Maybe she *was* special.

They would be expecting another attack, he thought. He had to come up with an all new plan. If he had to get both Lily and Shay alive, he needed a better plan and more vampires on his side. Lily and Shay now had the entire coven backing them. He had to get inside. He had to get coven vampires on his side. His two primary sources inside the coven were compromised. He knew Sarah would be punished for helping him to drug Lily. Brian would also be watched very carefully after failing to steal blood samples from McGoo's lab.

THE FIRST TEST

The next morning McGoo knocked on Shay's door. Vincent had finally brought in a human to make the change and it was time for Shay and Lily to change him. Shay answered the door.

"Hey, Doc." Shay yawned.

Her hair was a mess. She was wearing a satin blue robe that stopped at the knee.

"It's time," Jack told her.

Shay had a confused look on her face for a moment then it dawned on her what he was talking about.

"Oh, time to donate my blood. Right?"

"That's correct. We will be waiting in the lab. And don't forget to bring Lily," he smiled. As if Shay would show up without her.

Shay trudged back to the bedroom and plopped down next to Lily who was still sleeping. Shay pulled the sheet and blanket down and gently kissed Lily's neck. She kissed down Lily's chest and stopped at a breast. She pulled the covers off completely and kissed down Lily's stomach. She slowly spread Lily's legs apart then positioned herself between them. It didn't take long for Lily to wake up.

Lily moaned as Shay licked her slowly. She continued licking and sucking gently until Lily's legs began to shake. She moaned Shay's name as she grabbed a handful of the bed sheet. Her back arched and she came hard. Waves washed over her and she finally had to push Shay away. Shay only laughed and kissed her way back up Lily's body. When Shay was laying on top of her, Lily wrapped her arms around her and rolled her over onto her back.

"Oh no," Shay giggled. "I owed you one from yesterday."

"Didn't know you were keeping score," Lily said as she kissed Shay's lips.

Shay ran her fingers up through Lily's hair then ran her fingernails down Lily's back. Lily's back stiffened and she kissed Shay harder. Their tongues circled each other's and they kissed for a while. Finally Shay told Lily that they were wanted downstairs in the lab.

"Aww," Lily moaned. "Is it time already? So I take it Vincent came through on his human to change, huh?"

"Yup."

Lily rolled off of Shay and yawned then stretched.

"Couldn't think of a better way to wake up, though." Lily grinned as she stretched again.

"Get up, lazy, we have work to do."

They got up, took a quick shower together and headed downstairs. They walked to the elevator hand in hand. They kissed all the way down to the sub-basement.

When they walked into the lab where McGoo and Vincent waited, Vincent gave Lily a stern look then shook his head. He knew exactly what had taken them so long but he didn't say anything.

"Shall we get started?" McGoo finally said. "Lily, LaShay, this is Markus. He's from the Miami coven. He's been a feeder there for almost 40 years."

"Well that does explain the tan. I LaShay," she said as she reached out her hand to shake Markus's.

"Hello...?"

"LaShay," she repeated.

"LaShay, pretty name," Markus said.

"Thank you."

"Hello Markus, I'm Lily."

"Good to meet you Lily," Markus said.

"Shay, you can go here," McGoo motioned to a hospital bed beside Markus. He looked at Lily and motioned to the other empty bed.

Once they were laying down, McGoo raised the top half of the beds so Lily and Shay were sitting up. He left Markus in the flat position.

"Markus are you ready?" Vincent asked, walking over to his bedside.

"Are you *ever* really *ready* for this?" Markus laughed.

Vincent laughed, too. "I guess not."

McGoo connected the IV's to the machine then to Lily and Shay's arms and to Markus's neck, shoulder and thighs. Then he looked at Markus.

"Are you absolutely sure you want to do this? There is no going back and there is no stopping once it starts," McGoo said to Markus.

"Yes, I am absolutely sure," Markus affirmed. "But why two donors?"

"You will get only a pint of Shay's blood. This will... well, let me rephrase that. Shay's blood *should* prepare your blood for the change."

"I did tell you that it's an experiment, Markus," Vincent said.

"I know Vince. I'm just asking what the process is," Markus said.

"After Shay's blood, you will get a full transfusion of Lily's blood. The change should take less than five days. At least that's what we're hoping."

"OK," answered Markus. "I'm ready."

McGoo hung the bags of blood for Lily on the hooks then connected them.

"OK." McGoo took a deep breath and switched on the transfusion machine.

The machine clicked and whirred to life. After only about 10 minutes McGoo disconnected LaShay from the machine.

"Are you OK?" He asked. "Do you feel dizzy or sick?"

"No, I'm fine," Shay answered.

"Are you going to wait for Lily?"

"Yes."

Three hours passed before McGoo turned off the machine. That was it. It was up to the blood to do the rest. McGoo pulled the IV out of Lily's arm and placed a small square gauze pad over the small hole as it quickly healed.

"Take it easy for a few days, Lily," he told her.

"I know," Lily said.

Two and a half days passed and Lily and Shay were laying on Lily's couch watching a movie when the phone rang. Lily reached over and grabbed her phone from the coffee table.

"McGoo, what is it? Did he die?" Lily concluded before he even spoke.

Lily thought, *It's only been two and a half days, he must have died and all becau...*

"No Lily, I just called to see how the two of you are doing," McGoo said.

"Oh, we're fine," Lily told him. "Just relaxing and watching some television."

"Oh good. You're not busy then."

"What do you want Jack?" Lily sighed.

"I was just curious if I could possibly get a little more of Shay's blood."

Lily looked at Shay. "Do you feel like going to donate even more blood?"

"That the doc?" Shay assumed.

Lily nodded.

"Sure."

"We'll be there in a few."

"Thank you!" said McGoo before he hung up.

When they arrived at the lab, McGoo was all grins.

"What is it McGoo?" Lily asked flatly because she knew he was up to something.

"Come with me!" He nearly giggled.

They followed Jack to the room where Markus had been. He was sitting up on the bed. Eyes wide open and staring at his hands in his lap. He looked up at Lily and smiled a big toothy grin, but no fangs. He tried, but it was just too early. Lily and Shay stared in awe.

"Two and a half days?" Lily shrieked.

"Two days and thirteen hours," McGoo confirmed.

"Holy shit!" Lily yelled.

"I know!" Markus added. "When I woke up I thought something had gone wrong. It didn't seem like it had been that long. I mean the pain was... the pain was excruciating but I was figuring on it being a whole lot worse."

Lily and Shay couldn't believe it. All Lily was thinking was that it would only take two and half days to change Shay. If her blood helped make the transformation for a human that quick, she should change even faster. She could certainly survive two and a half days. But Vincent. There was no way Vincent would let her change Shay. But what if Eric came back? What if she or Erica wasn't there to save her? She had to talk to Vincent. She had to convince Vincent that her blood alone would save the vampires. Her blood only took 5 days. That was seven or eight days faster than his blood could make the change.

Alexa and Vince were at home in the penthouse. It's a good thing that no one else lived on their floor.

"Vincent, you have to let us change LaShay. You know damn well that Eric will kill her if he gets a chance! He doesn't really need Shay and he knows that," Alexa yelled for the fourth time that day.

"I'm not going to change Shay! Lily will just change her mind like she has three times before," Vincent countered.

"Shay isn't like the rest, Vince. Can't you see that? Lily almost died on that roof. And she'd do it again if she had to."

"The answer is still "No"!

"Dammit Vincent!" Alexa yelled. "You're not listening! Eric will *kill* Shay. If Shay dies do you know what happens to Lily? The hell with them changing vampires for you. If something happened to LaShay do you think for one second that Lily would give a shit about restoring the species? Think about it Vince!"

"Lexa," Vincent sighed. "If I let Lily change LaShay into a vampire and Lily decides that she doesn't love Shay anymore, where does that leave Shay? I'll tell you! It leaves Shay immortally in love with someone that has moved on to someone else."

"No Vincent! Lily is *in love* with Shay. This is the one, Vince. There will not be another for Lily. I promise you."

"I can't Lexa. For Shay's sake, I just can't."

"For Shay's sake? Shay is going to end up dead if you don't. You know the lengths he'll go to get Lily. Shay means nothing to Eric and killing her is just a means to an end. Then once Shay is gone, Lily won't care what happens to her. Do you want Eric to have the means to create his own vampire army?"

"Of course not!"

"Then let Lily change Shay. If not for Lily, do it for Shay!" Alexa yelled very loudly.

Vincent didn't say anything else, he simply walked off. He was tired of arguing with his wife about a subject that was just way too touchy for him. He knew Shay would be safer as a vampire but he had the entire vampire species to think about. With her blood, their numbers could grow again. Without the lingering effects of the change Shay's blood could change women just as easily as men. That had always been a problem before. More men wanted to be vampires than women. But with a transformation period of less than three days… Vincent thought of all of the possibilities. He also thought about Eric getting his hands on her. He didn't think that Eric would kill her because he needed her, but at the same time, Lily's blood could do it in six days, which was what it once took for his blood to make the change.

Alexa walked out onto the balcony off of the living room. The view was spectacular. The penthouse overlooked Central Park from the west at 84th Street. The building took up half a city block, with the main entrance on Central Park West and side entrances on 84th and 85th. On the corner, above the balcony was one of four gargoyles. They sat perched on large spheres at each corner and was said to be the first guardians of the vampires. They were each twelve feet tall with tails that snaked across the rim of the building. Intricate stonework cast shadows onto the roof from huge spotlights placed on each side of the building, just below the balcony.

Alexa was fuming, but what could she do? She knew where Vince was coming from. But how could he not see that this time was different? Lily had never stayed away from the coven for anyone, much less nearly died for them. There was only one thing that she knew to do.

Vincent walked out onto the balcony off his bedroom on the 85th Street side. He looked over toward the park and tried to figure out a plan that would work for everyone. If he changed Shay, he would lose the catalyst in her blood that sped up the change. If he didn't change Shay, it was a good bet that Eric would either try to take her or try to kill her. Eric hated Lily enough not to care about Shay's life. But how badly did he want Shay's blood? Would he be content just having Lily's? Vincent didn't know the answers. He just never knew what could possibly be going through Eric's twisted mind.

Alexa walked out onto the balcony with Vince.

"Vince, we have company," she said very seriously.

"Who?"

"Luther."

"Oh shit, what do they want?"

"What do you think they want?" Alexa asked rhetorically.

Luther, Rex and Flynn waited in the living room. They were the leaders of the Guardians. They all wore black custom suits and shiny black wingtips. Their hair was cropped short and Flynn sported a five o'clock shadow. They looked like a bunch of FBI agents from the 1990's.

"Luther, Rex, Flynn, what can I do for you gentlemen?" Vincent asked, trying not to be too formal.

"Eric has committed his final act of treason against this coven," Luther said. His voice was deep and raspy. "He attacked this coven and threatened the lives of individuals within it. That is a capital offense and we are here to see that justice is served."

"Do you know where he is?" Rex asked.

"No sir, I do not," Vincent answered. "He disappeared into the Underground and no one has seen him since. I have trackers on him but they're coming up empty."

"We'll find him," Flynn assured.

"Would you like to stay for a drink?" Alexa asked.

"Scotch," Luther answered.

Alexa nodded and walked over to the bar against the far wall of the living room. Above it was an original Warhol. She turned over five glasses from the top and poured the drinks. She took two at a time to her guests and husband.

"Sit, please," Alexa offered.

"Thank you, Alexa," Flynn said.

They all sat around the large living room. Flynn and Rex sat on the couch and Luther sat in the chair opposite them. Vincent sat in the chair next to Luther and Alexa sat on the arm of his chair. They all sipped their drinks for a moment before anyone spoke.

"So we hear that Lily and her lover have the answer to the vampire's transformation problems," Luther said out of nowhere.

How in the hell do they know that already? Was the first thought that went through Vincent's head. He had no idea that the Guardians knew about Lily and Shay.

"Unproven," Vincent said casually. "We have a working theory but we have yet to prove it."

"I thought so," Flynn said rudely. "How can a girl have more powerful blood than her makers? It just wouldn't make any sense."

Apparently the secret of Lily's birth had remained a secret all these years. But then again, why would they question it? They would never believe that Lily had been *born*. They didn't know about all of Dr. McGregor's experiments, either. They were completely unaware of the breakthroughs McGoo had made in recent decades.

That was because they really didn't care about Jack. They had turned their back on him a century earlier after he confessed to the Whitechapel Murders. The only reason they didn't kill him was because they were able to divert suspicion away from McGregor and the vampires. They told Jack he would never again be associated with the Guardians. And Jack was perfectly fine with that. He didn't like their stuffy attitudes anyway.

The Guardians had to hear of Lily and Shay through their sources in the Underground. They had sources everywhere. But, luckily for the coven, the Underground gossip is just that, gossip. No one could prove anything. The only people that had seen Mark and Markus change would never go to the Guardians. Although the vampires in the Underground may have seen Mark or Markus, it was only Eric's word and they really wouldn't know how the new vampires were made. But it still raised questions. There hadn't been a new vampire in decades.

We have to keep them away from Lily and Shay. There's no telling what they would do with the power to create at will. Armies would only be the beginning, Vince thought. *As long as they think it's nothing but rumors, the girls will be safe.*

Fortunately, the Guardians didn't have any more questions about them. They just assumed that Vincent was telling the truth about the unproven theory and Vince couldn't be happier about that. If they knew what Lily and Shay could do, they would not hesitate to take both of them. Vincent wouldn't allow that, regardless of who the Guardians were. And he didn't need a fight with the Guardians.

After a brief casual conversation, the Guardians left. Vincent escorted them out of the building. He didn't want them taking any detours on the way out.

Vincent closed the door to the stretched limo and waved goodbye.

"Whew," he sighed.

Eric was now also the responsibility of the Guardians. With the coven trackers and the Guardian trackers after him, Eric won't be able to hide for very long.

TURNING SHAY BLACK

When Vince got back to his apartment, Lily was waiting in the hall for him. The look that she gave him let him know that this was going to be serious. "Come in," he said.

Once inside, Lily said hello to Alexa, who was sitting in one of the chairs, still sipping on her scotch. Then Lily turned to Vincent.

"If this is about Shay, the answer is still no," he said.

"Vincent! Come on!" Lily yelled. "Vincent, you have to let me turn Shay. If you don't, Eric will kill her! You know it as well as I do."

"I'm not turning her, Lily," he said calmly.

"How else can I prove to you that she is my one true love? I would've died for her on that roof and I never even thought twice about it. I didn't care about the sun or about the burns or about dying. All I cared about was her. Why can't you see that?"

"You've known her less than three months Lily and she's safe here. No one is going to let Eric within fifty feet of either of you."

"Vincent..." she pleaded.

"No, Lily!"

Lily stormed out of the room and slammed the door behind her so hard that the Boccioni sculpture on the mantle shook. She ran down the hallway to the elevators. She punched the down button and waited. At her apartment, Shay was waiting. Lily walked in the front door and Shay knew from the look that Vincent had said no again.

"He'll come around," Shay reassured.

"Come on," Lily said holding out her hand. "Let's go talk to someone else."

"The Doc?" Shay asked.

"Yes, but first I have to tell you what he's going to tell you if he agrees."

She took Shay's hand and pulled her into her chest.

"First of all, I love you, Shay, and if I didn't fear for your safety, I would not be pressing this issue so hard. Eric is just evil and he will not stop until one of us or both of us are dead."

"Yeah, I know. He almost succeeded, remember, still pretty fresh in the memory. You lying burnt to a crisp on my couch, a knife to my throat then blood, everywhere."

"Right. I didn't die, see! Neither did you," Lily said, pulling Shay closer and hugging her tight.

"OK, what is McGoo going to tell me?"

Lily pushed Shay away until she was at arm's length then held her shoulders. "He's going to try explaining just how painful being turned is going to be. He'll ask you if you've ever had surgery. Then he'll ask you to imagine that you've had a heart transplant. The doctors cracked open your chest, moved around the other organs, cut out the heart, put the new one in then put everything back together. Now image that the doctors replaced everything. Shay, baby, in all seriousness, are you sure that you're ready for this?"

"Yes, for the fifteenth time, yes. I've seen, and felt, what Eric is capable of and next time we may not be so lucky. Another five minutes on that roof and you would not be here. And if Erica hadn't been here... my throat was slit, Lily. I want to know that I can fight him, too, if I need to. And I'm not going to lose you, Lily. I can't."

Shay put her hands on Lily's cheeks and kissed her lips softly.

"I love you so much," Shay whispered.

"I can't lose you either but what I'm about to ask someone to do, could kill you. I want you to understand just how hard this is going to be, for both of us. There will be nothing I can do for you once the procedure is started. There is no going back and there is no undoing it. You will either become a vampire or you will die. There is no halfway here."

"Baby, I know. We've been over this a dozen times. All I know is that I love you enough to know I will pull through. I know why I'm doing it and that will give me the strength to fight through it. I will not leave you willingly, Lily. I promise."

"You have no idea how hard this is," Lily said.

"Yes, Lily, I do. I was there when you almost didn't make it. I know how it feels to think you might lose the most important thing in your life. I almost lost you, Lily, and I will not just stand by and let Eric do that again. Trust me, I know what you must be feeling right now, but I will make it through this."

Lily took a deep breath and wrapped her arms around Shay.

"I love you so much, Shay," she said.

"Let's talk to the good doctor," Shay said.

They took the elevator down to the sub-basement, hand in hand. When they got there they headed toward the lab. They knew that was the most likely place he'd be. When they got there he was hunched over a microscope.

"Jack," Lily said.

"Well, well, well. It's about damn time you came to see me," Jack said, still looking in the microscope.

"Why don't you use the monitors?" Lily asked him.

"Old school, darling, I prefer doing things the *right* way. Old school. There's nothing like really seeing the stuff for yourself, you know."

"Old school?" Shay quizzed. "What is 'old school' and why is it *right?*"

Lily laughed and explained to Shay that old school was the way things were done before the more modern inventions.

"So what can I do for you?" he asked.

"As if you don't already know why we're here," Lily answered.

"Yup, I know. But..." he began before turning around. "But I'm one step ahead of you. We, my dear, are first going to have to get as much of Shay's blood as we possibly can. I'm sure I can synthesize it, but it's going to take time. In the meantime, your blood alone will have to suffice.

"But Jack..." Lily began but was interrupted.

"Ah! Wait," he said and held up his finger. "I believe that your blood will change her faster than Markus, simply because her blood is special. Instead of giving her a little bit of the catalyst, she has a whole body full of it."

"That makes sense," Lily said with a head tilt.

"It only stands to reason," Jack said.

"Which means what?" Shay asked.

"I don't know yet. But, I do know that your blood is more likely to change you in less than two days. The only drawback being... Vincent is going to be furious."

"And what if it doesn't change her in less than two days?" Lily asked.

"Then it will take as long as it takes and everyone is none the wiser," Jack answered matter-of-factly.

Lily shook her head and kissed Shay on the cheek.

"You are absolutely sure about this?" Lily asked Shay.

Shay just nodded and kissed Lily gently on the lips. "I'm sure."

"Shay, dear, I assure you this is going to be much harder for Lily to endure than it will be for you."

"I know," Shay said softly. "See, Lily, I'm going to be fine."

"Well, come on, what are you two waiting for?" Jack urged.

"You're going to do it now!?" Lily asked, surprised. "We can't do it *right now.*"

"Why not, everything is ready. Shay is here, you're here, I'm here... What's the hold-up?" he asked.

"But right now!" Lily said nervously.

"She will be fine. I've seen it a million times. Your bond is strong enough to overcome even death. Trust me, you two, it's strong enough. I can see it when you look at each other. The way the sides of your mouths curl up the tiniest bit. The way you watch each other across the room. The way you would die from sun exposure rather than let her be hurt by Erica's evil twin brother. I can see it. It's very obvious if you know where to look. Trust me, young Lily, your love will survive this."

"I guess we're doing this now," Lily sighed. "Shay?"

"I'm ready. I promise I will come back to you," Shay replied.

They walked into the experimental procedure lab and everything was already set up. There were bags of blood lying on a cart next to the transfusion machine. Syringes were lined up next to the lines of tubing on the cart on the other side of the table.

"I set everything up about twenty minutes ago. Weren't figuring on you arguing with Vince so long. Are you ready Shay?" Jack asked.

"What about Vincent?" Shay asked Lily.

"He's probably going to disown me, but he still needs my blood to change humans to vampires," Lily answered.

"This is true. He can't exactly kick you two out. Alexa and Erica would not allow that. They both are all for changing Shay. Neither one of them trust Eric. They're afraid that he'd kill her the first time he got a chance."

McGoo handed Shay a hospital gown and turned to leave.

"I'll give you two a few minutes," he said before leaving the lab.

Lily helped Shay out of her clothes and into the gown. Shay hopped up on the bed and sat with her hands in her lap. Lily placed her hands between Shay's knees then spread them apart. She slid her hands up Shay's thighs and around her hips as she stepped in between her legs.

"I will be right here," Lily told her. "I'll be here the whole time. From what I've heard, you probably won't even know anyone is around, but I will be. I'll be right here, ok."

Shay looked into Lily's eyes and smiled.

"I never believed that I would feel love like this. I've waited all my life to feel butterflies in my stomach every time I kissed someone and that someone is you, Lily. I promise you, I will make it through this," Shay said teary eyed.

"I love you, Shay. I wish I could tell you that once it starts you'll be a vampire in a few hours and that was it, but like over half of the people that start this, you can end it if the pain is too much to take. If you give the word, they will drag me away kicking and screaming and someone else will stop the process, because I will not be able to. I won't."

"I won't do that," Shay stated.

"You just never know," Erica said to Shay as she walked into the lab.

"Jack will be the one to do it if you do decide the pain is too much. I love you Shay, you know that, but this is going to be just as hard, if not harder, for Lily. I wish there was an easier way, but there isn't. Shay, all I can tell you is that Lily loves you more than you will ever know and you'll have an eternity to learn just how much."

"Wait. If I want to *end it*? What do you mean *'end it'*?" Shay asked.

"I'll take this," Erica said to McGoo. "Your version is just hard to hear."

"But it's factual," McGoo countered.

"Humph!" Erica snorted. "There is a point at which the change will make you immortal, but the transformation will not be complete. You will still be in extreme pain, but even if you mentally give up, your new body will not. So after that point, if you choose to have your life ended the only way to do that is to have someone end it for you. It used to be by beheading but these days, a scalpel, rib splitters and the removal of the heart is the only permanent way to end the life of a vampire."

"Oh," Shay said flatly. "Lily told me about the point of no return."

"But no," Lily interrupted. "I didn't tell you about being able to be put down after that point. I figured that if you made it that far, you would be able to pull through the rest of the way. Well, I hope, anyway."

"I will pull through I promise," Shay reassured.

"I don't think there is anything else we can do to prepare you, Shay. Do you have any questions?" McGoo asked as he picked up a syringe.

Shay shook her head and kissed Lily. "I love you," she said then took a deep breath. "I'm ready."

Lily sat on the bed next to Shay and McGoo connected all the IV's. He hung up the blood for Lily and then looked down at Shay.

"You're going to be just fine," he told her, then flipped the switch.

As soon as the blood entered her veins she could feel it. It was cool, not cold, but just slightly cooler than her own blood. She felt it travel up her legs and down her chest then it exploded out in every direction from her heart. It went into her lungs and that's when the pain started. Her lungs began to sting, like alcohol in a papercut.

"Wow," she said as she reached for Lily's hand. "Here we go."

Shay had told Lily a few dozen times that she was ready to be changed into a vampire. Had told her that she was ready to endure the pain of the transformation so she could help fend off Eric if he ever tried to pull another attack. She nearly lost Lily that day on the roof and she almost lost her life less than a month later. She swore to do whatever it took to never be in that situation again.

Her lungs began to burn then she felt the cool blood disperse through her brain. She saw flashes of color and heard sounds she could never have even imagined before. She could feel the electricity in her brain as the neurons fired all at once. Then she felt nauseous as her head began to spin faster and faster.

She could feel the muscles in her arms tighten so much, it felt like they were going to rip in two. She yelled out in pain and held tighter to Lily's hand.

Then her insides begin to burn. Her liver, her kidneys, stomach, intestines and heart began to get larger, squeezing against her ribcage and billowing out from her lower torso. Then she heard a horrible crunch as her spine split open from her neck to her waist.

Her fingers and toes swelled to twice their size as the claws and shafts formed. New tissues and muscles connected to bone and the bones grew thicker, denser.

The skin on her arms began to peel away and she screamed out in excruciating pain. After what seemed an eternity all of her skin had peeled away from the muscle and fat below and a stringy, sinuous covering began growing like ivy vines up her legs and arms. Then the vines covered her neck and chest, then her stomach and back.

After the white vines covered her whole body, a new set of vines, growing at opposite angles of the first began covering her, starting from her toes and fingertips and weaved its way through the vines that were already there. This had to be the vampire skin that Lily always referred to as Kevlar. Bulletproof and knife proof.

Next, another layer of pinkish tan skin covered the white vine layer; human skin.

She has human skin, like me, Lily thought. *She's going to be like me.*

Her insides still felt like someone was trying to rip them out with fish hooks. Her heart thumped so hard in her chest that she could see her own chest rise and fall with every heartbeat.

Lily squeezed her hand every time she would yell or scream. Lily would run her fingers through her hair when she was still enough for her to do it. She never let go of Shay's hand.

It took exactly thirty two hours and ten minutes for her to make the change. To Shay, it seemed like weeks. When all the pain stopped and she was able to move her new body, she sat up, wrapped her arms around Lily then kissed her for a very long time. She even tasted different. They would be together forever now. There was no question of how much they loved each other. Lily loved her enough to make her immortal. Enough to want to spend the rest of eternity together. And Shay felt the exact same way about her. Ever since she bumped into her at Baldwin's by 'accident'. They still laugh about that.

Shay looked at her hand and turned it over again and again.

"It feels different," Shay said softly. "Just moving my hand feels different."

Oh my God, I'm a vampire, Shay thought. *I'm a fucking vampire!*

Shay buried her face in Lily's neck and cried. She had made it through the change and was now Lily's equal although she did have a lot to learn.

Lily kissed her cheek and gently pushed her away so she could look at her face.

"God you're gorgeous," she said smiling.

"I don't look any different..." she stopped mid-sentence as Erica shoved a mirror in front of her face. "*Oh my!*" She literally looked younger.

The laugh lines around her eyes and mouth were gone. The furrow between her eyebrows had vanished and her skin was flawless except for the birthmark that was still on her neck. She no longer looked like she was thirty four. She looked twenty four.

Erica handed her some clothes then Shay gave Lily a peck on the cheek and hopped off the table. She stretched her arms over her head and arched her back. She could feel the skin pull tight over the new spikes in her back. She knew it had to be spikes because otherwise she figured her spine would not have changed, and there was something definitely different about her back.

She spread her fingers apart and tried to expose her claws. No luck. She curled her fingers and concentrated on the new feelings in her hand, but still, no claws.

"They're already broken," Shay said jokingly.

"Baby, don't expect to be able to be a fully functioning vampire just yet. Give it a week at least. It takes time to adjust to the new brain and how the new brain controls everything. It's all new. You've been rebuilt from the skeleton out and even had a few additions. So love, be patient."

"But I want to try it now!" She said eagerly.

Lily took a deep breath and looked over to Erica who was standing in the doorway. Erica shrugged her shoulders and walked back into the lab. She gave her a big smile.

"OK, Shay, you asked for it," Erica said.

Lily raised her hand and tapped her on the shoulder. Then she tapped harder, pushing her shoulder back.

"What are you doing?" Shay asked.

"You said that you wanted to try everything out now, so that's what we're gonna do," Lily said, hitting her in the shoulder. "The easiest way to trigger a vampire response of fangs and claws is through anger. So I'm going to try to make you mad so you'll see how your fangs, claws and maybe even your spikes work."

"Yes, I can feel the spikes under the skin on my back."

"OK, hit me," Lily said.

"Hit you?"

"Hit me!"

"I can't."

"Then your lesson will have to wait until later," Lily said.

"No wait," Shay pleaded, not wanting to give up so easily.

"OK. Before we start this, Shay, I want you to know that I love you. You know that. Everything I'm about to do is to get a reaction and that's all."

Shay nodded.

"I can help," Erica said as she walked up to them.

Lily made a slight motion with her head and stepped to Shay's right and Erica stepped to her left.

"Are you sure you want to do this now?" Erica asked. "This is the quickest way to get a vampire reaction, but I guarantee you will be mad at me and Lily when it's over."

"So the point is just to make me mad?" she asked.

"Yes, an anger response is the easiest to trigger."

Shay took a deep breath. "OK."

Lily jabbed her arm with her fist as Erica did the same thing. The first thing that Shay registered was that the punches should've hurt, but she barely even felt them.

Then Erica pushed her backwards so hard that she fell over the bed and crashed into the table on the other side then fell to the floor. That annoyed her, but she just couldn't get mad. It was Erica and she knew deep down that Erica would never really hurt her. She stood up, expecting something to hurt; her knee, her elbow, her head, something. But nothing did, she was just hurled over a bed onto hard tile and she didn't even feel bruised.

"Humm," Lily said out loud, then picked up a scalpel from out of a drawer.

She put the blade against her arm and pressed, making an indent in her skin.

"Lily don't," Shay pleaded.

She pressed harder.

"Lily, seriously."

The scalpel slid through the human skin and a trickle of blood rolled down her arm.

"Lily stop!" Shay demanded as she walked around the table toward her.

"Stop me!" Lily ordered then made a gash down the length of her forearm.

"Dammit Lily!" She yelled as she snatched the scalpel from Lily's hand.

Lily had a big smile on her face.

"What? Why are you so...?"

"Look," Erica interrupted as she handed Shay the mirror.

As she reached for the mirror she saw that her claws were out. Then she felt the fangs in her mouth. She took the mirror and looked at the three quarter inch canines protruding from her gums. She smiled.

I have claws and fangs, she thought. *Oh my God, I have fucking claws and fangs!*

"Now relax, sweetheart," Lily said, running her hand across Shay's cheek.

"Cool!" She beamed. "I have claws and fangs."

"Yes you do," Lily said. "And spikes may come later."

"Erica," Lily asked, "did Mark or Markus have spikes?"

Erica shook her head, "Not that we've seen."

"Well," Erica said, "Come on. You two better get out of here before Dad finds out. Mom already knows and I'm sure she'll tell him soon enough."

"I don't have to wait in quarantine?" Shay asked.

"No," Erica answered. "Mark and Markus don't have family or a mate here and they are way more likely to lash out in the first week after being turned. You, on the other hand, do have a mate and McGoo thinks that you will be fine with Lily. Onyx can help keep an eye on you, too."

The three of them rode the elevator up together. Shay kept looking at her hands and concentrating like every new vampire did. Lily stroked her cheek and Shay looked up at her. Lily was smiling at her.

"Hey! Guess what?" Shay asked Lily playfully.

"What?" Lily said.

"I am a fucking vampire!" Shay answered.

Lily laughed as Shay wrapped her arms around her and then kissed her.

"Get a room, you two!"

Lily flipped Erica off without even looking away from kissing Shay. Erica just laughed. When the elevator dinged for the fifty sixth floor Erica tapped Lily's shoulder. They looked up just long enough to step off the elevator into the hallway, then continued kissing. Onyx was waiting in the hallway outside Lily and Shay's doors.

"Good bye, ladies," Erica said smiling as the elevator doors closed.

The girls just waved in Erica's direction and never stopped kissing.

"Damn, and I thought I felt butterflies *before* the change," Shay whispered between kisses.

When they finally made it down the hallway to the apartment they kissed a few minutes longer then went into Lily's place. They sat on the couch to talk. Onyx lay down in front of the balcony doors. Shay was still getting used to the new hearing and sight. She could tell just by moving around that her body was stronger. It took so little effort to walk or lift her arms or legs. She had to adjust her motion in order to feel normal.

"Is it normal to feel like everything is moving too slow?" Shay asked as she looked at her wiggling fingers.

"Yes. You're faster, stronger, smarter. Everything will seem really heightened and... shiny, I guess is a good word. You'll notice details that you've never noticed before. Just wait until you go outside. But, all of the new vampires that I've known have gotten burned at least once. You have to remember that the sun is not a good thing for you. Your skin will probably be like mine and give you some leeway. I can be out in a hoodie and jeans and be ok. As long as I keep my hands in my pockets and my hood on and my head down. You'll probably be the same way. Don't worry, though, I won't let you forget the sunscreen. I keep it in the dresser if you haven't already noticed."

Shay laughed a little. "Yeah, I've noticed. You slather it on every morning after your shower."

Lily nodded and smiled. "You'll get used to doing it, too, love."

Lily reached for Shay's face and Shay leaned in toward her. Shay closed her eyes as Lily stroked her cheek and down her neck to her chest.

"I can feel trails from where you touched me. I felt them before but this is so much more intense. It's almost like your hands are hot and they're leaving marks on my skin."

Lily pulled her closer and kissed her. She parted her lips slowly with her tongue and they kissed for a while. Shay reached down and pulled Lily's shirt up. Lily's arms raised of their own accord and the shirt came off.

"Are you sure you're ready for this?" Lily asked.

You're damn right I'm ready for this! Shay thought.

"I've been waiting for this all my life," Shay said between kisses. "To want someone the way I want you. With sex, I could always take it or leave it. But now, I want you all the time. I've never felt this way before. And now, it's even stronger."

"That's the way I've felt since the first time I saw you," Lily confessed.

"How did you fight that urge for so long, without even kissing me? Without even *touching* me for months. I don't think I would have that much self-control."

"I've had a lot more practice at controlling it than you have. But lucky for you, love, you don't have to. Let it go," Lily said softly.

Lily pulled her close and kissed her slow and long. Then she pulled Shay's shirt over her head and unfastened her bra. She slid the straps down her arms and the bra fell to the floor.

Shay stood up, put out her hand and led Lily to the bedroom. The rest of their clothes were off by the time they reached the bed. Lily pushed Shay back onto the bed. She pulled her legs to the edge and knelt down. Lily spread Shay's legs and kissed up her inner thigh. It didn't take long for Shay to begin moaning. Lily knew what was coming and it wasn't just going to be Shay.

Lily licked and fingered until Shay was just seconds from an orgasm.

"Are you ready?"

"Yes," Shay moaned.

Lily went right back to it and after a few seconds, Shay's back came off the bed and both clawed hands grabbed a handful of sheets and mattress. Shay didn't realize what she had done and Lily didn't stop to tell her.

Three orgasms later, Lily finally let Shay get her breath and actually take a look at the bed.

"Oh shit! I did that?" Shay gasped.

Lily only laughed and kissed her full on the lips.

Shay was insatiable. After over five hours, the two finally collapsed on the bed. After catching her breath Shay stood up and put out her hand to Lily again.

"Shower?" Shay asked.

"Am I going to regret making you a vampire?"

"Probably," Shay smiled.

"Nah."

Lily got up and they showered together. A nice long, hot shower, complete with even more touching and kissing.

Lily kissed down Shay's body and lifted her leg to rest on the ledge in the shower. Shay leaned against the wall and let Lily spread her open and lick hard. Lily pressed her face into Shay and sucked her into her mouth. Her tongue circled the pink bundle of nerves then slid over the top. Licking up and down, faster and harder with each stroke. Shay's legs began to shake uncontrollably as she neared climax. Lily slid two fingers up into her and then twisted them slowly. Then she sucked Shay's clit between her lips and licked faster. Shay's legs shook even more as Lily licked harder, sliding her fingers in and out slowly and first then faster.

Shay screamed out as she came hard. Lily wrapped her arms around her thighs and kept sucking. Shay's body shook as the orgasm overtook her. Her back arched back then forward over Lily. Shay grabbed Lily's sides and dug her claws in as the stood up, still moaning and breathing heavy. Lily let out a surprised whimper but kept sucking.

The orgasm lasted almost three minutes. By the time Shay had calmed down, Lily's sides were almost healed but the blood in the bottom of the shower remained.

Shay finally opened her eyes and looked around. She noticed the blood and immediately looked at her hands. Her claws were out and there was still blood on her hands.

"Oh, my God, Lily! Did I hurt you?" She said as she kneeled in front of Lily.

"No, you didn't hurt me," Lily smiled and pulled Shay's face to hers. "That was incredible, wasn't it?"

"Oh my…" Shay breathed. "I have never had an orgasm like that. Not standing *or* one that lasted that long. My body is still shaking."

"And they only get better," Lily whispered in her ear.

They kissed and held each other for a little while longer before leaving the shower. They had only been out long enough to get dressed and pick up the mattress filling when they heard a knock on the front door. Onyx barked and was waiting at the door when Lily got there.

Lily took a deep breath. *I really hope that's not Vincent. Onyx, don't go far.*

Lily answered the door and it was Erica. Onyx went to lay back down.

"How is she doing?" Erica asked as she walked in the door.

Lily let out the breath she wasn't even aware she was holding. "She's great. Wasn't expecting the claws when she got them, though."

"You didn't warn her?" Erica laughed.

"You knew!" Shay yelled from the bedroom doorway.

"Well, you got a little better at controlling them, didn't you?" Lily smiled.

"Not really," Shay said under her breath.

"How are you feeling Shay?" Erica asked.

"I'm great! No sleep in over twenty four hours and still raring to go."

"Any success with the teeth or claws?"

"No, haven't really been trying either. Been busy with *other* things, ya know."

"Yes, I know," Erica said, smiling at Lily.

"So are you just here to check up on Shay?" Lily asked.

"Actually, no. I came by to tell you that Vincent knows."

"That was quick," Lily frowned. "What is he going to do?"

"I don't know. Mom said that he was going to talk to Jack first. I guess it depends on what Jack says."

"Even McGoo knows that they don't have to have Shay's blood. I can change humans in five days. And that's over twice as fast as before. Is there any way that he could just be happy with that?" Lily asked rhetorically.

"Looks like he's going to *have* to be happy with that," Erica said.

"There's still a chance that the Doc can synthesize my blood. He has plenty of samples. And he's smart. If anyone can, it's him," Shay piped in.

Just as Erica sat down on the couch, a knock came from the front door.

"That's my que to leave," Erica said quickly and stood up again.

Onyx was at the door before Lily. Lily looked through the peep hole and it was Vincent.

"Shay, go to the bedroom," Lily told her.

"No, I'm staying right here," she said and sat on the couch.

Lily opened the door and Erica stepped out. Vincent stepped aside so she could leave. As she walked away, she gave Lily a 'thumbs up' when Vincent wasn't looking.

"Hello, Vincent," Lily said.

Vincent sucked in air through his nose and blew it out slowly. He was pissed. Really pissed.

"You do know how furious I am, don't you?" He asked.

"I do," Lily answered.

He walked in and took a seat on the couch at the opposite end of Shay. Lily sat in the chair at Shay's end of the couch and Onyx stood beside Lily's chair.

"If I weren't afraid for both of your safety, I would banish you both from the coven for blatantly disobeying orders. I forbid you from changing Shay. I was very clear about that. But you changed her anyway. Not only did you disobey, you also contaminated the blood that could've saved our species. I have..."

"But...," Lily tried to interrupt but Vince stopped her.

He held up his hand. "I'm not done. I have spoken to Dr. McGregor and he is trying to synthesize the catalyst in her blood that speeds the changing process. He also made a very valid point. Her blood may speed the process, but you can only create a new vampire once every four to five days. Your body has to replenish your natural blood supply. And over time, your healing time could even decrease."

He sighed. "So even if we did have Shay's blood readily available, it wouldn't really matter. Except to the one that is changing. Jack has enough of Shay's blood to create three vampires quickly. He will save that for any female that may want to make the transformation. But it will only keep for a short amount of time. So lucky for you, you didn't completely leave us up shit's creek."

Shit's creek? Shay wondered. *Wonder where that is.*

"So my job now is to make a vampire every five to six days?" Lily asked.

"You're lucky you even have a place to live," Vincent reminded her.

Lily wanted so much to argue with him. Shay needed to be changed to protect her. But he was so against changing her because he still thought Lily wasn't in love. Lily didn't think that mattered now. Eric made sure of that. But if Lily had not loved Shay as much as she did, Shay would be dead. How could she possibly make him see that Shay was the one for her?

"Now that it's done, how are you adjusting Shay?" Vincent asked.

"I still can't expose my claws or teeth at will."

"It's only been a day," he said. "Give it at least a week. Lily isn't much help, she was born with fangs and claws. I still remember the first time I saw them. Pearly white in a dark cave.

Vincent thought for a moment of Lily crouched on a ledge in that black cave. The torch's light reflecting off the enamel of her fangs. Then he continued talking to Shay.

"If you need help just ask any other vampire. Except about the spikes. Only Lily and I have spikes. I rarely ever use mine anymore. Do you have any questions that I can answer?"

"Will the extreme attraction for Lily ever go away?" Shay asked.

"No. No matter what you do, you will always feel that love for her. Forever."

He looked at Lily and she knew what was going through his head. *Shay will love Lily for eternity, even if Lily decides she doesn't love Shay anymore.* Lily still had no idea how she could prove she loved Shay and only Shay, forever. She decided that only time would prove her love.

Vincent stood up to leave. Onyx walked to the door in front of him. As Lily was closing the door, Vincent stopped it with his foot.

"Oh, and tell LaShay that Jack wants to see her as soon as he can."

"OK," Lily told him.

SHAY'S SECOND LESSON

Lily closed the door and turned to Shay. Onyx went back to his place by the balcony doors. Lily walked over to the couch and put her hand out to Shay. Shay took it and stood up. Lily led her to the balcony and stepped outside. The night air was cool and the sounds of the city reverberated off the buildings below them. They were faint but some sound made it up to the fifty sixth floor where they stood.

"Close your eyes," Lily told Shay.

Lily walked behind Shay and then leaned her against the balcony railing. She wrapped her arm around her waist, moved her hair to the side and kissed the back of her neck.

"Listen," Lily whispered in her ear.

Shay listened to the sounds from the street.

"I can hear voices. Individual voices. Car engines revving. A dog barking. The wind whistling through the buildings."

"OK, now, look up at the sky."

Shay gasped. "Oh my God! Look at all the stars! I've never seen so many stars. And the park! It's dark but I can still see details instead of just shadows."

"Your eyesight is more adjusted to the night time. You'll notice that bright days will probably give you a headache, so I would always recommend sunglasses during the day. Now, take a deep breath through your nose. How many scents can you pick out?"

Shay took a deep breath. "Cinnamon. Definitely cinnamon. Basil. Soil. Trees. Onyx!"

Shay turned to see Onyx standing in the doorway to the balcony.

"Let's sneak out to the park," Shay said.

Onyx whimpered as if to say 'no'.

"It's nearly midnight," Lily reminded her.

"I know. We can sneak out through the garage. Take 86th through the park to Lex and play some pool at Baldwin's. No one will ever know."

"You know how much trouble we'll be in when Vincent finds out."

"I know, but I'm so tired of being cooped up here. Even before the change, I haven't been allowed to leave the building."

Lily thought about the consequences of leaving the coven after being told that it was forbidden. Her mind raced with questions. *If we go out, would Vincent send someone for us or just wait until we got back? How long would it take for him to find out we left? He will find out. What will he do to us? What if Eric is waiting for us outside? But what's the worst that can happen?*

"OK, but Onyx is coming with us," Lily said after a pause to weigh their options.

"I'm fine with that."

They both put on black hoodies, blue jeans and hiking shoes. They casually walked to the elevator, waved at the guard that poked his head out of the stairwell and waited for the steel doors to open. Shay looked at her new face in the reflective metal. Then she looked at Lily, touched her face and kissed her.

"Thank you," Shay said.

"For what?" Lily asked.

"For saving me. For loving me. For turning me. For everything."

"You are so welcome."

They rode the elevator down to the garage level. They strolled through the garage and Lily scanned her hand at the exit. Hopefully they would be halfway across the park before anyone realized they were gone. The tall, wrought iron gate opened for them to exit and they walked out. This garage exit put them out on 85th Street. They walked up one block then entered the park. With their hoodies pulled over their heads and a giant wolf walking with them, they couldn't have looked more suspicious.

They moseyed through the park at a leisurely pace. Shay took in the new sights and sounds and Onyx growled at a couple of people that he felt got too close. Then Lily remembered that Shay had never been close to a horse. She hoped that Shay would be like her and able to get close to them without spooking them.

Will she be able to go riding with me someday, Lily wondered. *Let's find out.*

"Come on," Lily said as she grabbed Shay's hand and took a ninety degree turn. "Come on Onyx."

"Where are we going?" Shay asked.

"You'll see," Lily grinned and walked faster.

Lily sniffed the air and turned in the direction of what she was searching for. They walked for about five minutes before Shay saw what Lily was up to.

Three police officers on horseback were conversing about forty meters ahead.

"Slowly," Lily whispered to Shay. "We don't know how they are going to react to you. You may be like me and able to get as close as you want without a problem, but if they smell more of the vampire on you, they'll run away."

"Aww," Shay pouted.

"Just let's wait and see," Lily told her. "Wait here, Onyx."

Lily made eye contact with one of the officers and he slid off of his mount.

"Can I help you ladies?" He asked. "It's awfully late to be out here alone isn't it?"

Lily turned around and motioned toward Onyx.

"We're not alone," Lily told the officer.

"We're just out for a late night walk. My friend has never seen a horse close up and we were wondering if it would be ok for her to pet it," Lily asked the officer.

"Sure," said the officer as he moved aside for the girls to get closer to the horse.

He was a huge horse, solid black with feathered feet and stood at least seventeen hands at the shoulder. He resembled a Friesian but was much bigger than any Friesian Lily had ever seen. When they approached, the horse was skittish. He lifted his head and backed away from them. Sometimes it took a moment, but Lily had always had a way with horses and was hoping that this horse would not be the exception.

"Easy," Lily whispered as she held out her hand.

After a few seconds the horse lowered his head slowly and sniffed the air once again. Again he lifted his head high and took a step back. It wasn't unusual for a horse to question its senses if it had never encountered a vampire. But this particular horse was trained to be fearless. It was in his job description. He had to deal with traffic, wolves, screaming kids wanting to pet it and countless other distractions on a daily basis.

"What's wrong with you boy?" The officer said as he pat the side of the horse's neck. "He's never jumpy."

"Let's just go," Shay said, not wanting to scare the horse.

"Give it a minute," Lily smiled.

After a little prodding from the officer the horse finally stepped forward and lowered his head to Lily's hand. She pat his nose and then rubbed the side of his neck. She wanted the horse to smell the vampire in her, so with her hand in her pocket, she slowly exposed her claws. The horses ears perked up and he pushed his nose into Lily's chest as if to question his senses but he didn't back away.

Lily took Shay's hand and lifted it to the horse's nose. He sniffed her hand and as if rejecting what he was smelling, shook his head and whinnied then snorted. But again, he didn't back away. His head bobbed up and down a few times before he lowered his head toward Shay.

Shay stepped closer and put both of her hands on each side of his head. He pushed his nose into her chest hard enough to cause her to step back. He snorted again and bobbed his head as he pawed the ground with one foot then the other. Lily was almost sure he was confused by what he smelled and sensed. He saw humans but still sensed a hint of the vampire predator in them.

"It's ok, boy," Shay said quietly.

After a minute the horse finally calmed and Shay continued to pet him. She smiled at Lily as she ran her hand down the horse's massive neck.

"He's beautiful," Shay said to the officer.

"Thank you," the officer answered. "His name is Mac and he's the best parts of a Friesian and a Percheron. He's only six years old but is the best horse on the force. He is absolutely fearless and will run head first into anything I steer him toward."

Shay put her forehead against Mac's nose then backed away.

"Thank you," she said to the officer.

The officer just nodded at the two and got back on his horse.

When they got to Baldwin's it was just after 1 AM. Lily told Onyx that they would exit out the back so he went to the alley to wait.

Lily and Shay went to the bar and ordered a drink. Scotch on the rocks for both.

The place was empty except for a few regular drunks at the other end of the bar. Lily and Shay went to the back to play pool. The tables were empty and the balls had already been racked. Lily took a pool stick off the wall and broke. The twelve ball and the four ball went into pockets.

"Solids," she called.

Shay got a stick and took her shot. Lily walked around the table to Shay and put her arm around her waist. She kissed her. Shay kissed back. They got hoots and hollers from the end of the bar. That only made Lily want to do it more. So she grabbed Shay with both hands and pulled her closer. They kissed long and deep. When the hollers finally stopped, the girls picked up their game of pool.

During all the commotion, they failed to notice the four men that walked in mid-kiss. The men traded looks and the biggest of the four nodded and smiled. They were looking for trouble and the two lesbians in the back looked fun to play with, and they didn't want to play pool. The four sat at the bar, ordered drinks and waited.

Lily and Shay played another couple of games and decided that they should probably get home. This time they'd take a cab. Hopefully they could find a van at this hour to accommodate Onyx. If not, they would have to go back the way they came. When the girls left out the back door the four men followed, three through the back and one through the front. The two girls were halfway to the street when one of the men stopped them in the alley. He didn't notice the black wolf in the shadows.

"Hey," he said to Lily and Shay. "Wanna play?"

Lily was in defense mode instantly as the vampire's survival instinct kick in. Shay felt Lily's claws against her hand as soon as the man spoke. The other three men caught up quickly and one had a crowbar in his hand. Onyx silently stepped out of the shadows behind the three men. The man that went out the front door saw Onyx and turned and ran. The others laughed and joked about how big of a pussy he was. Then Onyx growled.

Lily turned around, eyes glowing red in the dim light and walked toward her would be attackers. The man with the crow bar kept coming toward Lily and Shay. The other two thought they had heard a dog growling and turned around to face Onyx's two inch canines. His head was down and his ears were flat against his head. The hair on the back of his neck and back stood up. The alley was narrow and dark. Lined with trash cans and dumpsters so they literally had nowhere to run. The man in front didn't see Lily's claws until it was too late. One swipe across the chest and he went down to his knees grabbing his chest and soon his hands were covered in blood.

Shay smelled the blood immediately. She felt her gums start to move as the muscles attached to her teeth reacted involuntarily. Then she felt her eyes burn and suddenly her fisted hands hurt. She looked down to see her claws had cut through her palms. She stepped up to where Lily was standing and grabbed Lily's hand. The smell of the blood was almost too tempting to the new vampire. Lily looked at Shay and squeezed her hand tight.

"Fight it, Shay," she whispered.

The two men that were left standing turned to run from Onyx but Lily and Shay were waiting. The men turned back toward the huge wolf and then froze. There was nowhere for them to go.

Lily thought about the repercussions of killing three men in an alley. Whether they deserved it or not. Lily grabbed Shay's arm and pulled her toward her then stepped to the side.

"Let him pass," Lily said calmly.

Shay looked down at her hands and then back to Lily.

"I know, love, but this is not the time to be testing your new weapons. If you were to drink from them, it's forbidden and the Guardians would be at the coven in hours. Even though it would be easy to do and dispose of the body, that's just not what kind of vampires we are. Even if the ass holes deserve it. But I'm sure they realize that they made a big mistake at this point. Don't let him see your claws or teeth. Just let him pass. Let Onyx take care of the other two. His attack can be explained. Ours can't."

Shay just nodded and tried to relax.

The man that Lily had clawed had four large rips in his dirty gray tee shirt. The flesh was ripped and bleeding heavily but the gashes weren't deep enough to kill him. He was going to need medical help, but he would live. He got to his feet still holding his chest, blood dripped off his fingers and down his arm. The girls stepped behind a dumpster. They just let Onyx chase the men out of the alley.

Lily's claws and fangs retracted and she focused on Shay.

"Deep breaths, babe," she said softly. "Come here."

Lily took Shay into her arms and held her tight. She rocked her back and forth trying to calm her. Onyx came back down the alley and sat down beside the girls. He knew it may be a minute.

"Shhhh," Lily cooed. "Deep breaths. This was not supposed to be your second lesson. I'm so sorry."

LaShay leaned away from Lily. "For what? It was my idea. And you had no way of controlling what happened. Don't be sorry."

Shay leaned back into Lily's arms and put her head on her shoulder. After a few minutes, her eyes slowly lost their burn and she felt her claws and teeth retract. She took another deep breath and stepped away from Lily.

Onyx put his head against Shay's waist and pushed gently.

"I'm OK, big guy. Thank you," Shay said and rubbed him behind the ears.

They ended up walking back through the park to get home. It was nearly four AM when they finally made it back to the fifty sixth floor of the Crown Building. They showered together and finally went to bed.

It was barely seven AM when Erica knocked on Lily's front door. She was just going to 'sleep through' it, but the person at the door was persistent. Lily fumbled to the door and poked her head out. She was still naked and was hoping to make the visitor go away. No such luck. Erica pushed the door open and came in.

"Get dressed," she told Lily.

"I haven't even been asleep for an hour," she whined.

Erica ignored her and knowing there was no arguing with Erica, Lily went to put on clothes. Lily went into the bedroom and returned wearing an oversized tee shirt and a pair of old shorts.

"So how was your venture out last night?" Erica asked as Lily sat on the couch.

The look on Lily's face was priceless. A look of shock, embarrassment and being caught all at once.

"It was great," she gulped. "I guess."

"You do know that there are cameras and scanners in the garage, right?" Erica questioned.

"Of course. I was just hoping we'd be long gone before anyone noticed."

"Well, you were noticed. And I, for one, am pissed that you left the building. Lily, what if Eric had been waiting with his band of Underground brothers? You and Shay would not have stood a chance."

"Onyx was with us," Lily interrupted.

"Pft! So there were three against a possible horde? Not good odds, Lily."

"Shay wanted to go out. She's been cooped up here since she moved in a week and a half ago," Lily pleaded.

"I thought she was going to work?"

"Nope, she's been here the whole time."

"That's still no excuse for you two to leave the building."

"Erica, we can't be cooped up in this building forever."

"It's not forever, love. It's just until Eric is out of the picture."

"And how long is that going to be?" Lily asked. "Weeks? Months? A year even?"

"I honestly don't know, hon, but you know what he's capable of. And now that Shay lives here he knows she's important, at least to you. And you know he'll kill her if he gets a chance."

Lily opened her mouth to speak but Erica put up her hand before anything came out.

"And just because she's a vampire now, doesn't make her safe. You either. Especially outside these walls. He won't kill *you* because he needs you, he knows that. But he'll kill Shay just for spite."

Lily knew Erica was right.

"I'm sorry," Lily told her.

Erica stood up and so did Lily. Erica gave her a big hug and kissed her cheek. "I'll be sure to tell Vincent that you've been reprimanded."

"Thank you," Lily replied.

"Now go back to sleep. You have twenty four hours to catch up on sleep and to be with Shay. Then McGoo gets to begin more experiments. Maybe we can synthesize both of your blood and give you and Shay some peace."

At seven AM, almost exactly twenty four hours later, McGoo was already knocking on Lily's door. Shay had been up for about half an hour but decided to let her sleep until Jack arrived. Shay was dressed in one of Lily's old *Stefi G* tee shirts and leggings. She knew she was going to spend the day in the lab and she wanted to be comfortable. She greeted McGoo and let him into the apartment.

"I'll go wake up Lily. We weren't expecting you until a little later," Shay admitted.

"That's fine. You have coffee?" He asked.

Shay went to the kitchen and started McGoo a cup of coffee. "Coming up," she said as she walked through the living room.

McGoo went to the kitchen to wait.

Shay woke Lily with a kiss and a stealing of the covers.

"Paybacks are hell," Lily said as she rolled out of bed.

"I let you sleep as long I could," Shay told her. "The Doc is waiting."

"OK," Lily said as she walked toward Shay.

Lily put her hands on each side of Shay's face and kissed her.

"I'll just be a few minutes," she told Shay and walked into the bathroom.

MCGOO'S DISCOVERY

Lily and Shay followed Jack down to the labs. He sat them both is chairs in his blood lab. They both looked at each other and gave a weak grin. Today was going to be a long day. At least they had plenty of sleep over the past twenty four hours. Well, mostly sleep.

"So ladies. How are you this morning? Thank you for the coffee, Shay. Today we are going to test your blood against each other's. My hope is that Shay's blood is as strong as yours," he said pointing to Lily. "Since Shay has spikes my thought is that her blood is the same. If it isn't, I can only hope that it contains the specialized white blood cells that her blood carried before. That's why I let you change her, because I believe that your blood will be similar. Your arm please, Shay."

Shay lifted her arm, palm up, and let McGoo draw blood. Then he reached for Lily's arm and he drew her blood. He immediately took the vials to the microscope counter. He grabbed a dropper from a drawer and placed a drop of Shay's blood on a slide and covered it. Then he grabbed another dropper and did same with Lily's blood. He placed each slide on a separate microscope and adjusted the focus. He flicked a couple of switches and the two samples came up on the monitors that were suspended on arms from the ceiling. McGoo tapped some keys on the keyboard that sat between the two microscopes and both slides came up side by side on both monitors.

Lily and Shay looked at the screens for a moment then looked at McGoo.

"So?" Lily asked.

"They look the same," Shay said.

"Yes they do. The content looks the same. So let's get a better look."

McGoo placed Lily's sample into the electron microscope. Then he brought the image up onto one of the monitors. It looked like a bunch of red flattened balls with dipped centers. With the occasional large white snowball looking structure and the tiny vampire virus. Visible as a ball with dozens of spikes. In the blood, there were also clusters of stem cells, purplish balls with a visible nucleus. There weren't as many platelets in vampire blood as there was in human blood. Next he loaded in

Shay's sample then brought it up on the other monitor. They were only slightly different. Shay's blood still had the same occasional red dots on some of the white blood cells.

McGoo just smiled and stared at the monitors.

"Doc," Shay called, interrupting his moment. "What are we looking at? They look exactly the same to me."

"Almost," McGoo beamed. "See this here? This is your specialized white blood cell. It still exists in your blood."

"What does that mean?" Lily asked.

"It means that Shay's blood should make a vampire in less than two days. Either with a little of her blood and the rest yours, or all of hers. Either way it should decrease the transformation duration by two to three days, versus yours, Lily. Ten to fourteen days versus Vincent."

"Doc?" Shay said. "With everything you can do, why didn't you just concentrate Vincent's blood to make more vampires?"

"We did. That's how we changed the last two vampires decades ago. The problem was that it took so much of Vincent's blood that the samples would go bad before we had enough to make the transformation. We need almost a gallon and a half of blood to transfuse a large man. The average male human has about five point five liters of blood. That's just shy of one and half gallons. That's a lot of blood. And in order to concentrate it, we needed about three times that. Vincent can't replace his entire blood volume that quickly. We tried freezing the samples, but it damaged them in the process. Freezing the samples apparently kills the virus. And we tried administering the concentrated blood in three intervals, but that didn't work either. The humans died."

"OK, I get it," Shay laughed.

"So that means that Shay and I both can make vampires," Lily added. "So Eric and the Underground will be after us both. The good news is, he'd be stupid to kill you now."

"Not reassuring, love," Shay smirked.

"Sorry, but I'm just saying."

"Here, I want to try something, Lily. Give me your arm."

Lily lifted her arm to McGoo and he injected her with Shay's blood sample.

"What was that?" Lily asked.

"That, if my theory is correct, will give your blood the same specialized white blood cells that Shay has."

"But I've given her my blood before, shouldn't she already have them?" Shay questioned.

"The day you gave her your blood, she needed the specialized cells to heal her. Therefore she used them all up during the healing process," McGoo explained.

"At least that's what I think happened. Because her blood doesn't have the cells although she was exposed to them. It could also be that it wasn't introduced intravenously. I'm not exactly sure why they didn't stay in her blood."

Outside McGoo's lab, Brian stood just out of sight. He had heard everything that the good doctor said. He tossed his hood over his head, looked at the floor and walked to the elevator. He left through the garage and went straight to the Underground fight club. Eric was in the ring sparring with Matt. Matt was huge, with bulging arms and thighs. He had a chest that was nearly twice as wide and twice as thick as Eric's. Eric was faster but Matt was stronger.

Eric ducked and turned in the time it took Matt to throw a punch. Eric took a swing at his face but Matt caught his hand and squeezed. Eric went down to his knees as Matt bent his wrist back and down toward the floor.

"OK!" Eric yelled.

Matt just laughed and let go. "I win again," he sneered.

"We're just playing around."

"Sore loser."

"Fuck you, Matt."

"Eric," Brian called from the floor.

"What do you want, Brian?" Eric spat.

"I have some news that you certainly want to hear," Brian told him.

"Then tell me." Eric leaned on the ropes and bent over toward Brian.

"Not here," Brian said.

Eric let out an irritated sigh and climbed through the ropes. He and Brian walked outside the fight house and sat at one the empty tables.

"So what's this big news?" Eric asked, rolling his eyes.

"I was eavesdropping on the good doctor when he brought Lily and LaShay down to his lab. I figured he wanted to do testing of some kind so I snuck over and waited behind the door. He took blood from Shay then from Lily..."

"Get to the point, feeder boy," Eric interrupted.

"Shay's blood is just as strong as Lily's. But Shay's blood is special. It makes the change in like two days. Lily's, without the addition of Shay's, takes five days."

"So I can get either one and be able to change vampires," Eric concluded. "Great. Have you recruited the security guards yet? The ones on Lily and Shay's floor?"

"Yes, but what about the wolves and Onyx? There's no way the wolves would betray Lily. Vincent would put them down in a heartbeat and they know that. So what do we do about the wolves?"

"We drug them," Eric said. "I have a good supply of horse tranquilizer. That should put them out for a while. Long enough to grab the girls, anyway."

What Brian didn't know, and failed to tell Eric, was that Shay was now a vampire.

"What do you want me to do?" Brian asked.

"Nothing," Eric told him.

"Nothing? Why?"

"You may be a feeder and able to heal faster than a human, but you're still mostly human. One swipe from a vampire or one bite from a wolf and you're dead, buddy."

After all I've done for this ass hole and now I'm just pushed to the side, Brian thought.

Brian was disappointed that Eric didn't want his help. Now that Brian really thought about it, *Eric has never appreciated anything I've done for him. Maybe I should just go tell Vincent what Eric is planning. Maybe I'll tell Lily and Shay, too.*

Brian had already bribed the security officers on the fifty sixth floor and two more in the lobby. But Eric didn't know how Brian bribed the guards. He had promised them that Eric would turn them into vampires after they had Lily.

Eric made some phone calls and within ten minutes, vampires from the Underground began showing up in front of the fight club. After about thirty minutes, Eric began telling them his plan.

"Last time, Vincent was able to get security to Lily's floor faster than I had anticipated. We should've been gone by the time they arrived. But Erica knew too fast. Shay must have called as soon as Lily passed out. We're not going to get away with drugging Lily again either. So our plan is to get as many vampires to Lily's floor as possible. You will wait in the stairwell until I give the signal. Once I give the signal, you will meet me at the elevators. The plan is to sneak in and fight our way out. In the early morning hours, most of the vampires are in their apartments getting ready for the day. Either going to bed or doing something inside. The security is light until seven AM. And the doorman and Guardian wolf at the front door aren't there until seven AM as well. So if we show up at six, there will be less chance of being seen.

"There is a guard in the lobby that will let us in the front door. Once we get past the lobby, it should be smooth sailing. The only person we need to take out is Author, the guest elevator attendant. He'll be there at six AM just like he has been for the past seventy years. Aaron has a silencer for him. No flashing your guns, claws and teeth around either. The wolves will take the staircase and make sure that security can't get upstairs. We'll be nice and quiet and we'll be fine.

"Any questions?" Eric asked the group.

"Who's going to be with you to get the girl?" Matt asked.

"Girls, plural. That would be you and Aaron," Eric answered.

"Wait, you want both of them now?" Matt asked.

"Yes," Eric said flatly. "The plan is to get them both."

"When are we doing this?" asked someone from the back of the crowd.

"Tomorrow morning," Eric answered.

The girls were in McGoo's lab all day. He would take a fresh blood sample every hour from them both. Finally at the end of the day, he had concluded that the specialized white blood cells were now present in Lily's blood. Meaning that both Lily *and* Shay could create a vampire in less than three days. When Jack gave Vincent the news he was ecstatic. The vampire numbers would come back.

McGoo finally let the girls leave about six o'clock.

The girls hadn't been home ten minutes when someone knocked on Shay's door. She went to answer it thinking that McGoo wanted something else and just swung open the door.

"Doc, we...," Shay began but stopped. "Dad? What are you doing here?"

"You haven't been at work and you're not returning my calls."

"I'm sorry, I've just been really busy, Dad," she admitted." Come in."

Lily poked her head out of Shay's bedroom as Martin and Shay were walking into the living room.

"Would you like a drink?" Lily asked as she walked into the room.

"Yes, thank you," Martin answered.

Martin stared at Shay for few seconds with a strange look on his face.

"You look incredible, hon. What have you been doing?" he asked Shay.

"Uh... Nothing in particular," she stammered.

"Wow," her dad said. "You look almost ten years younger. I guess the Crown Building is really working out for you."

"Maybe it's Lily. So, Dad, what are you doing here?" Shay asked, changing the subject.

"I was hoping to talk to Vincent."

Lily nearly dropped the three glasses of scotch as she was putting them on the table.

"Vincent?" Lily asked. "What do you want with my granddad?"

"Well, I was doing a little research and learned that this building is owned by the Crown Corporation. Do you know what that is, Lily?"

Lily looked at Shay and wondered where this conversation was going.

"Well, this Crown Corporation," Martin continued, "owns every prestigious address in every major city and at least one subdivision in every secondary city. The corporation is worth billions. And you said your grandfather owns the Crown

Building. Why does this corporation own only one property in every city? That makes no sense."

Lily did not want to have this conversation. She reached in her pocket, pulled out her phone and called Vincent. Luckily he was available and said he'd be there in a few minutes. Vincent had been afraid that Martin was going to look into the ownership of the covens. He was hoping that he wouldn't have to have this conversation with Martin. But since he was here, Vince had to come up with a good story to cover the covens, but he was coming up empty. Technically Vincent did own the covens. The Elders owned Crown Corp, but it wasn't like his name was on any of the documents that proved ownership. It was just understood that if the Elders were to die, Crown Corp would go to the Guardians. There would always be Guardians. Maybe not the same ones, but they would always exist as long as there were vampires.

Vincent knocked on Shay's door and Lily answered.

Martin stood to shake Vincent's hand when he entered the living room.

"So I hear you're looking into the Crown Corporation," Vincent said before he even sat down.

"Sit, please," Martin said. "I was just curious as to why you said you owned the building."

"I do. I'm the silent CEO of Crown Corp. The corporation's funds are distributed over several hundred properties. Each property is independently operated but abide by the rules and regulations of the Corporation."

"Silent CEO?" Martin questioned. "What is that exactly?"

"It means the corporation is self-sufficient. It's been in operation...,"

"Forever, it seems," Martin interrupted. "There is no 'founded' date for the corporation. It's like it's been in existence forever."

"It has, for the most part."

"So if I dig deeper into the Crown Corporation, what will I find?" Martin asked.

"Depends on where you dig," Vince countered. "You'll find a lot of properties that house honest, hard-working individuals and families. That's the only thing Crown owns, housing properties. It was begun hundreds of years ago by the King of some little known country, hence "The Crown". Its sole purpose was to house the wealthy and their servants during hard times. It owns properties in every country on earth.

"If you dig long enough and hard enough you will find that in the 12th century Britain, the Easterling family, now abbreviated to "Sterling", was among the first to obtain residences at these properties."

"As in Vincent *Sterling*," Martin said.

"Yes." Vincent stood up and put out his hand. "Feel free to dig as much as you'd like. The Corporation is legit and has never been associated with any wrongdoing."

Martin stood and shook Vincent's hand.

"The 12th century, huh," Martin quizzed.

"Yes, it goes back a very long time."

"So why is it that it's so hard to get into the properties?" Martin asked.

"Residency is passed down from generation to generation. One can marry into one of the families," Vincent nodded toward Shay who was intent on hearing this story, too.

"Married?" Martin looked at Shay.

"No, Dad, were not married, yet," Shay said. "I would've told you."

"So there's going to be a wedding?" Martin questioned.

"We haven't actually talked about it, Dad."

"Then how did you get into the building?" Martin asked, looking at Vincent.

"Special request by my granddaughter. You know how hard it is to say no to your granddaughter, right Martin?"

"I suppose," Martin confirmed.

Vincent handed Martin a business card that only had his name and a phone number on it. "If you should have any more questions, feel free to call me. No need to interrogate the children."

Martin just nodded his head.

Vincent gave Lily a hug and kissed her on the cheek. "Stay out of trouble, dear," Vince told her.

"Yes, sir," she replied.

After Vincent and Martin left, Lily and Shay finally took a deep breath. They had no idea where that meeting was going to go. Martin had started asking all the right questions that would lead him to every vampire coven in the world. And if he kept digging, he'd find the Underground and all the vampire's secrets. Vince was hoping that the inquiry was over.

"So what was *that* all about?" Lily asked Shay.

"Whew! I have no idea. But I'm glad Vincent was here so quick."

"I know."

It was a Saturday, and the girls decided that they wanted to spend the day on the couch together, just relaxing and watching movies. So that's what they did until someone knocked on the door about four o'clock.

"Dammit," Lily cursed. "Who the hell is it now? Your dad has been here already, Vincent has already been here, McGoo has already taken all the blood that he possibly could... So who is this?"

Shay walked to the door and peeped through the hole. It was Shane.

"Shane? How did you get up here?" Shay asked as she swung the door open.

"Well I didn't fly to the fifty sixth floor. The elevator was much safer," he joked.

Shay gave him a hug and invited him in. Lily was still laying on the couch. She was thinking that she had wished that Shay's dad was back. Anyone except Shane.

"Hello, Lily," he said politely.

"Hi, Shane," she said.

"So, seriously, how did you get in the building?" Shay asked.

"I walked in and went to the information desk, you know, the one beside all of the Egyptian stuff, and told them I was here to see LaShay Black on the fifty sixth floor. You told me that you got an apartment across from Lily, and I remembered that she was in fifty six A. I never forgot that for some reason."

"So they just let you in?" Shay asked.

"Well, I got sniffed by a really big dog. Oh my God, that one is even bigger," he gasped when he saw Onyx stand up by the balcony doors. "Holy shit what do you feed your dogs in this place?"

"He's a wolf, Shane, not a dog," Shay corrected.

"He's massive! Does he bite?"

"If you give a reason to," Shay smiled. "He'll let you pet him, if you want to."

Shane walked over to Onyx and Onyx sniffed him then sat down. Shane petted him for a few minutes before he sat on the couch next to Shay.

"He's really big," Shane reiterated. "Beautiful though."

"Thank you, he's Lily's,"

"No, love, he's ours," Lily said. "He belongs to us both now."

"So you like have joint custody or something?" Shane laughed.

"Well, we're always together and if not he's in the hallway where he can monitor us both," Lily said.

"Like he really knows that," Shane smirked.

"You'd be surprised," Shay told him.

"So Shay, what's it like living in the Crown Building?"

Shay just shrugged her shoulders and tilted her head. "Just like living in my old apartment, except it's a lot higher up."

"With ridiculous security in the lobby, giant guard dogs, I mean wolves, and there are even guards in the stairwells. They thought I didn't see them poke their heads out when I got off the elevator. There are two more wolves in the hallway. Is Lily like some sort of Princess or something?" Shane joked.

They all laughed.

"No, she's not a Princess, but her grandfather does own the building."

"No shit! Really? Wow! I'm in the company of royalty."

"So what are you doing here, Shane? I thought you hated me," Lily asked.

"Weeell, I gave it some thought and if Shay trusts you enough to move here, I guess I should try to trust you, too. I would hate to lose my best friend over something like that. Shay has always been a good judge of character, so I figured I should trust her judgment."

"Would you like something to drink?" Shay asked.

"You know it! Something fru fru please."

Lily stood up and went to the kitchen to make drinks.

"So how are things? How are things with Lily?" Shane asked.

"Better than I could've ever imagined," Shay beamed. "It's like I have an entirely new life. I'm truly happy for the first time. I really never thought I could be this happy."

"Is the sex that good? Because damn girl, it sure looks good on you," Shane teased.

Shay hit him in the arm. "Shut up! And yes, it is."

"Ooooo!"

"Well, you asked."

"You look incredible, by the way," he added. "So her grandfather really owns the building?"

"Yup. Been in the family for centuries," Shay told him.

"This building has been here for centuries?" Shane quizzed.

"Well, no. But the land has belonged to her family for a very long time."

"Oh, I see," Shane said.

There was a whirring sound from the kitchen and glass clanking. In a few minutes Lily walked back into the living room with three drinks. They were on a little tray and she was trying not to drop them. She sat them down gently on the table and then sat back down opposite of Shay. Shane picked up the one closest to him and took a sip. Strawberry daiquiris.

"So Lily, what's it like to be the granddaughter of the owner of the most prestigious address in the city?"

"Well, Shane, I guess I've never really thought about it," Lily answered truthfully. She has always lived in the Crown Corporations properties so it's never been a big deal to her.

"Shay tells me that you two are doing great. I'm glad to hear that." Shane looked over at Shay and then patted her knee. "I've never seen her so happy. Or looking so young."

The three of them sat and talked for about an hour and a half before Shane said he had to leave. He too had met a new guy and was eager to get to his date.

"Taylor doesn't like to be kept waiting", Shane smiled. "He lives in this building, too, you know."

Shane had no clue what that meant. Lily and Shay just looked at each other and smiled.

"What," Shane asked.

"Nothin'," the girls said in unison.

The girls walked Shane to the door and said their goodbyes.

THE COVEN VS THE UNDERGROUND

hay leaned back against the door and Lily put her arms on Shay's hips. Shay wrapped her arms around Lily's neck and kissed her. Shay ran her fingers up through Lily's hair and pulled her closer. They kissed all the way as they stumbled to the bedroom.

Around midnight they finally came up for air. Shay was walking to the coffee table to grab the melted drinks they had left there when Onyx's ears perked up. He stood and walked to the front door. Shay had almost gotten to the bedroom door when Onyx barked. Lily jumped out of bed and threw on some clothes.

"Hurry up, get dressed," Lily said as she passed Shay on the way into the living room.

"What's wrong?" Shay asked.

"Onyx?" Lily called.

He barked again and the fur on his back and tail stood up. His ears flattened against his head and a low growl rumbled in his chest. He stood with his head lowered facing the front door.

He took a step back from the doors just as they flew off the hinges. Lily heard the crack of wood and came running down the short hall from the living room. Onyx was already on Eric. Two other vampires grabbed Onyx and threw him into the hallway. Eric was in Shay's apartment and this time he had brought backup, a lot of backup. Eric and his two vampire friends multiplied to six then eight. Shay walked out of the bedroom to see Eric and two others grab Lily. Lily got off two good swings at Eric but it didn't even slow him down. He didn't wait for his other six friends who had orders to grab Shay. Eric dragged Lily down the hallway, past the dining room and out the busted double doors. There were more vampires waiting in the hallway.

Shay felt her teeth shift and her fingers stretch. Her eyes burned and she took a clawed swipe at the first vampire to get to her. Then took another.

"She's a vampire!" One of them said.

"She's supposed to be human!" Another called out.

Eric didn't hear them. He and two others were dragging Lily down the hallway. She saw the two Guardian wolves laying on the floor just past the elevators. They weren't moving. The two guards from the stairwell were standing guard by the stairs just beyond the wolves. Eric hit the elevator button and then hit it again.

When the door opened, Vincent and Venom were facing Eric and Lily. Eric was so stunned, Lily was able to elbow him in the ribs and slip away. She punched one of the other vampires square in the chest cracking his sternum. He fell forward grabbing his chest. Lily took a clawed swipe at the second vampire and caught him across the cheek. Blood splattered the wall and he too went down. Venom made sure he didn't get up.

When Lily made it back to the apartment, Shay was being dragged out the door by three vampires. Onyx had taken out two and Shay had taken down one of the other six that were left in the apartment. Shay was struggling against her attackers. Suddenly the vampire directly behind her let go and grabbed his chest with both hands. Before he even realized what had happened he was on the floor. The vampire on Shay's left suddenly let go of her, too. He looked down at his hand to see two gaping holes. The vampire on the right did the same. They looked at each other, then at Shay. Her spikes were clearly visible through her gray and black shirt.

Lily made it to Shay just as Onyx stepped back into the apartment. Lily took out the vampire on the left and Shay took the one on the right. Onyx made sure neither one of them got up again. Lily wrapped her arms around Shay and recoiled when the spikes nearly stabbed her arms.

"You have spikes, love," Lily smiled.

As quickly as the spikes appeared, they were gone. Shay could feel the spikes retract and the holes heal.

"Wow, they come in handy, don't they?" Shay said. "Not so good for the shirt, though."

Venom went back toward the elevators. He lunged at Eric and knocked him onto his back, hitting Eric's head hard against the wall. Vincent grabbed Eric by the throat and lifted him off the floor. The two stairwell guards rushed at Vincent but were stopped by Venom. The gray and white wolf stood with his head down and his teeth bared in front of Vincent. The guards turned and ran down the stairs.

Another elevator door opened and off stepped Erica and her wolf, Apollo. On orders from Erica, Apollo ran to Shay's apartment. Onyx was dragging dead, headless vampires out into the hallway when he arrived. Shay and Lily were fine so Apollo headed back to Erica.

Erica grabbed Eric's arm and threw him toward the elevator door just as it opened. Steven and four security guards caught Eric as he stumbled in. Another elevator dinged and opened. Four more of Eric's vampire friends were about to step out when Venom and Apollo cut them off. The four took a step back and let the elevator doors close in front of them.

When Eric got his footing on the elevator, Steven shoved him back toward Vincent and Erica. Each grabbed an arm and they all stepped onto the elevator behind them. They waited for Venom and Apollo to load in. Vincent pushed the button for sub-basement three. Three floors below the parking garage.

Vincent and Erica escorted Eric to the far end of one of the hallways. Through thick, steel double doors there sat two large cages with thick steel bars.

"Wolf cages? Really! You're going to put me in a wolf cage?" Eric whined.

"You're lucky you're still alive!" Erica told him.

Eric knew that they would put him there if he were caught. He already had a plan to escape. He had found more entrances into the sub-basement from the Underground tunnels. They must have been escape routes for the vampires long ago. They were unfinished and falling in, but they were passable. Eric's vampire buddies already knew to come for him if he didn't make it back to the Underground with Lily and/or Shay.

Erica rode the elevator back up to the fifty sixth floor. Workers were busy carrying dead vampires down to the incinerator on the maintenance floor of the sub-basement. It was used to heat the building in the winter, but under the circumstances, there were an excessive number of bodies that needed to be disposed of.

Lily and Shay had gone to Lily's apartment while workers repaired the door and cleaned the carpets. Shay was still pretty shaken and was having a little trouble with her fangs. Lily was trying to comfort her when Erica came in.

"Lily? Shay?" She called from the hallway.

"In here," Lily called back.

"How are you two doing?" Asked a very concerned Erica.

"Kind of shaken up," Shay said with a weak smile to show her teeth.

"That's understandable," Erica said. "Some sleep would probably be the best thing for that. Not 'sleeping together', sleep!"

Shay laughed. "You know what it's like to be a new vampire. It's just never enough. How did you get past that?"

"I was single at the time," Erica grinned quaintly.

"Oh," Shay replied. "Sorry."

"No worries," Erica laughed. "But seriously, Lily you know what calms you down."

When Lily was young, she had near complete control of her claws and teeth, but sometimes, after one of the many fights with Eric, she would have some trouble with her teeth, too. Anger and fear are the two main triggers and sometimes when tempers were flared, Erica would have to calm Lily down. She did it by brushing Lily's hair. It always worked to calm her and thought it may work for Shay.

"Lily, scoot down," Erica told her. "Shay, lay down and put your head in Lily's lap."

Lily began to run her fingers through Shay's long dark hair. Within fifteen minutes Shay was asleep. Erica winked at Lily and waved good-bye then let herself out.

Shay woke Lily up about two hours later. And they went to bed.

It was just after six AM when Eric's vampire friends broke into the sub-basement. They had used an entrance on the far end of one of the unfinished hallways. Most of the basement was white tile, drop ceiling and florescent lighting. But at the far end of some of the tunnels, tunnels that extended far past the floors upstairs, the tile ended and there were only the solid walls of Manhattan bedrock. Unlike the other tunnels that were supported by old timbers, these tunnels were solid. Harder and louder to dig through but easier and safer to escape through.

Zeus and Raven were guarding Eric's cage and four security guards were at the door. The guards had machine guns and enough armor piercing ammunition to start another world war. They saw the vampires coming from the clear view down the long hallway. Three canisters came rolling up to the guards. Smoke and fumes began bellowing out of the canisters. Within seconds the smoke had obstructed the view so the guards just began firing in the direction on the incoming vampires. A couple of the vampires were hit but none were fatal. The gas masks that the vampires wore protected them from the sleeping gas.

By the time they had made it to the doors, the guards, the wolves and Eric were all out cold. For good measure, one of the vampires shot both of the wolves with a tranquilizer dart. The vampires went to work on the cage. One sprayed the padlock with a freezing agent and another smashed it with a sledge hammer. They walked into the cage, put a gas mask on Eric and dragged him by the arms out of the cage and down the hall. The smoke was still thick when more guards came on the scene. One by one they too, were knocked out by the lingering gas.

It wasn't until eight AM that Vincent got word that Eric had escaped the cage.

"Dammit!" He yelled and threw his coffee cup against the kitchen wall. "How in the hell did he get out?"

"Gas canisters and tranquilizer darts," said the voice on the phone.

"God dammit!" Vincent yelled again, slamming his hand down on the counter.

He hung up the phone and called Erica. He told her what had happened and she was just as furious.

"I'm sending more trackers after him and I'm notifying the Guardians of his actions here last night. They'll send out their own trackers and they won't hesitate to put him down when they find him." Vincent said.

"I'll go tell Shay and Lily that he's out," Erica told him.

"Thanks."

Erica woke Steven and let him in on what was going on. Then she went downstairs and knocked on Lily's door. She waited but no one answered. She knocked on Shay's door but, again, no one answered.

She immediately called Lily. It went straight to voicemail. Then she called Shay. It went to voicemail too. Erica ran to the elevator and waited. When the door opened she ran in, pushed the sub-basement three button and called Steven as she waited.

"They're gone," she told Steven.

"Who's gone?"

"Lily and Shay, they're not here!" She said frantically. "I'm going to the basement now to see if they went down there."

"OK, I'll check the blood bank and let Vincent know they're missing."

Steven knew that Erica's phone would have poor reception in the basement. That's what Erica was hoping, too. That the girls had gone down to see the cage or see McGoo and just weren't getting any reception on their cells. She reached the basement and called for the girls. Her call echoed down the empty halls. She went to where they had kept Eric but they weren't there. She went to McGoo's lab, but only McGoo was there, working on his blood samples.

"Jack, have you seen Lily or Shay?" Erica asked.

"Nope," he said without even looking away from the microscope.

Erica ran back to the elevators. She met Steven on the thirteenth floor at the blood bank.

"They're not here, either," Steven reported. "I called Vince and he's going to have Parker check the cameras to see if they left the building."

Erica decided that she'd be more comfortable waiting with Vincent and Alexa. There was nothing she could do until they figured out where they went. The girls were thinking that Eric was no longer a threat.

Shay had been asking about the Underground and Lily thought that since Eric was locked up, that they would sneak down to the fight club and Lily would show Shay around. Since Shay was a vampire now and had proven she could protect herself, Lily figured that they would lay low, see the club and get back before anyone realized they had left.

They entered the tunnels through a restaurant on Amsterdam. At first they were dimly lit but about fifty yard in, around twists and turns, it got brighter. The farther they walked, it seemed like the brighter it got until they got to the main open space by the fight club. When they walked in, everyone stopped to look at them. Some even took a few steps toward them but Onyx was there to make sure that no one tried to hurt them. Brian's back was toward them in the sitting area, but he knew who was there. He took out his cell and dialed.

Ellen walked out of the fight club and saw everyone staring at Lily and Shay. She knew that they could make vampires and she forbid anyone from touching the girls or they'd be banned from fight club. After a few minutes, everyone went back to what they were doing.

"So Miss Lily, I hear great things about you. Aren't you a little frightened to be down here alone?" Ellen asked.

"We have him," Lily said, petting Onyx on the head. "So, are there any fights scheduled for today?"

"You're in luck," Ellen said and looked toward ring number two.

Sid and Walter were climbing into the ring. They squared off and waited for the referee and the buzzer. The ref climbed through the ropes and stood between the fighters. He looked over and the buzzer went off. The ref stepped back and the fighters stepped toward each other. Sid swung a right hook at Walter's head. Walter ducked and punched Sid in the chest. Sid stepped back to catch his breath but Walter was there with another blow to the chest. Sid gasped and the referee pushed Walter into the ropes.

"No more chest shots," the ref told him. "We are not trying to kill our opponent."

Walter nodded and waited for Sid to come at him. Sid came up swinging and kicking. A full round house caught Walter across the face. The kick turned him into the ropes and he grabbed the top one to steady his head. Sid punched him the side twice. Walter turned around swinging. His claws caught Sid across the face and blood splattered the concrete floor of the ring. Sid swept Walter's feet from under him and Walter went down flat on his back. He rolled out of the way of a stomp to the chest by Sid.

"No chest shots," the referee repeated loudly.

Sid gave Walter a chance to stand up and shake it off before going at him again. Sid went in swinging again. First a left then a right then another right. Two of the three landed solid on Walter's cheeks. He came back swinging. An uppercut to the gut then a right jab to the face. Sid kept swinging through the punches. A right was blocked then a kick. Walter landed a rock solid punch to Sid's nose and he staggered backwards grabbing his face. Blood poured from his nose for a moment before the busted vein in his sinuses healed itself. The buzzer rang.

"Fight goes to Walter," the referee called.

"Damn!" Sid said under his breath.

"And that my dear, is fight club," Lily told Shay.

"So that's it? Two vampires in the ring duking it out. Over what? What's the incentive?"

"Rank," Lily said. "Bragging rights."

When Lily and Shay turned to leave, they saw a group of vampires standing outside Ellen's door. Onyx stepped in front of the girls and lowered his head. A growl rumbled in his chest as he walked slowly to the front door. The group showed their claws and fangs and didn't move. Then the group made an opening and Eric stepped through the crowd.

From the back of the crowd, Eric heard Erica's voice.

"Do you want to fight?" She asked.

Eric turned around and Erica was walking up through the crowd of vampires. They took two steps back from her as she walked through to make room for Apollo on one side and Venom on the other. In the back of the crowd, Eric saw Vincent and Alexa. And behind them, members of the coven were showing up in groups of three and four.

When Erica reached Eric she slapped him across the face.

"That's for being such an ass hole," she said.

Then she swung a full hand of claws across his other cheek.

Eric dove into her, knocking her on her back. Apollo grabbed Eric by the arm and threw him into his crowd of vampires. They all moved out of the way and let him hit the floor. He stood up and went for Erica again but Apollo blocked his way.

"Get them!" Eric yelled to his friends.

In an instant everyone was fighting everyone else. Claws cut through clothes and flesh. Vampire blood splattered the floor and storefront. Vincent made his way toward the club doors. Fighting off vampires with swipes of his claws and turning to attack with his spikes. His spikes were a lot longer than Lily and Shay's and sharper. Vampires would come running toward Vince and he would simply turn around and allow them to run into him. Often the spikes found the vampire's heart and they went down only to get their chests crushed by Vincent's booted foot. The wolves would make sure they were all dead.

Eric and Erica exchanged blows again but she was overtaken by four vampires from the crowd. That gave Eric a chance to run inside.

Onyx stayed inside the fight club with Lily and Shay and was waiting for Eric when he came through the front doors. Onyx jumped on Eric, with his paws on Eric's shoulders, Onyx took bites at Eric's face. Eric turned just in time for Onyx to bite the side of his head, instead of his face. Onyx bit down and turned his head. A large piece of flesh fell from Eric's head. The skin was barely connected. Eric threw Onyx off of him and lifted the flesh back onto his skull. It healed almost instantly but not before blood ran down his neck and onto his white polo shirt.

Onyx was back on Eric right away. This time, Eric grabbed Onyx by his hide on both sides of his chest and flung Onyx through the storefront window. He landed hard on his side outside the fight club. Onyx was cut up pretty badly from the thick window glass, but he was back on his feet and after Eric. He jumped through the broken window and followed after Eric.

Eric had chased Lily and Shay to the second room of the fight club. The room that had two raised rings with concrete floors.

"Get in the ring," Eric demanded.

"No, I'm not fighting you," Lily said.

"Oh, yes you are!" Eric told her. "You either fight me, or Shay fights me."

Eric still didn't know that Shay was a vampire. Although he should've known that Lily would not have brought a human to the Underground.

Onyx limped into the fight room.

"Onyx, wait," Lily told him.

"If I beat you in the ring, Eric, will you leave us alone?"

"Fine," Eric smirked.

Shay grabbed Lily as she was stepping up to the ring.

"Lily, you know he won't fight fair," Shay said.

Lily only nodded and winked at Shay. Lily wasn't planning on fighting fair either. Lily knew that Eric wasn't aware that Shay was a vampire. And if he wanted a fight, he was sure going to get one.

Lily ducked through the ropes and waited for Eric. Erica walked through the doors into the fight room and made her way to the ring.

"Lily, what's going on," Erica asked.

"A fight to the death," Eric said. "We'll see once and for all who's the best fighter."

"Absolutely not!" Ellen and Vincent said in unison at the door.

"Too late," Eric said and took a swipe at Lily's face.

Lily wasn't even looking at Eric when he took the shot. Five gashes lay across the side of Lily's head. Blood trickled down to her blue and white shirt. It took half a second for Lily to get her bearings. Then she was on Eric. She pinned him against the ropes and continued to claw his arms and side as he tried to block her swings. He was able to get an arm free and grab one of Lily's arms. He grabbed her and flipped her around. With his free arm he hit her in the side just above her hip. She writhed in pain and swept her right leg under Eric. He fell and barely caught himself before landing on his face. Lily stomped on his back and he gasped for air. She went to stomp again but he rolled out of the way just in time.

He stood and looked around the room. The entire room was packed full. Erica, Vincent, Alexa and Steven all stood just outside the ring. On the opposite side, Eric's vampire friends were all gathered together. Before Lily was able to get to him, he bent through the ropes and took something from the hand of one of his friends. Eric stood up and waved the small object in front of him, then he pressed the button. Electricity coursed between the tongs of the Taser.

"Eric!" Vincent yelled and tried to get into the ring but Eric's friends blocked his path then dragged him backwards.

Eric's friends blocked all sides of the ring and wouldn't allow anyone near, except Shay. None of them thought that she was a threat. They all still thought that she was human. None of them thought to question the lack of a human scent in the Underground.

Eric and Lily circled each other in the ring. Eric would waive the Taser back and forth in front of his face, daring Lily to come closer. Then he lunged. Lily went down instantly. Every muscle tightened and as she hit the concrete floor. Eric began kicking Lily before she even stopped seizing. When she was able to move, he hit her with the Taser again and down she went. He hit her in the head repeatedly and kicked her ribs and stomach.

Once again he pushed the Taser into her skin. He backed up against the ropes and watched her writhe. Lily was trying to stand up when Eric got a strange look on his face.

Eric felt a sharp pain in his back. He turned around to see Shay standing behind the ropes on the ring platform. He raised the Taser to her waist but before he was able to touch her, the Taser fell to the floor. Eric looked into Shay's hazel and red eyes before he looked down at himself. Shay had reached into Eric's abdomen, up through his diaphragm and her hand wrapped around Eric's heart. She squeezed then pulled. Eric saw his own heart clutched in Shay's claws just before he hit the concrete.

Shay slid through the ropes and rushed to Lily. She was just standing up when Shay got to her. Eric's blood covered Shay's hand and forearm. Lily took Shay's hand and held it in front of her. Eric's heart was still clutched in Shay's claws.

When she realized exactly what she had done, she dropped the heart and looked into Lily's eyes. Shay was terrified. She hadn't even realized she had done it. Then she noticed the burn in her eyes and the fangs in her mouth. She turned to look at Eric's body lying on the ring floor.

The crowd began fighting again. The Underground vampires that had sided with Eric were quickly subdued. Erica and Alexa climbed into the ring with Lily and Shay. Alexa gave Lily a big hug. Erica hugged Shay and rubbed her back.

"Shhh," Erica cooed. "It's alright. It's all over now. You did what any vampire would've done"

Alexa and Erica let Lily and Shay go to each other.

"You saved my life," Lily said and pulled Shay closer.

Shay wrapped her arms around Lily and just held her until she calmed down enough to retract her claws and fangs. When Shay finally let go, the fight club was almost empty. They had already come to get Eric's body and most of the coven had gone home.

Erica was still in the ring, leaning over the ropes and talking to Steven. Apollo sat on the floor beside Steve. Onyx had healed and was standing by the door. Lily kissed Shay and ran her fingers through her hair.

"Uh hum," Erica interrupted.

Lily put her pointer finger up and continued kissing Shay.

"OK you two, we'd like to go home now," Steven said impatiently.

Shay couldn't help but laugh.

They all walked through the Underground and exited on the corner of West 90th and Columbus. The four of them along with the two wolves walked home with their hats and long sleeves.

Back at the Crown Building, they entered through the main entrance on Central Park West. Shay looked out from under her hoodie and saw a familiar face. Shane was leaving the lobby.

"Shane?" Shay said as he nearly walked by her.

"Shay! Hey girlfriend! What are you doing?" he asked.

"Uh, nothing was just out for a walk. Beautiful day, isn't it?" she said.

"Don't know, haven't been out. Hello On-ix," Shane said like he was talking a baby, then he scratched Onyx behind the ears.

Surprisingly, Onyx let him.

"So Shane, what are you doing here?" Lily asked.

Just as she said that, Taylor, one of the fighters from the fight club, walked off the elevator and caught up with Shane.

"Are you ready?" Taylor asked Shane.

"What took you so long?" Shane asked.

"Had to do my make-up," Taylor answered and then winked at Shay and Lily. They knew that he was putting on sunscreen. He was in cargo shorts and a tank top with a white baseball cap.

"Great foundation," Lily joked with Taylor.

"Thank you," Taylor replied. "And we are off like a dirty shirt! See you ladies later."

"Bye," the girls said.

Lily and Shay both laughed as they watched Shane and Taylor walk hand in hand out of the Crown Building.

"If he only knew," Shay said as they were waiting for the elevator.

When the elevator doors opened, three men on black suits and black wingtips were waiting.

www.ingramcontent.com/pod-product-compliance
Lightning Source LLC
Chambersburg PA
CBHW070819120626
46556CB00002B/573